TOO GOOD
TO BE TRUE

What Reviewers Say About Leigh Hayes's Work

Providence

"[O]ne of the most refreshing and sexiest romance novels I've read in a long time. The two leads had sizzling chemistry, the power dynamic between them was exciting and erotic, the romantic storyline was not formulaic in any way."—Melina Bickard, Librarian, Waterloo Library (UK)

"I've never stared at a book cover for so long. And Leigh Hays's writing is equally a showstopper in her debut lesbian romance *Providence.*"—*Lambda Literary*

"Are we sure this is a debut book? It's Fantastic! I thoroughly enjoyed Providence. It was an edgy storyline with a fresh take on romance. When you start this book, you think it's going to be a romance; then you realize it's erotica with some light BDSM and then you're back to love but not before the author throws in a little drama. I was in a lesfic tailspin by the end...and completely loving it!"—*Les Rêveur*

"I liked how this was written. The settings were vivid, the chemistry well done, and their emotional journeys were a highlight. ...It's a solid debut book and it left me thinking for days after I finished it. I'd recommend it if you like books with tortured characters and I'll be looking out for more from Leigh Hays in the future."
—*Lesbian Review*

Visit us at www.boldstrokesbooks.com

By the Author

Providence

Too Good to be True

TOO GOOD
TO BE TRUE

by

Leigh Hays

2020

TOO GOOD TO BE TRUE

ISBN 13: 978-1-63555-715-2

This Trade Paperback Original Is Published By
Bold Strokes Books, Inc.
P.O. Box 249
Valley Falls, NY 12185

First Edition: November 2020

CREDITS
Editor: Barbara Ann Wright
Production Design: Susan Ramundo
Cover Design By Tammy Seidick

Acknowledgments

This book's draft was due a few weeks before the COVID-19 crisis hit our area and suddenly I was working and homeschooling from home. An extra thank you for Barbara for giving me a little extra time on the edits.

Sandy, Radclyffe, Ruth, and the small army of people who make the books happen at BSB. I continue to learn and grow with your guidance.

As always, my co-workers who've supported me through this process. This year has been a ride.

Aurora Rey who earned her bottle of bourbon through the first rough draft and providing her own unique blend of cheerleader, task master and mentor.

My wife for finding space in our life for me to write and picking up the pieces that I let slide when I'm in the midst of it.

My son. You are so patient and supportive when I'm doing this work.

Dedication

For T. There would be no Jen without you.

CHAPTER ONE

A warm breeze blew in off the ocean, and the setting sun bathed the wedding guests in golden hues. It was so perfect and picturesque that it almost overwhelmed Jen Winslow's natural cynicism. But not quite. It was, after all, the best wedding money could buy.

Jen finished watching her niece dance with her new husband and then headed to the patio bar to order a scotch neat. It was smoky with a subtle finish. Her sister had good taste. She turned and spotted her mother engaged in conversation with several men a few years younger than her. She couldn't remember which of them was her date. She took another sip, grateful that she was alone for the night.

Then she accidentally made eye contact with her mother.

She looked for a diversion and spotted her old college roommate, Erika, moving toward the patio. She downed her drink and intercepted her. "Erika, so good to see you."

Erika stopped and stared. A vague smile appeared. "Likewise. How are you?"

Jen knew that expression. She had no idea who she was. "You don't remember me."

Erika's smiled faded. "No, I'm sorry."

"Jen Winslow. Yale. First semester roommate."

Erika's brows knitted together, and then she smiled. "Jen, of course. You look great."

Jen knew she was faking it. She read people for a living. However, she could sustain small talk for hours, another job skill. "So do you. Where are you working these days?"

"I'm the Jane Barnes Chair of Social Work at Smith." Seriously, did she need the whole title? Pretentious asshole. She made no move to ask about Jen.

In for a penny, in for a pound, Jen said, "That's great. I work at Brown."

Erika's interest picked up. "Really? Which department?"

"Development." Jen raised money for the college. Not a skill particularly admired by pure academics, even though they benefited from her work. They tended to think she threw parties and had lunch with rich people. While that was a part of her job, she specialized in principal gifts, the big money donors. Her connections went deeper than that.

And just as quickly, Erika's interest waned. "Oh."

Just why was she here anyway? Did her family have some connection with Erika? Annoyed and yet unable to stop herself, Jen persisted. "Last year, I brought in twenty million dollars." Why was she justifying herself to this woman?

Erika's eyes widened. "Wow. That's...impressive." She made a show of glancing at a nonexistent watch. "I'm sorry, I've got to go."

"Oh, of course. It was good to see you."

"You, too." Erika called over her shoulder as she walked into the house.

"Prick," Jen muttered under her breath. Her mother sauntered up to her. It had all been for naught. "Hello, Mother."

She leaned in and air-kissed Jen's cheek. "You look lovely. Are those my pearls?"

Jen glanced down at her necklace and black sleeveless sheath dress. She covered the pearls with her hand. "You mean Gran's? Yes. They are."

Her mother pursed her lips. "She was supposed to give them to me."

The Winslow fortune had seen better years. In fact, her mother was the last recipient of a trust fund. There had been no money left by the time their grandmother had passed on, and she had insisted on gifting her jewelry to her two granddaughters. Their mother had never let them forget it.

Her mother switched tactics. "Are you here alone? Where's Rachel?"

"She's with Carter this weekend." She shared her house and custody of her ten-year-old son with her ex-partner. A situation she thought would make their separation easier on Carter but much to her dismay, had become semi-permanent as their separation dragged on with no end in sight.

"Why didn't you bring them? It doesn't look good to come alone."

Jen shrugged. "Probably not. But I don't care." The thought of an entire weekend alone had sounded lovely. But now she realized another person would have provided a buffer.

Her mother twisted her lips and opened her mouth again.

Jen held up a hand. "I'm heading to the restroom. I'll be right back."

It didn't surprise her that her mother had asked to see her ex-wife first. Rachel had been the perfect answer to her mother's perpetual disappointment in both her career and her sexual orientation. It was obvious early on that Jen wasn't going to marry their way out of "poverty." But Rachel was an up-and-coming folk singer who performed well both professionally and personally. She satisfied her mother's needs for status and wealth. Unfortunately for Jen, it was the day-to-day living where Rachel failed to meet expectations.

She stopped thinking about her mother and focused on finding a bathroom in the grand estate her sister had rented for the weekend. Lost in the maze of halls, she started randomly opening doors and found Erika cornering a woman against an antique armoire.

'Oh, excuse—" Jen paused when something about the way the woman's hands were positioned alerted Jen to her distress.

She'd dealt with enough academic bullies in her day-to-day work to know how to deal with them. Not one to shy away from a fight, she walked in and said, "Oh, hey, Erika. I'm glad I found you."

Erika pulled away, and the other woman inched toward the door. "Now's not a good time."

"Oh, am I interrupting?" She moved closer, blocking Erika's access to the other woman. Jen got a better look at her. Mid-twenties, dark purple hair, a look of relief on her face.

"Yes."

"No. I was just leaving," the purple-haired woman said.

"Madison, wait." Erika went to follow, but Jen stepped between them.

Growing up, Jen had always been on the shorter side, but during her last year of high school, she'd hit a growth spurt and shot up to five-ten. With heels, she stood close to six feet. She had six inches on Erika, and she was using them. "I don't think she wants to talk with you."

Erika's eyes narrowed. "It's none of your business."

Jen folded her arms and stared. She let the silence grow.

Erika huffed. "Are you going to keep me in here all night?"

Jen shook her head. "No. Just long enough for her to make a clean getaway."

Erika growled and pushed past. Jen let her, pleased to have pissed her off.

Half an hour later, Jen's sister, Elizabeth, found her nursing another scotch and lounging in a leather wingback chair. Elizabeth collapsed in the chair opposite. "Are you hiding from Mom?"

Jen raised her glass. "Guilty as charged." She took a sip. "Why is she even here?"

There was no love lost between Elizabeth and their mother, either. "Jess wanted to invite her."

Jen snorted. "As if the bride ever gets to see anyone at their own wedding."

She waved toward Jen's glass. Jen passed it over. She took a sip and said, "You can blame Bill and all his family-centric bullshit." Elizabeth sounded harsher than she probably felt. She loved Jessie's new husband, but the extended family bit was not their scene.

Jen watched the party through the open doors. Guests mingled on the stone patio next to the bar, but the bulk of the party was happening under a white tent closer to the water. "Speaking of guests, what the fuck is Erika Robson doing here?"

Elizabeth sighed and took another sip. "She's married to Annelise. One of Bill's cousins." Bill's family was huge, with seven siblings in his father's generation and six in his own.

Jen snatched her drink back. "Really? How long?"

"Maybe sixteen years."

Jen took another sip and shook her head. "She's still the same dick from college. Pretentious and manipulative. She was totally making a pass at someone else when I barged in."

Elizabeth groaned. "Fabulous. Let me guess. Mid-twenties?"

Jen nodded, the purple hair hard to forget. "Yes, she was. I gather it's not her first time?"

Elizabeth shook her head. "Nope. She collects a student once every few years."

That explained the scene she walked in on. Whatever Erika's previous relationship with the woman had been, she was pretty certain it was over now. She knew a thing or two about women who couldn't let go. Jen frowned and finished her drink. "What an ass." She stood and held out her hand. "I need another drink."

They split up at the bar, wedding duties calling Elizabeth away. Tiny white lights and paper lanterns lit the way to the tent and encompassed it on all sides, emitting enough light to drink and dance by. Jen scanned the tent, looking for someone to pass the time with until the event ran its course. Across the room, she spotted Madison sitting in a group of other twentysomethings, laughing. Her table boasted two other colors of the rainbow. Her purple hair complemented another man with dark green hair and another person with bright orange. But the dark purple stood out as an elegant spark of individuality. The contrast intrigued Jen. A flicker of not quite desire but definitely not platonic feelings stirred inside her.

Madison glanced over and caught Jen staring.

Taking a bigger sip than she had intended, she choked as it burned its way down. When she looked up from her coughing fit, Madison was gone.

"Shit," Jen mumbled, wiping down her chest with the cocktail napkin. Slightly embarrassed, she grabbed her drink and found a set of chairs facing the ocean. Looking out at the water, the onshore lights cast the sea in shadow, and she silently laughed at herself for getting flustered by a woman's gaze across the room. But even as she did that, she felt disappointment at a missed opportunity.

"There you are."

Jen glanced up at a shadowy figure backlit by the reception's lights. The voice sounded familiar, but she'd only heard it once. A shiver went through her body that had nothing to do with the temperature, and she tilted her head to get a better look.

Madison smiled down at her.

Still a little off-balance from her coughing fit, her comeback lacked her usual finesse. "Here I am."

Madison took the chair opposite. The light outlined her face. "I wanted to thank you for rescuing me."

Rescuing. Like some knight in shining armor. Jen preened a little, and then, before her mind caught up with her, she said, "Does that make you a damsel in distress?" Ah, fuck, was she flirting?

Madison smiled, and a hint of playfulness emerged in her tone and posture. "For the right person."

"I'll keep that in mind." Okay, what the fuck was she doing? It wasn't the scotch. She hadn't consumed any more than she would at a work function. No, it was a mix of pride and the flattery coming from an attractive woman. Because Madison was attractive. More than a decade younger but still attractive. *Go with it.* She held out her hand and said, "I'm Jen."

Madison reached out and said, "Madison."

Her hand was rougher than Jen was expecting but warm, and she looked right at her as they held hands. Jen smiled and opened her mouth, but whatever flirty comment was about to come out died on her lips when she heard her mother's voice. She groaned.

Madison looked confused and pulled her hand back. "What?"

Jen's shoulders slumped. "It's my mother."

"Jennifer, what are you doing lurking in the shadows?" She looked at Madison and then back at Jen. Jen saw the exact moment the purple hair registered by the slight curl of disapproval on her lips. "Isn't she a little young for you? I mean really, how old are you?"

Madison answered without missing a beat. "Old enough to know what I want."

Jen choked on a laugh. She liked this woman. She set her drink on the lawn and held out her hand. "You're right. I am lurking. Come on, darling, let's dance."

Madison let Jen lead her to the dance floor. Her hand was warm, her grip solid, confident, as if she didn't care who saw her. Not like Erika, whose every touch was furtive and hidden. Seeing her had brought up old feelings of doubt. Even now, she expected Jen to let go once they were safely out of her mother's range, but she didn't. Instead, she slipped an arm around Madison's waist, picked up her other hand, and led her into a dance.

Madison's surprise must have registered on her face because Jen paused and loosened her grip. "Is this okay?"

Her poise and confidence both alarmed and attracted her. Jen was totally her type—older and self-assured—and that alone would lead to trouble. Erika had been her type, too, and that relationship had ended in heartbreak for her. All the apprehension from seeing Erika flared up before she pushed it back down. An interesting woman wanted to dance with her, and she wasn't going to squander the opportunity. Fuck Erika.

She nodded and squeezed Jen's hand. "Yes." The song was soft and slightly up-tempo. Madison recognized it as "Dream a Little Dream of Me."

Jen turned out to be a good dancer, and Madison said so. Jen twirled her and pulled her back in. "Years of etiquette lessons in my youth. It always felt awkward until I realized I was trying to lead."

Madison laughed, and the music shifted to another old standard with the same tempo. Jen showed no signs of letting go, so Madison kept dancing. It felt strange to follow. She was usually the taller woman and often the one who led, but Jen had a few inches on her even without the heels.

Jen kept eye contact, drawing Madison in with her attentiveness and presence. Delighted to be in the spotlight, she relished Jen's open admiration and appreciation. She couldn't remember the last time she'd danced with another woman. And not grinding in some club. It felt good.

"You're not so bad yourself." Jen grinned at her, and her brown eyes crinkled when she smiled.

"Ballet in grade school. Theater in college."

"Ah, a drama major." Jen held her close, and Madison missed a step. Jen caught her effortlessly. All too aware of the woman holding her, she mumbled an apology and cursed herself for getting distracted. The music morphed into another, slower, more romantic song. Jen continued to guide her at a slower pace. Their bodies came closer but didn't quite touch.

Madison could smell her perfume, something subtle but distinct. It suited her. "More like drama adjacent. I dated a theatre major."

Jen chuckled, and Madison felt it throughout her body. She suppressed a moan, imagining that velvet sound surrounding her in a more intimate environment. "I've known a few people who specialized in drama." Her tone made it clear that she wasn't talking about the stage.

Madison willed herself to relax and stay focused on the conversation. "Like your mother?"

Jen groaned and threw her head back. "She has a fucking master's."

Madison imagined leaning in and kissing along the column of her neck. It would be so easy to turn their physical familiarity more intimate. Without thinking, she pulled Jen against her.

Jen looked down as if startled, and then a slow smile spread across her face. Her hands settled on Madison's hips. Their conversation stopped, and they spoke with their bodies. Giving in to the fantasy of something more, Madison slung her arms around Jen's neck. They moved with the music but focused on each other. Madison had never danced so well with another person. Jen's hands were sure and deft, feet smooth and precise.

When the music stopped, she stayed in Jen's arms. Jen's eyes stayed on hers, flickering briefly to Madison's lips. Madison leaned in.

A raucous dance beat thundered through the speakers. Jen hung her head.

Madison laughed and leaned in to shout. "Total buzzkill."

Jen rolled her eyes and stepped away. "Totally. Come on. Let's get a drink."

Madison followed her off the dance floor and across the lawn to the outdoor bar, watching the way her hips swayed in that black dress.

"What are you drinking?" Jen called over her shoulder.

She suppressed the urge to say you and instead came up with the first cocktail she could think of. "A Cosmo."

"Of course." Jen laughed and got the bartender's attention.

Madison leaned against the bar. "Are you making fun of me?"

"For a pink drink?" Jen just grinned.

Madison crossed her arms. She wasn't sure if she was teasing or not. "Well, what are you drinking?"

The bartender arrived, and Jen ordered. "Scotch neat and a Cosmo for my friend."

Madison curled her lip. The one time she'd tasted scotch, she'd spit it back out. The astringent flavor had left a bitter taste in her mouth.

"It's an acquired taste." Jen collected her drink, and they waited for the bartender to finish Madison's cocktail.

Someone touched Madison's lower back, and she stiffened before her sister came up beside her. "Hey, I wanted to check in. I saw you on the dance floor." She extended a hand to Jen. "I'm Kayla. Madison's sister."

"Jen. Jessica's aunt."

Jen didn't ask how they were sisters since Kayla was black, and Madison was white. Madison had used that reaction more than once to weed out undesirable people. Instead, Jen sipped her drink and asked over the rim, "Are you checking up on her or me?"

Kayla grinned. "Both."

Madison slapped the back of her hand against Kayla's shoulder. "Stop. She helped me deal with Erika earlier."

Kayla beamed. "Well, in that case. Carry on."

Jen just laughed. Madison was beginning to like the sound. Resonant and alluring.

Kayla hooked her thumb over her shoulder. "We're going to hit the pool in a bit. Care to join us?"

"Maybe later." Madison looked to Jen, who shrugged.

As she turned away, Kayla gave her a look and nodded. "Sure."

Handing the pink cocktail over, Jen nodded toward a pair of empty chairs. Madison followed her and sat. The half light made Jen's features more severe when she wasn't laughing or smiling. The effect was very intimidating. No wonder Erika had backed down. She smiled.

Jen slowly spun her glass. "You're smiling. What are you thinking?"

Madison grinned. "That I've never seen Erika back down so quickly."

Rolling her eyes, Jen sipped her scotch. "That's because you didn't know her in college."

"And you did?" Madison finally tasted her drink. It was exactly what she'd wanted.

Jen snorted. "I fucking lived with her for a semester."

"Harvard, right?"

Jen laughed. "Oh, hell no. We went to Yale. I mean, we both did grad work at Harvard. It's only the last degree that matters."

Madison couldn't help herself. "What was she like?"

"Pompous, insecure, with bouts of charisma and charm."

Pretty much the same person whom Madison met six years ago, without the insecurity. But Erika had needed a lot of attention, so maybe the insecurity had always been there, too.

Jen held the glass against her forehead. "Why do you want to know?"

Good question. This was the first time she'd run into Erika since breaking things off two years ago. Their affair had started in her second year of grad school and had ended about six months after graduation. Seven months into the relationship, Erika had already reneged on her promise to leave her wife. Madison had believed her excuses and had stayed a year longer than she should have.

"Just curious." Now, Madison feigned nonchalance.

Jen hummed. "Are you still seeing her?"

Madison recoiled. So much for playing it cool. "No. This is the first...Is it that obvious?"

"Not to anyone who didn't walk in on you."

Madison took a deep breath. "I broke it off a few years ago."

"Good. You could do better." Jen drained the last of her scotch.

Madison coughed, her indignation coming through in her tone. "You don't even know me."

"I don't have to. She's a dick." Undeterred, Jen shrugged and put her empty glass down.

But Jen didn't know enough about her or Erika to say that. A little irked by this woman's dismissive arrogance, she felt the need to defend her choices. "She wasn't always a jerk."

Jen covered Madison's hand. "Oh, they never are. That's the problem. You get sucked in."

They weren't talking about Erika anymore, and that immediately softened Madison's response. "Who are you thinking of?"

Jen glanced at their joined hands and then back up. She shook her head. "My ex. She wanted all these things, and then she didn't."

Madison stared. The pleasant buzz of sexual arousal had faded, and she was left wondering if it had all been in her head. Sadness and regret were in the twist of Jen's lips, and her dark eyes focused beyond Madison. A little surprised by the shift in Jen's mood, Madison pulled back. Jen didn't try to stop her.

Sensing the evening was over but not wanting to lose her company on such a sour note, Madison tried to salvage their connection. "Do you want to join me at the pool?"

Jen's smile alone eased her insecurities. "Maybe. But I should go check in with my family."

Confused by the way their conversation ended, Madison tried to hide her disappointment, but some of it must have showed.

"Are you staying here at the estate?" Jen asked.

Madison nodded, a tiny spark of hope igniting.

"I'll save you a seat at breakfast." Jen winked and walked away.

Not sure how to take that statement, she swallowed her regret and satisfied herself with watching the way Jen's hips swayed as she headed back to the house. She struggled to figure out where it'd gone wrong. She'd never been impulsive but she wished she'd been a little more direct. She was sure she could have had something more tonight if only she'd known the right way to ask.

CHAPTER TWO

An hour later, Jen returned to her room and kicked her heels off. Her feet hurt more than she was willing to admit. The dancing might not have been the wisest choice with her shoes. She grinned. But totally worth it.

She slipped out of her dress and hung it up. She paused at her bra and considered Madison's invitation. She'd let thoughts of Rachel ruin her evening earlier than she'd planned. Fuck that. She'd come here alone on purpose to do what she wanted with who she wanted. At this point, she wasn't sure if the scotch was talking, but she didn't care. She wasn't drunk; all her faculties were intact. She could still make sound decisions, but the more cautious side of her had already left the building. She didn't have a swimsuit, but that didn't matter. It would feel good to soak her feet in the pool. She pulled on a pair of shorts and a dark blue T-shirt before palming her room key and leaving her phone behind.

The pool was empty and the patio quiet. She suppressed her disappointment and then considered why she felt that way in the first place. What was she hoping would happen? A quick wedding hookup with someone half her age? The less reserved side of her responded with a resounding yes. And why not? She deserved a little recreation. She worked hard, and she was essentially a single parent. Considering the fact that her last two relationships had crashed and burned, having sex with no repercussions felt like a great idea.

The more conservative side reminded her that women in their twenties came with a lot of baggage, the kind she had already packed up ten years ago. She rolled her eyes at herself and muttered, "It's only baggage if you pick it up."

"Are you looking for Madison?"

Startled, Jen pulled her eyes from the rippling water and turned.

Kayla hefted a pair of sandals. "Sorry, didn't mean to scare you. We're inside. Why don't you join us?"

Jen wavered. "I don't want to intrude."

Kayla shook her head, and the beads in her hair clicked together. "You're not. Come on."

Jen took a deep breath and followed her.

Over her shoulder, Kayla said, "So you're Jessie's aunt?"

Jen caught up and said, "Yes. How do you know Jessie?"

"She dated my ex-boyfriend. When he dumped her the same way he dumped me, we became friends."

Jen smiled. "Booty buddies. I can relate."

Kayla laughed. "I'd never called it that, but it works." She breezed through the French doors and opened her arms, holding her shoes aloft. "I return victorious."

A round of cheers and whoops greeted her. Jen surveyed the group, mostly mid-twenties, more women than men, more people of color than white. Madison lounged in the circle. Jen watched her face change from amused to interested when their eyes met. Smiling, she scooted over and opened up a spot beside her.

Jen returned the smile and walked over.

Madison looked up. "I thought you went to bed."

"I'm not that old." Jen settled beside her. The cushion dipped and pushed her closer.

"I didn't say you were."

Kayla dropped on the other side, and the cushion dipped farther. Jen steadied herself on Madison's thigh. Madison shifted, and Jen pulled her hand away. "Sorry."

Madison moved her arm and slung it behind Jen along the couch. Jen slid closer, and Madison leaned in. "Much better."

Smiling, Jen shook her head and listened to the conversation around her. She felt comfortable in a crowd. She could make small talk with anyone. This particular group was a bit younger than her normal crowd. Not that it bothered her in the least. Occasionally, Kayla or Madison would give her some context. But she kept quiet for the most part, content to soak up the feeling of Madison's body against hers. About twenty minutes into another story and she'd gotten no further signals from Madison except that damn arm around her shoulders. She could feel the day catching up. She'd hit the bathroom and stay for another ten minutes before making her excuses.

She stood, and Madison asked why with her eyes. Jen leaned in and whispered, "Bathroom."

Madison pulled back with a half smirk and nodded.

Puzzled by her reaction, Jen walked away. She had just finished on the toilet and was mid-wipe when the door opened, and Madison walked in.

"Oh!" Madison's face turned red, and she backed right out of the room.

"Fuck." Two simultaneous thoughts occurred to her. One, she'd forgotten to lock the damn door and two, Madison had thought Jen was sending her a signal. Suddenly, her odd look made sense. Jen shot off the toilet and yanked her shorts up in one motion, her balance a little more off than she was accustomed to. Opening the door, she stuck her head out. Madison was making her way down the hall. "Get in here." Madison turned, and Jen waved her back.

Madison shook her head. "No, it's okay. I'm sorry. I thought—"

Jen summoned her authoritative voice. "Now." There was a moment when she thought Madison's embarrassment might win out, but then it was gone.

Shutting the door behind them, Jen moved in front of Madison and turned on the sink. She washed her hands. Madison was staring at her in the mirror, a slight blush to her face.

Jen held her gaze while she dried her hands. "I think we need a little clarity in our signals."

Madison shifted to give her more room, but Jen stepped into her space. Without her heels, they were almost the same height. Throwing her arms on Madison's shoulders and tucking her hands behind her neck, Jen pulled her closer. "Is this what you want?"

Madison put her hands on Jen's hips. Her eyes dropped to Jen's lips. "Yes."

"Then ask."

"Are you as skilled a lover as you are a dancer?"

Jen's breath caught at the question. Now that it was out there, there was no doubt where the end of this conversation would lead. Her heart rate sped up, and her voice came out much softer than she was expecting. "Do you want me to show you?"

Madison leaned in and breathed the word, "Yes," across Jen's lips before she kissed her. It was clumsy at first, finding the right tilt of her head, but then Jen moved one way, and she moved the other. And the awkwardness faded, replaced by a growing desire as her mouth moved of its own accord, nipping and pulling at Jen's lips until Jen opened her mouth. Madison's tongue dove inside and swirled around before pulling back. Jen took the lead then, moving in and out of her mouth as their hands roamed.

The door began to open just as Madison touched Jen's stomach. Madison pulled back and threw her hand against the door, shutting it. She fumbled for the lock. "There's someone in here."

They listened for a moment, and then Jen opened the door and looked out. Grabbing Madison's hand, she said, "Come on. Let's go somewhere else."

Madison followed her upstairs, her tongue slightly sore from the intense kissing session. Still holding Jen's hand, she paused at the threshold of Jen's room, unable to move forward. It was one thing to fantasize about sex with a stranger and another thing to go through with it.

Jen turned. "Are you okay?"

"Yeah, I'm good." She forced a smile and stepped into the room, closing the door behind her.

Jen stared. "Are you sure?"

Madison swallowed, trying to figure out what was holding her back. It wasn't her first time, and yet it had that same weightiness to it. A beautiful woman wanted to have sex with her, and she was paralyzed. Seeing Erika had brought up all her insecurities. She needed to get over herself and quick if she wanted this to happen. She kicked off her shoes and opted for a half truth. "Just a little nervous."

Smiling, Jen hooked her hands into Madison's belt and pulled her closer. "So I'm not another notch on your bedpost?"

Madison laughed. She'd only slept with three people. Only one of them was a onetime deal, the other two were long-term relationships. She didn't hop into bed with people, even though she wished she did. It would hurt less when they dumped her. She was more concerned about being a notch on Jen's bedpost, but she didn't say so. "No."

"Good. I hate being just a number."

"You're not." Silencing her doubts, Madison pulled her closer and started kissing the line of her jaw up to her ear.

Jen groaned and tilted her head back. "That feels nice."

Madison smiled against her neck and slid her hand under Jen's shirt. She brushed against Jen's bra strap a few times before she decided to take it off for an unobstructed feel.

Jen lifted Madison's face and met her in a messy kiss. She pulled back halfway through, leaving Madison chasing her lips as Jen yanked her shirt and bra over her head. Madison paused and looked at Jen's breasts. Her eyes widened at the intricate tattoos along Jen's shoulders and upper chest. Jen had worn a fairly revealing dress earlier, and not a single tattoo had shown through.

"They're my secret." Jen stepped back and turned around. More artwork covered her back, centered along her spine and fanning out to the edges.

Madison brushed her fingers along the ink. "It's gorgeous." Bright bursts of color mixed with deep black lines in stylized patterns. She leaned in and placed a light kiss along a red blossom.

Jen reached behind and tangled a hand in Madison's hair. She moved closer, trailing kisses along Jen's shoulder blades. Jen leaned back and sighed. "You have a tender touch."

Madison's ego swelled. Erika had told her she was too clingy. Nuzzling Jen's neck, she wrapped her arms around Jen's waist and squeezed.

Jen turned and tilted Madison's face toward her. "Did I say something wrong?"

Madison shook her head. "No. I've been called clingy."

Jen's mouth set, her features severe and foreboding. "Erika?"

"It doesn't matter."

Jen stopped her from pulling away. "It does. You're a beautiful woman, and I want you to show me who you are."

Jen's words sank into Madison's heart, and she pulled her into a searing kiss. Jen matched her intensity, and they moved back toward the bed, never letting their mouths and hands stray too far from each other. Madison yanked her shirt over her head and tossed it across the room. Jen shimmied out of her shorts and let them fall where she stood. Jen popped Madison's button and unzipped her pants. Madison pushed her boxers down with her pants, toeing off her socks at the same time and kicked the whole pile off to the side.

Jen had her hands poised to take off the last bit of clothing between them when Madison reached out and said, "Let me." Slipping her hands into both sides of the black lace panties, she pushed them down and sank to her knees. She helped Jen lift one foot and then the other before she took the panties and held them. "These are very nice."

"Yeah. I picked them up in Chicago. They were a really good deal." She rattled off a few other random details.

Madison glanced up and smiled. Jen's face was flushed, and she had lost all the severity of her features.

She frowned. "What?"

"Do you always babble when you're nervous?"

Jen made a face. "I do not babble."

Madison twirled the panties in her hand. "So I really needed to know the whole history of these underwear."

Jen bit her lower lip. "Probably not."

"Sit down."

Jen sat on the edge of the bed. Madison palmed her thighs and pushed her legs apart, revealing a dark tangle of hair and pink inner lips. She looked up at Jen and deliberately licked her own lips. Jen swallowed and clutched the side of the bed. Leaning in, Madison nuzzled Jen's wiry hair and took a deep breath. Jen shifted in her hands, and her breath hitched.

Sticking out her tongue, Madison opened Jen's outer labia and took a tiny lick.

Jen gasped and rocked forward. Madison moved closer and took another lick. Jen's breath stuttered. Madison liked that sound and wanted to hear it again. She took successively longer and longer swipes, punctuated by breaks and that breathy sound Jen made.

Jen gripped her hair and forced her to look up. "Stop teasing." Her whisper ended in a tone bordering on a beg. "Please."

Madison felt her own wetness increase with that one word. Lifting one of Jen's legs over her shoulder, she leaned in and licked her entire labia, running up and around the outer petals. She made a few passes across her clit once, twice, before moving down toward her opening. Jen's insides clutched at her tongue, holding it in place before letting it go.

Madison licked Jen's center, up and around again and again, while Jen's hips rocked toward her. Madison moved faster, trying to keep up. Pulling almost painfully on Madison's hair, Jen gasped and convulsed under her hands and her lips. Madison kept licking until Jen muttered, "Stop."

A little worried, Madison pulled back. "Are you okay?"

Jen groaned. "Yes. Just too much. Come here."

Too much? She climbed up on the bed and laid next to her. Did she not like it? Jen had her eyes closed, taking deep breaths. Did she wear her out? She was older. Madison was so lost in her thoughts she jumped when Jen rolled over and threw her leg across Madison's body.

"Did I startle you?" Jen smiled and inched closer.

Madison turned and faced her. Jen's brown eyes traveled up and down Madison's body, as if looking for ways to uncover her secrets. She shivered in anticipation.

Running her hand down Madison's side, Jen's eyes darkened and she said, "Tell me what you like."

Madison closed her eyes at the touch. "I like your hands touching me."

Jen shifted and straddled Madison's hips. Her fingers splayed across Madison's stomach and moved toward her breasts—featherlight touches that soothed and aroused. Madison lost herself in the sensation, growing wetter with each touch that moved lower and lower. "What else?"

Madison struggled to recall what she was asking.

"What else do you like?" Jen persisted.

"Your mouth—" She gasped when Jen's lips captured her nipple and sucked. She arched her back. Jen switched nipples, sucking and pulling before alternating kisses with light nips down Madison's torso. She kissed along her lower stomach, and Madison jerked her hips. Running her hand up Madison's body, she cupped Madison's breast and squeezed. She kissed her center and then opened her up.

Jen's tongue touched her everywhere, lingering licks and quick flicks, gentle suction and hard pulling. She lost track of individual touches, succumbing to the overwhelming sensations, and her orgasm grew until it crashed out and over her.

Jen crawled up her body and kissed her. Madison tasted herself on her mouth, which turned her on more. Jen pulled back with a grin. "What else do you like?"

"Fuck. Fuck. Ah…" Jen came with three of Madison's fingers inside her and flopped back on the bed, pulling Madison with her.

"Whoa, wait." Madison slid out of her and slumped against her.

"Umph." Jen groaned.

"Sorry." Madison moved on to her stomach, worried she'd hurt her.

Jen glanced at her. "So not graceful."

Madison felt mildly embarrassed but didn't care. Hours of nonstop sex had her endorphins pumping overtime. "I didn't hurt you?"

Jen sighed. "No, I'm good." She chuckled. "You're good." She yawned, and Madison followed suit.

Madison lay on her stomach and drifted half-awake, half-asleep. In that twilight state, soft kisses brushed along her spine, and she hummed. "That feels nice."

The movement continued up toward the nape of her neck. Fingers brushed her hair to the side, and Jen whispered in her ear. "I like this color. It suits you."

Smiling, Madison started to roll over, but Jen held her still. Leaning in to kiss her, Jen said, "I want you like this."

Madison shuddered at Jen's voice, the tone and the command behind them. Jen's hands slid down her back and over her ass, gripping and massaging her cheeks. She clenched her ass, anticipating her next move. Her sleepiness faded and left her with a different and deeper arousal than before. Vulnerability gave way to desire. The feeling of Jen hovering over her increased her awareness as Jen's fingers moved down toward her opening. Lying along her back, Jen kissed her just below her earlobe and pushed a finger inside her. "So wet."

Madison groaned and bucked her hips.

Jen thrusted and added another finger. "Is this okay?"

Madison arched her back and gripped the sheets. She nodded.

"Good, because I want to fuck you." Jen kissed her shoulder blade and pulled away.

Jen kept up the pace, pushing in and out, in and out, with a speed that left Madison unable to focus on anything but the fingers inside her. Jen's other hand slipped around Madison's waist and brushed along her clit.

"Oh yes." Madison curled into Jen's body.

Jen kissed her ear. "Do you like that?"

She nodded, eyes closed now, and said, "Don't stop."

Jen pushed her back down, and her fingers twisted inside and set up a corkscrew motion that made her toes tingle. She came hard and quick. She tried to move, but all her strength had left her. She tried to speak, but the words would not come. She fell asleep to the steady sound of Jen's breathing.

She woke to a shrill ring and a muffled hello. The mattress dipped, and Jen got out of bed. She closed her eyes and started to drift off again.

But she woke up at the words, "I'll be home in an hour." Totally disoriented, she tried to match the words with the voice. Erika always had to be home, but this was Jen. Suddenly, everything about the night before felt suspect.

Jen touched her back, and she pretended to be asleep. She heard Jen sigh.

Her heart sank while she listened to Jen quietly pack up. Who did Jen have waiting for her at home? She felt so stupid, pretending that this one night was the start of a different pattern, a new her, but it was just the same old reality. She should have known better; all her life she'd been second best. She waited until Jen left before she got up.

In the bathroom, she found a note tucked next to the soap. Even Jen's handwriting was a reflection of her, bold and sharp. "Sorry I had to leave. My son is sick. I had a good time, and I'd love to go dancing again."

She'd left her number. Madison read it twice. Son. After Erika, anyone with a family was a nonstarter. She crumpled it up and tossed it in the trash.

Chapter Three

Madison weaved her way through the pile of boxes in her living room just as her father walked up the stairs.

"Where do you want this?" He hefted a box labeled kitchen.

Madison reached out. "I've got it." He passed it over and headed back downstairs to get more. She stacked the box on the pile next to her mother, who was elbow deep in the cabinets with a washcloth and spray bottle.

When things had fallen apart with Erika, she tried to stay in Northampton, but after she'd lost her field placement, she'd called her parents in a panic. They'd taken turns talking her down until finally her mom had said, "We're coming to get you."

Lost and alone, she hadn't even bothered to protest. They'd arrived two days later and slept on her couch, buying her groceries, cleaning her apartment, and feeding her while they'd helped her decided what to do next. And like always, they'd left her feeling stronger than she was when she'd first come to them.

"Mom, you don't have to do that," she said, knowing she'd lose the argument before it began.

Her mom glanced over her shoulder and smiled, an iron will waiting in plain sight. "I know."

Her dad walked in again. "I've got a kitchen one."

Her mom glanced up and waved him over. "Bring it here."

"I thought I was supposed to be doing the cleaning," he said as he set it down on the cabinet.

Her mom pointed at a bucket of cleaning supplies. "As soon as Kayla gets here, the oven's all yours. Until then, don't lift anything too heavy." She pointed toward the door and the rest of the boxes.

"Come on, Pop." Not wanting her dad to haul up the heavy boxes, Madison led the way downstairs. They were halfway through the truck—Madison carefully curating which box her dad got and which one she carried—when Kayla pulled up in her white Honda Accord. Seeing Kayla made the move feel permanent and less like her college days.

Madison watched her look around the neighborhood. A quiet road off Blackstone Boulevard with huge houses and manicured lawns. Two- and three-story Colonials in neat rows with their two and a half kids and cars. The kind of neighborhood where white people called the cops when Kayla showed up.

"Dad knows several people on this block." Even though it was closer to her new job, she'd initially ruled it out because she wanted a place where her sister would feel safe.

Kayla visibly relaxed and tilted her head toward the garage. "You know, when you said garage apartment, I was thinking something less grand."

Madison glanced at the gabled roof of the two-car garage and grinned. "I know, right? It's cheap, too." Originally designed as a mother-in-law apartment where the mother-in-law in question was not ready to move in, her landlords wanted to rent to someone that they knew and were willing to go below market value for a good tenant. After spending the summer at her parents' house, she was looking forward to her own space. "Come on. I want to show you around."

"You made it." Her dad met them at the bottom of the stairs.

Kayla hugged him. "Sorry I'm late."

"Don't worry, we saved the furniture for you and your mom." Both of them worked for the Providence Fire Department, Kayla as a paramedic, and her mom as a fire station captain. They were trained to carry heavy loads.

Madison laughed, and Kayla groaned. "Really? I just got off shift."

"Did you honestly think you weren't going to work?" Madison teased.

Her mother came down. "I thought I heard you." She clapped her hands, all authoritarian. "Good. Let's get to work."

The sun was just starting to set when they finally sat down to dinner among the boxes. Madison listened with half an ear while Kayla and her mom talked shop.

"Penny for your thoughts?" Her dad asked while Kayla went off on city politics. Her mom had her own thoughts on the subject, considering her budget went up and down with each election.

Madison shook her head. "Just thinking about all the stuff I've got to do before work." She had less than two weeks before she started, and her mind was occupied with all the things she wanted to do before school started in full session.

"Anything I can help with?"

She considered his offer. They'd already done so much for her that she was reluctant to ask for anything else. Besides, she didn't really need any help just time to get set up. "I don't think so."

He smiled. "Are you nervous?"

Again, she thought about his question. Not so much nervous but a little anxious. "Yes and no. I've got all these local contacts which is great. And the principal is awesome. But I'm the only social worker on site. There are three hundred kids from four to eighteen. It's a wide range of stuff I could be dealing with."

"You can handle it." He said it so matter-of-fact that Madison believed him. Not only had Erika been a blow to her personal esteem, but she'd also taken an ego hit professionally. Erika had been her faculty advisor and her primary professional reference. After their breakup, all of Erika's connections dried up, and Madison had found herself isolated both personally and professionally in Northampton and Boston. After her parents' visit, she'd finally come clean with her secondary advisor, and he'd helped her escape Erika's professional stranglehold. Providence was only an hour and half south of Northampton and an hour from Boston, but in terms of Erika and her influence, it was an ocean apart.

He slung his arm across Madison's shoulders. She leaned into the contact. "I'm so glad you're back home."

Her mom smiled. "I agree. I'm happy that all my kids are back in town."

Surrounded by her family in her own apartment with another job lined up, her life was finally back on track. She smiled, feeling the perpetual knot in her stomach starting to fade. "Me, too."

After dinner, her dad volunteered to return the moving van, and her mother went with him.

"Are you sure you don't want us to come back?" Her mom leaned against her car door while Madison shook her head.

Grateful beyond words, she said, "You guys have done more than enough." And not just the physical labor. She'd already lost the fight about paying for the moving van.

"I don't want to crowd you or your sister, but I'm hoping that we can do a Sunday dinner once a month after you get settled in your job."

Madison's heart swelled. "Oh, Ma, that would be awesome."

She watched them pull out, hope blooming in her chest. She was finally home, and everything was going to be all right. Three weeks ago, when Kayla had insisted she'd come to Jessie's wedding, she'd been in a bad place. And then she'd come face-to-face with Erika again. But she didn't crumble. In fact, she'd walked away. Sure, Jen helped her, but she didn't fall apart. And even though Jen had turned into a brief but pleasant blip, she symbolized Madison's return to normal, and for that, she was grateful.

Taking a deep cleansing breath, she pushed aside her thoughts, opened her eyes, and headed back upstairs to unpack.

"How many mugs do you own?" Kayla held one up for show.

Madison shrugged. "I don't know. Too many?"

Kayla tilted the box toward her. "You could go two weeks without washing one and still have clean ones available."

Madison cringed. "That's too many." She sat on the floor next to her and pulled over another box. They unpacked for an hour, talking about science fiction and fantasy books and television, the familiarity both a comfort and a joy. Their shared nerdiness had been the bond that held them together when it seemed they had little else in common.

Kayla was shelving some of Madison's books when she said, "We should do a gaming night again."

Madison smiled. Kayla didn't mean Pictionary or Cards Against Humanity. She meant tabletop role playing. "I'm not sure I want to do D&D again."

Kayla glanced back at her. "There's so much more out there. I've been wanting to run a big old space opera. Kind of *Firefly* meets *Star Trek* but all black. Some straight up Afro-Futurism stuff."

"Can I still be queer?"

Kayla looked at her. "As if you've ever played anything else."

Madison laughed. Even the boys she'd played ended up gay or trans. "I guess not. Is anyone still here?"

"Celia works at a law firm downtown. And Beck's working at RISD. I haven't seen Vanessa since high school. There are a couple people I know who might be interested. What do you think?"

She'd played in a few groups in Northampton but nothing that stuck long-term. For her, gaming groups were as much about the people she played with as the game or its setting, and no one had come close to Van, Celia, Beck, and Kayla. They gelled and played off each other in ways that a pickup game just couldn't match. An interesting setting and her old group would also help her feel normal. "I think I need to unpack my dice."

They finished her bookcase and found her old DVD collection.

"Oh, I loved this show." Kayla held up a box set of *Farscape*.

Madison glanced at it and around her room. Most of her essentials were unpacked, and what was left in the boxes could stay in the boxes. Each object she pulled out carried with it memories of her time away, and right now, the idea of curling up on her couch and watching a few episodes seemed far more inviting than unpacking. "Want to hook up the Xbox?"

Madison made popcorn while they debated which episode they wanted to watch. They finally settled on "The Locket." "I think that John and Aeryn are my favorite straight couple in all fandom."

Kayla laughed. "That's because Aeryn's totally your type."

Madison sat and handed her the popcorn bowl. "Emotionally distant?"

Kayla rolled her eyes. "No that's an unfortunate side effect to some of the women you've dated. I mean super confident and competent."

Madison nodded. An accurate assessment. She did like her women to know what they wanted and how to get it. It just sucked when it wasn't her.

"Oh, no. None of that."

Madison looked at her. "None of what?"

Kayla waved around. "That look. Forget Erika and what she did to you. She didn't deserve you. You can do better. And you will."

"I know." Madison grabbed the remote and pressed play. Jen had said something similar at the wedding. Not for the first time, she wished she'd kept her phone number, and now it felt like the moment had passed. Even if it wasn't meant to be, Jen had helped restore Madison's confidence. And maybe she'd be able to start dating again.

Jen woke to the quiet burr of her electric mower outside her bedroom window. No one else in her neighborhood owned one. She knew Carter wasn't mowing, which meant…

She crawled out of bed and looked down into her yard. Rachel. "Damn it."

She suppressed the urge to throw open the window and shout at her. Furious at the early wake up, she dressed quickly and quietly shut Carter's door on her way downstairs. Pausing at the bottom, she glanced to her right, and the coffee maker calling her name. She decided that no amount of coffee would make this situation any less irritating, so she cut through the kitchen and went out the side door.

She positioned herself on the walkway and waited.

Rachel gave a little wave and parked the mower. Pulling out her headphones, she smiled at Jen and sauntered over with that half grin and easy sway to her hips. Wearing cargo shorts and a tank top, her lean and lanky body was on full display. Jen mentally facepalmed herself. What the fuck was she doing? Her wedding fling with Madison had definitely reignited her sexual desire but there was no reason to ogle her ex-wife.

Rachel wiped her hands on her shorts, the grin becoming a smirk. "Hey."

Like she was chatting her up at the bar. Oh no, time to nip this in the bud. Jen crossed her arms. "What are you doing?"

Rachel's face showed an utter lack of understanding. "Mowing the lawn."

"It's not your weekend."

Rachel shrugged. "Does it matter? I have time now."

Irritated, she sighed. "Yes, it matters."

Rachel rolled her eyes. "Why? It's my house, too."

"Not when I'm here." How many times could they have this discussion?

Throwing her hands up in the air, Rachel said, "This is ridiculous." She stuffed her headphones into her pocket and walked away. "Fine. You do the lawn. I'm only here for another month anyway."

"What's that supposed to mean? Another month? Are you going back on tour?" Jen followed, dreading the answer.

Rachel stopped and turned. "Yes."

Her heart sunk as she realized the next progression in their conversation. "You haven't told Carter."

Rachel bit her lip, a gesture that got Jen to move mountains before but now only irked her more. "I was hoping you would tell him."

There it was. The setup and she'd walked right into it. Jen covered her face with her hands. "Rachel..."

Rachel touched her arm, and Jen lowered her hands. "It's been five years. I need to get back out there. For my career." She pleaded with Jen. "For my sanity."

Jen knew that Rachel would eventually head back out. She'd limited her concerts to weekend festivals and spent most of the time working on her new album, but this past year, she'd spent more time on the road. But that didn't mean she couldn't woman up and tell their son. "He needs to hear it from you."

"I know, but it's going to break his heart."

"He's going to want to come." Carter's first three years had been spent on the road and then again from age five to seven. Exhausting, exhilarating years. He still talked about those years.

Rachel moved toward her. "Then let him. Jeremy's bringing Lana and Zach." Rachel's longtime bass player toured with his wife and son. And they weren't the only members of the band to bring family.

Jen raised an eyebrow. "Really? You think you can parent and tour?"

"I've done it before."

Jen rolled her eyes. "With me."

"Then come."

It always came back to this push-pull, and she was so tired of it. Jen sighed. "We're not together anymore."

Rachel moved even closer. "That can change, you know. Just say the word."

Alarmed and frustrated, she stepped back from Rachel and the circular nature of their conversation. She wasn't going to change her mind so she gave up. Holding up her hand, she said, "Do what you want. Mow the lawn, leave it, I don't care. I'm getting coffee."

Jen went inside and fixed herself a cup. The mower started up again while she read the paper on her tablet and considered what to make for breakfast. She was halfway through the international news when her ten-year-old son plodded downstairs. "Morning."

Carter yawned and opened the fridge. "Morning." He closed it without taking anything out. "What's for breakfast?"

Jen smiled. "I don't know. What are you making?"

He opened the fridge again and said from inside, "Eggs?"

"Sounds good." She continued reading while her son pulled out the ingredients. Scrambled eggs was the first meal she'd ever taught him to make, and he had been making them alone for almost two years.

"Do you want toast?"

She shook her head. "I'm good." His legs were finally catching up to his feet. Rachel was his birth mother, so he didn't get his height from her, but with those feet, he was definitely going to be tall. She sometimes forgot that he was not her little boy anymore. Maybe he'd be okay with Rachel's decision. She hadn't wanted to push things with Rachel in an attempt to make co-parenting easier, but Rachel kept blurring the lines.

He put a plate in front of her and sat next to her. Shoveling a big bite into his mouth, he asked, "Is Mama mowing the lawn?"

Jen set her tablet aside and grabbed a fork. "Yes."

"Why? Isn't it your weekend?" He talked with his mouth full.

Jen harrumphed. "That's what I said."

"Can we go school shopping today?" And just like that, the subject shifted.

"Sure. Do you have a list?"

"I want a new backpack. And another set of pastels."

She nodded. She'd log into the school's site and see what he actually needed for the year before they left the house. He was growing, but he still needed her guidance. "Let me take a shower, and then we can head out."

They finished breakfast, and Jen went upstairs to get ready. Stepping out of the shower, she glanced out her window and saw Rachel and Carter on the lawn. Carter's body was angled toward the house, and she could see the rapt expression on his face. He was going to be crushed that she was going on tour without him. It would be the first tangible evidence that his parents were separated.

Although it had already been three years since their breakup, they still split their time at the house with Carter, each of them living somewhere else during their off weeks. Even though Jen didn't want to admit it, Rachel had made an effort to stay in Carter's life and co-parent with her. But she couldn't shake the feeling that Rachel would make her the bad guy for insisting Carter stay here. How could she compete with a life on the road?

After getting dressed, she rummaged in her jewelry box for a set of earrings. Spotting her grandmother's pearls, she remembered the last time she'd worn them and the woman she'd met at Jessie's wedding. It was not the first time she'd thought about her in the past few weeks. Memories of her would crop up at odd hours and more than once while masturbating. She'd left a note but hadn't heard from her. It had only been three weeks, but there'd been a connection—well, that was one word for it—that she wanted to explore. Her relationship with Rachel was so complicated. Madison had been easy. She could do easy. She'd almost asked Jess for more details but had stopped short, not wanting to admit to an attraction to someone in her niece's peer group. She just knew that she'd enjoyed the way Madison felt in her arms.

Chapter Four

A white pastry bag appeared on Madison's desk, followed by a green and white Starbucks cup. She glanced up and smiled as the scent of caramel traveled to her nose. "Is this some sort of apology?"

Eamon grimaced. "That bad?"

Nodding, Madison took a sip. Eamon had set her up on a blind date that had gone south pretty quickly. Ashley had picked her up late, taken her to a chain restaurant where the burgers were dry and the fries soggy, then proceeded to talk about herself for the next hour and a half. She had feigned a work emergency and took a cab home.

"David knows another woman—"

She held up her hand, not caring that David was Eamon's partner. There was no way she'd go on another blind date. "No."

His shoulders sagged. "I'm just trying to help."

"I know, but I've got it." She put the pastry bag in her desk drawer and nodded toward the clock.

He glanced at his watch. "Oh crap. I got to go. I'll see you later?"

She nodded and spent the morning reading up on the students she'd be working with that week. Almost one month into her time and she was already getting a handle on the culture at the school. The students at Anne Hutchinson's were a fairly homogeneous group. Affluent, mostly white, from two parent, professional households. They were the children of Brown faculty members, old Providence money, and state politicians. Recent years had seen a shift toward a more diverse class composition in the lower grades. In particular, there had been a move to extend more aid to lower income students. Food insecurity had started to increase among their students, and she wanted to see if she could find a way to make sure everyone had breakfast and lunch. She'd sent along a proposal to her boss, Kathleen, a week ago and was waiting to hear back.

The electronic bell rang for recess, and she walked outside. The school occupied a small city block with three brick buildings clustered together and bounded by playgrounds and green fields. The administrative offices where she worked were located in the primary school building. The staff shared responsibility for watching student interaction on the playgrounds and fields. Madison positioned herself near the primary students. She liked being outside on the warm days.

She watched the ebb and flow around her and thought about her nonexistent love life. Ashley had been her third attempt since summer to connect with someone new. It had failed miserably. She was considering taking a break from looking. The only bright moment in her dating world had been the wedding and Jen, and it wasn't even a date.

"Ms. Hewitt, Ms. Hewitt." A curly headed boy ran up to her. "Carrie is not sharing the tube." The playground had lots of interesting sensory toys for the kids to play with. Inevitably, one of them became the high value object. Today it was the tube. Tomorrow it would be something else.

She crouched. "Have you tried talking to her?"

"Yes. I told her to share. She won't listen."

Madison smiled and said, "Let's go see if we can solve this." She helped them negotiate terms and crisis averted, returned to her spot a few minutes later. She liked working with the primary kids. Their issues were straightforward and solvable. If only her secondary students' problems could be resolved so easily.

Kathleen caught her on the way back from recess and spoke with her usual quick efficiency. "I got your email. It's a good idea. I'm passing it along to the fundraising committee."

They turned the corner to the administrative suite, and leaning across the counter, smiling at Kathleen's administrative assistant, was

Jen from the wedding. Shock ran through Madison, quickly followed by jealousy over the intimacy of Jen's stance with her coworker.

Jen's tailored work clothes looked almost as good on her as that dress from the wedding.

"Speak of the devil." Kathleen nodded at Jen.

Still grinning, Jen looked up, and those sharp features smoothed out in surprise.

"I was just talking about you," Kathleen said while Madison struggled to pay attention. What were they talking about? Her lunch program proposal and the fundraising committee? Her stomach dropped. Jen was on the fundraising committee?

"Madison Hewitt, meet Jen Winslow. Jen's one of the best fundraisers I know."

Jen pushed away from the counter and winked. "Just one of the best? Darling, I can make it rain money."

Jen's voice brought back all those memories that had been on replay for weeks but had no business in her workplace. She could do this. Maybe Jen picked up women all the time and wouldn't even remember her. That was it. Pretend they hadn't met. Ignoring what that swagger did to her, Madison straightened her deep blue V-neck blouse and projected her best professional tone. "Pleased to meet you."

Jen held out her hand. "Likewise." Jen held her hand a fraction of a second too long, and Madison worried she'd say something more. She was so close, Madison could smell her perfume, a rich scent that brought her back to that night. She felt heat rise in her face.

Kathleen cleared her throat, and the rest of the room came back into focus. "Jen, can I see you in my office for a minute?"

Jen didn't move, and Madison held her breath. What was she doing? *Please don't remember me. Not here, not now.* She bit her lip, and Jen slowly smiled.

Kathleen paused on the way toward her office. "Are you coming?"

Jen started to follow, then paused. "I…" She shook her head, and Madison knew that she'd changed her mind about what to say. "It's good to see you."

Madison answered without thinking. "Yeah. You, too." Crap, she did remember. She stood rooted to the spot, her eyes drawn to the way Jen's hips swayed, reminding her of a similar walk:

"Are you trying to get rid of me?" Jen had laughed while Madison lounged in bed.

"Maybe I just want to see the back of you." Madison had slipped off the bed and...

Her face burned as the rest of the explicit memory surfaced.

Jen threw a knowing look over her shoulder as the door closed, and Madison knew she was in trouble. Staving off her panic, she went back to her office.

That night had been a fluke, residual intimacy after Jen had rescued her from Erika. She'd been vulnerable and had reached out to the nearest person who showed her compassion. The dance had been fantastic, and it felt good to be wanted. She needed to get a grip if she was going to work with Jen, but the memory of that walk, that look, and—she sighed—those hands, kept her unfocused for the rest of the day.

Jen barely had time to reflect on the cosmic irony of running into her wedding fling at her son's school before she walked into Kathleen's office and shut the door. Seriously, as if her life needed that kind of complication.

Kathleen leaned back against her desk and folded her arms. "So you and my new social worker..."

She'd known Kathleen for almost fifteen years. Several years before she became the principal of Hutchinson's. Jen arched an eyebrow. "Yes?"

"Want to tell me about it?"

Jen scratched her neck. "We met at Jessie's wedding."

Kathleen's eyes widened, and Jen regretted telling her about her hookup. "She's the woman..."

"Yes." She was only slightly embarrassed at being caught picking up one of Kathleen's employees.

"Oh, Jen, when you branch out, you jump right out of the tree."

Jen heard the defensiveness in her voice. "Well, it's not like I thought I'd see her again."

Kathleen laughed. "True. It's been a while since I saw someone take the wind out of your sails."

Annoyed at being so transparent, Jen snorted. "I was just surprised. I had no idea she worked here."

"Obviously." She sighed. "I wish I'd known before."

That sounded interesting. "Why?"

"I have a project I wanted you to consult with her on." She waved and moved behind her desk. "I'll get someone else to work on it."

She didn't want to give up on seeing Madison again so soon. "What project?" Wasn't she just thinking she didn't need complications? Apparently, not all of her had gotten the memo, especially her mouth.

Kathleen shook her head. "If there's history there, I can't ask her to work with you."

Jen sprawled in a chair. "It's not bad history." An image of a smooth back, dark purple hair spilling down its length, crossed her mind. She smiled.

Kathleen pointed at her. "That is exactly why I don't want you anywhere near this."

Jen knew she'd been caught in a fantasy and came out defensive rather than embarrassed. "Come on, Kathleen. I'm a fucking professional. If I can't keep it in my pants, I won't do it."

Kathleen made a face. "Crude but noted."

Unconcerned with Kathleen's judgment, Jen pressed on. "Now what is it?"

Kathleen held up her hand in warning. "If she so much as breathes a no, I'm giving it to someone else." She outlined a plan to offer free breakfast and lunch to all students, so no child would feel the stigma of free food.

"Tell me how much money you're looking for." When Kathleen threw out a number, Jen tapped her finger against her chin. "It's not an outrageous sum. But it would require some work to sustain it. Why not roll it into the financial aid package?"

"Not with the endowment as is. Besides, I want to offer to all students not just the need-based ones."

Since Hutchinson's was a private school, they didn't receive federal funding. It survived on tuition and an endowment that Kathleen's predecessor had mismanaged. Kathleen had asked Jen to come on the board to help stabilize and grow the endowment. Jen hated to suggest this because it affected her directly, but it was the most direct method of fundraising. "How about raising the cost of tuition?"

Kathleen shook her head, and Jen could almost hear the door close with that idea. "Not for a single program."

Not bothering to wonder why she felt compelled to do it other than if it was important to Madison it was important to her, Jen leaned in to close the deal. "How badly do you want this?"

Kathleen steepled her fingers, making Jen wait before she finally said, "It's a good idea. But I need you to focus on the endowment."

Jen's ego spoke before she was ready. "I can do both." She waited, thinking she might have overplayed her hand, but then Kathleen took a deep breath and said:

"Fine. But not a word of this until I okay it with her."

Jen mimed buttoning her lips, downplaying the thrill of seeing Madison again. "Understood. I'll bring it up at the next board meeting." She didn't anticipate any resistance.

Kathleen grabbed a notebook and said, "Okay, tell me where we're at."

Jen got down to business, but half her mind was occupied with how she'd approach Madison and not just about the project. Should she bring up that night? She wanted to—did she ever—her body still tingled when she'd replay that night in her head, but now that she'd volunteered to work with her, it might not be the best idea. Fuck. Maybe this wasn't such a good idea. Well, she was committed now.

Chapter Five

K athleen knocked on Madison's half-open door and asked, "Do you have a minute?"

She nodded. "Sure. What's up?"

Kathleen walked in and closed the door. "I wanted to check in and make sure you were okay working with Jen."

Her stomach roiled. Oh no, did Kathleen know? After her unexpected run-in, Madison had done some discreet digging around about Jen. Eamon told her that Kathleen recruited Jen to the board, and they were friends. But were they the kind of friends who shared sex stories?

Something in her face must have shown because Kathleen moved closer. "Jen's a formidable woman. I know there's"—she cleared her throat—"history between you. I won't ask you to do this if you feel uncomfortable."

Fabulous. Her boss knew that she'd fucked a board member. She wanted to sink into the floor. "It's fine. Jen and I..." Jen and her, what? Nothing she was going to say was anything she wanted to share with her principal. "I'm good. We're good." A mortifying thought crossed her mind. "Did she say anything?"

Kathleen pursed her lips, clearly uncomfortable with the question.

How much more high school could this get? "I mean, does she know she's working with me?"

Kathleen exhaled. "Yes. She does. In fact, she volunteered."

"Really?" Madison didn't bother to hide her surprise. She figured that her brush-off both after the wedding and when she pretended not to know Jen at school would have deterred her from further contact. But Jen wanted to work with her. She wasn't sure how to feel about that. Did she want to continue where they'd left off? The idea of seeing her again generated a mix of anticipation as she remembered that night, followed quickly by dread as she recalled how things with Erika ultimately worked out.

"Let me know what you decide."

Sensing the opportunity slipping way, she dismissed her doubts and said, "I'll do it."

Madison held the hood open and stared at the engine of her Honda Fit, trying to decipher why it wouldn't start. Nothing obvious stood out. No leaking hoses, smoking parts, just a black and gray engine.

At 6:15 on a Friday night, the lot was mostly empty. She had twenty minutes to get home, change, and head out to her gaming group. Should she just leave it and come back tomorrow?

"Do you need a ride?" a familiar voice asked.

She almost dropped the hood. Jen.

Jen's hand shot out and grabbed it. "Sorry. I didn't mean to startle you."

"Thanks. I've got it." Not wanting to look as incompetent as she felt, Madison gripped the hood with both hands, and Jen let go. She let it drop and pushed to make sure it was closed.

Jen folded her arms and glanced at Madison's car. "Won't start?"

She'd just agreed to the project a few days ago and still hadn't sorted out how she was going to deal with Jen yet. Feeling silly for even opening the hood without a clear idea of what to do, she said, "No."

"Did you figure it out?" Jen pointed to the hood.

Madison cringed inside and confessed. "Uh, no. I have no idea how to fix a car."

Jen laughed. "Then why did you open the hood?"

She shrugged, embarrassed. "I was hoping it was something obvious."

Jen held out her hands and gestured for her keys. "It never is. Do you mind?"

"Do you know cars?" Hope sparked along with a bit of nervous anticipation.

"A little. I've got about twenty years' experience on you."

Madison did some quick math. There was no way Jen was in her fifties. "Just how old do you think I am?"

Smiling, Jen gave her a once-over. Madison felt her face flush. "About twenty-five."

"I'm twenty-eight." She fumbled with her keys and handed them over.

Still smiling, Jen opened the driver's door and got in.

"How old are you?" Madison asked, trying to stay focused on the conversation and not her proximity to Jen.

Jen started the car and nothing happened. She popped the hood and got out. "Forty-two. Do you have jumper cables?"

She shook her head.

Jen brushed past her and used the metal bar to prop the hood open. Leaning over, she looked inside.

"Careful of your clothes." Madison winced as the cuff of Jen's jacket brushed against the engine. Her casual business suit looked dry-clean only.

Jen pulled away. "I'll be right back." Her oxford shoes clicked as she walked across the asphalt.

The age conversation bothered Madison. Jen was not the first older woman she'd found herself attracted to. She'd often had crushes on older women. That was how her relationship with Erika had begun. Madison had enjoyed the flirtation. But the moment it had become real, something changed, and Madison had fallen hard.

Now she found herself unaccountably annoyed that Jen thought she was so young. Did that mean Jen thought less of her? Did young mean unequal? And what did it matter? Why was Madison worried about it? It wasn't like she was planning on a long-term relationship. She just needed to work with her.

That was it. If she was just a kid in Jen's eyes, how would she prove she was professional? Of all the things Erika taught her—and she taught her a lot—it was the danger of crossing personal and professional relationships. If she wanted her project to succeed, she needed to let the attraction to Jen go. It just sucked that she actually needed her help right now with her car.

Jen drove over in a black sports car. She parked in front of Madison's car and with the engine idling, popped the hood. "Can you prop the hood up?" she called as she went to the rear of her car.

Madison hurried forward and saw a boy in the front seat, no doubt Jen's son. She smiled and waved.

He waved back.

"Is that your son?" She found the hood's latch. Her eyes fell on the gold horse emblem—a Porsche—before she finished opening the hood.

Holding a set of jumper cables, Jen looked back and smiled. "Yeah. Carter." She brushed past her and connected them to Madison's car. She moved with expert efficiency, her hands flexing. Madison's world narrowed to those hands, the smooth knuckles and long fingers, tracing across her body, holding her down. She closed her eyes against the memories, but that only made it worse. When she opened them, Jen's smirk said it all. She'd caught Madison staring. So much for keeping it professional.

Jen patted the hood and winked. "Try it now."

Flustered, Madison got into her car. But instead of nothing, a grinding sound started.

Jen waved her hand frantically and shouted, "Stop!"

Madison pulled her hand away from the ignition and got out. "What was that?"

Jen shook her head. "Nothing good. Do you have AAA?"

Madison glanced at her watch. Waiting for a tow truck would take time she didn't have.

"Are you late?"

Nodding, Madison reached for her wallet and cell. "Yeah, I have to be somewhere at seven."

Jen hooked a thumb over her shoulder. "I can take you."

Madison shook her head. "I need to go home and change before I get there."

Jen waved. "Come on. I'll take you home at least, and then you can get ready for your date."

"Oh, it's not a date." She felt compelled to clear that up.

"Oh, okay." Jen's expression stayed blank.

An awkward moment passed between them, and then Jen pulled the jumpers off both cars and started coiling them up.

Madison grabbed her stuff from her car and locked up. She turned back to see Jen leaning into the car and talking with her son. Madison's body warmed. Jen could sell cars looking like that in her tailored pants and dark shirt.

It took her a second to realize Jen was now talking to her. "Where to?"

Madison rattled off her address as Carter crawled in the back, and they got into the car.

"This is my son, Carter. Carter, do you know Ms. Hewitt?"

Madison reached back and shook his hand. He had a grip like his mother's, firm but relaxed, with just the right amount of hold to it. "Nice to meet you."

"Hello." He leaned back.

Grabbing the seat belt, she buckled up. "Thanks for doing this."

Jen started her car and reached toward Madison's head. Her fingers moved toward Madison's face, coming within an inch of her before she panicked and squeaked, "Jen?"

Jen frowned and held up her hand. "Sorry. Just..." She tapped Madison's headrest. "Backing up."

Madison laughed at herself and squelched her nerves. "Of course." She tried not to think of how close Jen's hand was to her neck. If she leaned back and over, Jen's fingers would brush her nape.

"What's wrong with your car?" Carter asked, an effective bucket of cold water.

Madison looked back and bumped into Jen's arm before she pulled it back and shifted into gear. "I don't know."

Jen glanced into her mirror. "Probably the alternator."

"She should bring it to Nat's place."

Jen chuckled. "Nat doesn't work on cars like that." She leaned over, drawing Madison in with a whisper. "She does classic restorations."

Madison stumbled over her thoughts. Were they still talking about cars?

"But she works on yours."

Jen shrugged. "Not always."

Carter kept asking questions, and Jen answered, occasionally looping Madison in. But for the most part, she just listened to them, relieved to no longer be the center of attention.

The conversation flowed from one topic to the next, but Madison wasn't listening to the words. She was hearing the subtext between them and the respect they had for one another that went beyond mother and son. They liked each other and understood if not shared each other's interests. Madison worked with many parents who did neither. That easy rapport Jen had with her son, with Madison, and she suspected with other people, was probably the reason she could "rain money." Despite her outrageous claim, Jen had the goods to back it up. It also made Madison nervous. If Jen was like this with everyone, then Madison was the rule and not the exception.

Jen pulled into her driveway, and Madison opened the door. She said, "It was nice meeting you, Carter."

"You, too." He climbed out and took her place up front.

Shouldering her bag, she glanced at Jen. "Thanks for the ride."

"Of course. Anytime."

Madison was halfway to her door when she heard the car door shut and footsteps behind her. She turned, and Jen stopped in front of her.

Tucking her hands in her pockets, Jen spoke softly. "Hey, if we're going to work together, we should clear the air."

Her stomach dropped. She couldn't do this, not right now. What if Jen wanted more, what if she wanted less? She panicked and took the quick way out. "There's nothing to clear. It was a onetime deal."

Jen's expression was unreadable. "Yeah, of course. That's why I wanted to talk about it. We're on the same page." She spread her arms and stepped back. "We'll set up a time. Get coffee and strategize next steps."

And just like that, they were in professional mode. Madison could do professional mode. "Sounds good."

After an awkward round of great, good, and good night, Jen pulled away, leaving Madison in her driveway, sad and relieved that they'd settled that so quickly. If she was going to work with Jen, there was no way she was going to screw up another job with sex, no matter how hot Jen was.

CHAPTER SIX

Madison turned the corner to her office to find Jen lounging against the wall with two cups of coffee in hand. She wore a more toned-down business casual than last week, but it was still a better outfit than anything Madison owned: a navy and black, glen check coat over a fitted black shirt, with white slacks that ended in a pair of black Chelsea boots. Madison traced Jen's contours and regretted her decision to keep it professional. She knew just how those dips and curves felt.

Jen pushed off the wall and offered her a cup. "Hi." Jen had emailed her the day before to set up the meeting, so Madison felt mentally prepared but apparently not physically, judging from her immediate response to Jen's presence.

Great. Hoping she'd get over it, she forced a nonchalance she didn't feel and took the cup. She caught a whiff of pumpkin spice. "Hi. Sorry I'm late."

Jen's smile was easy and relaxed. "No worries. Is this a good time?"

Madison nodded and stepped back. Just two colleagues working together, nothing to see here. With a calm she didn't exactly feel, she said, "Of course. Come in."

Jen pointed at Madison's drink. "I took a chance. If you don't like pumpkin spice, I'll take it."

"I love it. But if you want it." She paused and handed it back. She didn't want to take the better drink.

Jen recoiled and hefted her own cup. "Oh no, I'm good. Straight up latte."

Madison's insides warmed at Jen's thoughtfulness and her willingness to drink something she obviously disliked also scored points in her book. So much for getting over it quick.

Jen shrugged out of her coat and laid it across the table.

"Let me take that." Madison knew she'd spill her drink if she didn't move that jacket. She hung it on the back of her door and turned to catch Jen staring at her ass.

Jen's eyes widened, and she held up a hand. "I'm so sorry. I... there's no excuse."

Both flattered and relieved that she wasn't the only one still harboring lustful thoughts, Madison cleared her throat and sat. As much as she wanted to put it behind her, this undercurrent between them couldn't go on. She wasn't willing to feel this unsettled each time they met. "Okay, this is awkward."

Jen looked right at her, her expression warm and open. "Then we should talk."

She nodded. "Right."

"Right."

But neither of them spoke. Finally, Jen laughed and extended her hand. "Hi, I'm Jen Winslow."

Madison shook her hand and played along. "Madison Hewitt. It's nice to meet you. I've heard so much about you."

Jen crossed her arms, clearly warming to the act. "Really? And what have you heard?"

Was she flirting? In the spirit of new beginnings, Madison decided to take the question at face value and ignore any subtext. She debated what to tell her. Kathleen may have dubbed her a formidable woman, but Madison's other colleagues had less diplomatic words for her. Everything about Jen said she knew the impact she had. Still Madison's unexpected desire to protect her made her hesitate.

But her hesitation answered Jen's question. "I see my reputation precedes me." Jen chuckled.

She waggled her hand. "Kind of. They say you don't beat around the bush." And that she had a foul mouth.

"And?"

"You're not afraid of coarse language."

Jen burst out laughing. "Coarse language. Is that a polite way to say I use the word fuck in meetings?"

Madison smiled. "Pretty much."

"You don't seem too fazed by me." Jen propped her head in her hand.

Madison shrugged, finally relaxing. Intimidating women were her forte. "Fuck doesn't bother me. Besides, I met you before I knew who you were."

"Yes, you did."

The weight of that memory hung between them. One that Madison had daydreamed about in the weeks since the wedding. A fantasy where they met again at another event and picked up where they had left off. Only this time, Madison didn't toss out her number. But it was a fantasy that did not include Jen showing up at her work for a meeting or having a son attending Hutchinson's. Resigned to the fact that she'd been seeing Jen at her workplace and not in her bedroom, she ended her fantasy.

Pushing aside what could have been, Madison forced a smile. "Let's talk about my proposal."

"Proposal?" Jen's mind was still at the wedding and the last time they were alone together. Working together might be harder than she thought. *So we're not going to talk about the past. Got it.* She suppressed a twinge of disappointment before reminding herself that she wanted to avoid complications. Madison would be a big complication.

"Student lunches?" Madison frowned, her brow crinkling in the most adorable way.

"Of course, right. Yeah, let's talk."

But even with that stern reminder, she listened to Madison speak, trying hard to focus on her words and not the way she spoke with her hands. Hands that had gripped Jen's thighs while she went down on her. *Oh, okay, pay attention. Work here.*

Madison's proposal was good. She wanted to provide lunches for her need-based students. It was a small group; Hutchinson's didn't have the financial resources to offer substantial financial aid packages. At least not yet. Her initial idea was to work with local programs to arrange bagged lunches. Jen could think of at least two nonprofits to ask.

"But bagged lunches are not the most efficient solution, and it comes with its own stigma. Students will pick up on it almost immediately," Madison said.

"Yes, well, what you really need is a kitchen. But..." Jen stopped mid-sentence, her mind spiraling ahead of her mouth. Hutchinson's didn't have a kitchen, but what if they did? Then all students could get lunch, either free or paid for. They could set up an electronic system behind the scenes that all students could use, so no one would know if the lunch was paid for or not. She'd have to secure funding for a building or renovation and a project manager because no way in hell did Kathleen have time to oversee a project of this magnitude.

"Jen?"

Caught in a work daydream this time and not a sexual fantasy, she pulled her attention back to Madison. The small space and their proximity made thinking impossible. She needed a change of scenery. Holding out her hand, she said, "Let's take a walk. I have an idea."

Madison stared at her hand for a second before she took it. "Where are we going?"

Relief poured through her when Madison finally grabbed hold—maybe physical contact was not such a good idea—and then disappointment when she let go almost immediately. Did she really think they'd walk hand in hand through the hallways? She mentally rolled her eyes at her silliness.

Walking always helped her flesh out her thoughts, and seeing the campus with fresh eyes would put it all in perspective. Not bothering with her coat, they toured the campus together: an entire city block situated in the Wayland Square neighborhood with three main buildings—one for the elementary, another for the middle school, and another for the high school—connected to a library and a gym.

"I like your idea," Jen began. "I think Hutchinson's needs to show a social and cultural commitment to diversity beyond its meager financial package. Bagged lunches are a great start, and I can get you that money. Breakfasts will be harder, but there are nonprofits that can help."

She floated a few names and details, but that wasn't what she was looking for. At the edge of the soccer and baseball fields, she turned back and looked over the grounds with a builder's eye. *Yes, right there.* She pointed and delivered her final pitch. "But what if we had a commercial kitchen on premises?"

Madison looked in the direction. "A kitchen?"

"Yes." She held her breath. This was the moment, that edge of decision-indecision that she led so many donors through every year, so familiar and yet so new because it was Madison she was trying to convince, or was it herself? This was unknown territory for her, and it thrilled her.

Madison laughed.

Not the reaction Jen was expecting. Her enthusiasm evaporated. *Okay, back to the drawing board.* Not until she was faced with Madison's laughter did Jen realize that she'd hoped to impress Madison with her vision.

But Madison surprised her and grabbed her hands. "It's fantastic. Can you really do it?"

Jen smiled and squeezed her hands, excitement rushing through her. "Darling, I told you, I can make it rain money."

A few days later, Jen felt a drought coming on. She followed her boss back to his office. As soon as she crossed the threshold, she said, "If I have to listen to that asshole mansplain donor management one more time, I will set fire to his fucking Tesla."

Mark Calhoun motioned for her to close the door and settled behind his desk. Folding his hands in his lap, he leaned back and let her vent.

The he in question, Michael Harris, was their newest team member and ten years her junior. He was hired three months ago at the same level as her, but he was starting to behave more as her superior. "Do you know he won't meet with any women alone?" she asked. "Some kind of 'religious exemption.' That can't be legal. Is Brian really grooming him for his job?"

Mark leaned forward. "Where did you hear that?"

Jen paused mid-stride at the tone of his voice. She couldn't tell if he meant the meeting alone or the grooming bit. Although she had a feeling it was the grooming rumor. She recognized that particular blend of resignation and inevitableness. She lived with that feeling with Rachel and her never-ending arrangement for the past few years. She didn't need it at work. All the fire fled, and she dropped into a chair. "Mark, your poker face is awful."

He rubbed his forehead. "There's been talk."

She frowned. "That's your job."

He smiled. "I don't want it. I like where I'm at."

Mark was the VP for principal gifts. Principal gifts worked with gifts over one million dollars. Only Mark exceeded her skill at bringing in donors. But Brian was the VP for all the college's development units, including principal gifts.

"Michael doesn't have the qualifications for it," Jen said, not that her opinion mattered. Principal gifts was a boys' club, and she'd spent years bucking the system only to have the door slammed in her face again and again. "He's done less than three years in principal gifts and most of that at Penn."

"Yes, but in that time, he brought in more money than both of us combined in the last four years."

Jen snorted. "A point he's happy to make every chance he gets. But I did my homework. It all comes from his family. The Harris Foundation and its subsidiaries account for two-thirds of that two hundred and fifty million dollars."

He smiled. "Eighty-three million is still a lot of money."

She narrowed her eyes. "But not more than we raised last year. He's a one-trick pony."

"But with the right connections." He shrugged.

"And the right equipment." She tossed that one out there and waited for Mark to say something to defend the misogyny in her field. She had danced around this subject with him before, and he'd never come out and said it, but he knew the cards were stacked against women, particularly in principal gifts, where so much of the money rested with white men.

He surprised her by agreeing. "Yes. But Brian's a couple years away from retiring. You've got time."

She left his office an hour later. She couldn't shake the feeling that her work life was about to get much harder. Despite Mark's assurances, she didn't trust the old boys' network to ever work in her favor. She used the same tools and had her own family name and connections, but she always hit the gender wall. In a few years, she'd be hitting the crispy edge of burnout from fighting the same battles, and she was getting too old to work so hard for another idiot. Something was going to have to give. She needed to do something that felt good.

Something like Madison's project. Pulling out her phone, she texted Kathleen. *Drinks tonight?*

A few minutes later, she got a reply. *Sure. When and where?*

Kathleen put her drink down. "A kitchen? Are you serious? I'm desperately trying to hold the finances together, and you want to talk about an expansion? Not to mention the additional time it would take to manage a project of that magnitude. Then staffing it and getting it up to code. I just asked you to find some money for bagged lunches." Her words were more combative than her tone, but they were still on the edge.

Jen had invited her out for cocktails because she knew she had to get Kathleen a little bit buzzed to break the idea to her. Kathleen was under a tremendous amount of pressure, but the kitchen idea was a good one. Jen just needed to pull her back in and lead her there. "I can do this. You know I can."

Kathleen rubbed her forehead. "Jen…"

She leaned in. "Let me try it."

Kathleen shook her head. "It's too much. A new cafeteria? I don't have the resources for an expansion."

"I know. I will find a way to take care of that."

"What about the endowment?"

"They're two separate streams. I can manage them both."

Kathleen sighed. "And then maintaining it. There are food service regulations."

"We can outsource that. Kathleen, please let me try this."

Kathleen narrowed her eyes. "Why does this mean so much to you?"

Good question. Why was she so invested in it? She was already committed to helping Kathleen grow the endowment. Why add on work? Why not do something else? She could tell other people, including Kathleen, that it was the project that drew her in; she did believe in it, but she would not lie to herself. This was Madison's project, and that was the real reason. She'd seen the way Madison still looked at her when she didn't think Jen was watching. She didn't want to close the door on something more just yet. She just needed more time. "Because I can."

Kathleen stared at her for a full minute before she said, "This is a side project. Your first priority is getting a lunch program working with Madison. Once that's set up, you can do this."

She smiled, and Kathleen held up her hand. For a moment, she worried that her friend would call her on the real reasons behind the hard sell. She knew it wouldn't hold up to close scrutiny. "But if this takes away from the endowment, it ends before it begins."

Hopefully, her plan to get closer to Madison wouldn't suffer the same fate.

Jen arrived at school a few minutes before class let out. Unable to wait in one place, she moved through the sea of students and parents, keeping an eye out for Madison. A little giddy at the prospect of seeing her, she wanted to share the good news, but she didn't want to seem too eager. Casually bumping into her at pickup would cover her intentions.

A hand curled around her forearm, and she jumped. Apparently, she was more nervous than she thought. But before she could react, the woman behind the hand pulled her into a tight hug. "It's so good to see you. I've missed you."

Shawn. Jen had filed Shawn under "don't shit where you eat." Shortly after her separation, they'd had a brief relationship that had flamed out just as fast it began. Carter had told her that Delia, Shawn's daughter, was back in town, but she hadn't thought much about it. She had managed to avoid her for the first full month of school.

Jen extricated herself from the embrace and stepped back. A lead ball settled in her stomach, and all her anticipation at seeing Madison bled away. She forced herself to do the social niceties. "How was France?"

Shawn smiled and hitched up her purse. "Lovely. It was so good for Delia to experience it firsthand, you know what I mean? And the food, the wine. Of course, Kim worked the entire time."

Jen nodded. "Of course." She'd heard that line before. In the beginning, they'd bonded over distant partners. In hindsight, Jen knew she'd confused her loneliness and Shawn's sympathy for compatibility and love. Bringing up Kim as the emotionally unavailable partner might have worked in the past, but there was no way she was walking this road again.

"How's Carter? Are you and Rachel still sharing the house?"

Jen couldn't suppress a smile at the thought of her son. "He's good. He's happy to have Delia back." Even if Jen wasn't pleased to see Delia's parents again, she could acknowledge that. Delia was a good kid, and Jen had missed her, too. However, she wasn't about to answer the Rachel question.

Shawn moved closer. "And you? How've you been?"

Jen had the good sense not to shout, "Like you fucking care." Because in some small way, Shawn did, but only insofar as it got her into Jen's bed. Jen grinned and pulled her most professional persona from her bag of tricks. "I'm good. Really good. I met someone."

At first, it was a lie meant to push Shawn away, but then Madison appeared in her mind's eye. She had met someone. But it was a bit too soon to be sharing.

Shawn's face fell just a fraction, and Jen felt a sense of satisfaction that it had hit home. A sharper feeling jabbed her with guilt for using Madison as a weapon. In hindsight, she'd known Shawn hadn't loved her, but Shawn had definitely hurt her by going back to Kim. Shawn glanced around as if to see if someone had overheard their conversation. "Oh, good, good. Well, I should be going. We should get together. All of us. I'd love to meet your new…"

Jen didn't supply her with a term but instead nodded and said, "Sure. We'll see what the kids want." Like that was going to happen.

They parted in opposite directions. Jen shook it off, wishing once again that she hadn't slept with someone she would run into every day. Her desire to see Madison cooled somewhat with Shawn's arrival. She was a stark reminder of how close all the pieces of her life were connected and how mistakes in one area could affect another.

Carter found her a few minutes later. "Hey."

Jen turned and slung an arm over his shoulder. "You're getting tall."

"Stop." He bumped his shoulder into her stomach. But he didn't move away. She tucked him into her side, enjoying the closeness with him.

Halfway down the hall, Jen spotted Madison talking with a student. On the heels of her Shawn conversation, she wasn't so sure she wanted the two to see each other. Still, she couldn't ignore the spark of possibility she'd had imagining Madison as her girlfriend. But before she could move one way or the other, the student walked off, leaving Madison alone and looking right at her.

Jen panicked and pretended not to see her. She regretted it when Madison's smile faltered and faded away. Fuck. She should put on her big girl panties and talk to her; it was the reason she'd come to school early. Fuck Shawn and her mind games.

"Can I go over to Del's this week?"

Ignoring her rising guilt, she focused on her son. "I think so. I'll have to check with her mom."

Carter paused, and Jen did, too. He looked up and said, "His."

"Who?" How had she lost the thread of this conversation so quickly? She looked over, and Madison was gone. Damn.

"Del. He's a boy. He told me. He used to be a girl. But now he's a boy."

Jen digested that for a half second before realizing that her son was watching her reaction very closely. Time to woman up. "That's great. I'm so glad he felt he could share that with you." She wondered if Shawn was aware of her child's gender identity yet. There was no way she was going to be the first to tell her. She cared about Del, and she'd support him with whatever he needed. But she had her own shit to deal with without getting involved with Shawn again.

Chapter Seven

Madison waited outside the school, checking her app to see when her Uber was going to arrive. She'd accepted the ride without paying attention to who was giving it. Now she was staring at the driver's picture, and her heart froze. Travis Chambers, her birth father. What were the odds? Shit. She hadn't seen him in years, and there was no way she was getting into a car with him.

She turned and headed back into the school. She fumbled with her security card and finally opened the door. Her hands shook so badly that she dropped her phone, and it skittered across the tile entrance.

"Shit."

"Careful."

Of course, it was Jen. Madison hadn't been able to stop thinking about her since, well, since the wedding. But she'd disappeared after coming up with the kitchen idea last week, and Madison had no idea why. She'd kept a lookout for her during pickup times, hoping to get back on track. Talk about the project or maybe something else. But when she finally spotted her, Jen had turned away. She still felt the sting of rejection. Unsure of where she stood with Jen or the project, Madison avoided any contact. Let Jen do the work of connecting with her. It was a business relationship they had. But none of that mattered now that her birth father was coming to pick her up in his Uber, and she had no other way home.

Jen scooped the phone up and handed it to her. Her smile froze, and she said, "What's wrong?"

Madison shook her head, and her voice shook when she spoke. "My Uber. I'm not taking it."

Jen nodded, looking slightly confused. "Okay. You need a ride. I can take you home."

All of a sudden, it didn't matter if Jen had snubbed her. She was here now. Madison gripped her arms. "Thank you."

"Come on." Jen opened the door just as a tan Camry pulled up.

The window rolled down. "Hey, I thought that was you."

Madison froze. Travis Chambers looked exactly like he had when child services had pulled her from the house for the last time. Now in his mid-fifties, he still had her eyes and that ruddy complexion associated with chronic alcoholism. He opened his door and got out. "Hey, squirt."

She folded her arms, falling back on old emotional patterns, hiding her anger under ice. "I'm not your squirt."

He took in Jen's proximity and planted his hands on his hips. "Well, aren't you going to introduce me?"

"No." She spoke without hesitation, hearing how flat she sounded.

He extended a hand to Jen. "Travis Chambers. Madi's father."

Jen did not take it. Her hand against the small of Madison's back steadied her. She took comfort in her touch.

He frowned and pulled back.

Madison cleared her throat. "You're not my father."

Travis glanced at her, then back at Jen. "So what are you, her sugar mama?"

Madison ignored his question. "I thought you were working in Pawtucket."

He circled his car and patted the hood. "Still am. It's a busy night. Ready to go?"

Jen wrapped her arm around Madison's waist. The touch grounded her. Leaning in, she whispered, "I've got this, okay?"

Relieved and grateful, Madison nodded and stayed put.

Travis moved toward her, but Jen slipped between them. She pulled out her wallet and extracted a couple of bills. Folding them over her fingers, she slipped them into his palm. "I'm taking her home. Here's a little extra for your trouble."

He took the bills and glanced at Madison. "So that's how it's going to be."

Buffered by Jen's strength, Madison stared him down. "That's how it's always been."

"Suit yourself." Shaking his head, he slammed the door and drove out of the parking lot.

Madison sagged against Jen.

"Are you okay?"

Comforted by her warmth and calm confidence, Madison nodded. "I didn't expect to see him. I feel like an idiot. I should have paid attention to the app."

Jen rubbed along her back, and her tone soothed her. "You're not. How long has it been?"

"Years." Taking a deep breath, she pulled away from the security of Jen's hand. Why was Jen always rescuing her? She wasn't some damsel in distress, and she didn't want Jen to think that. She cared what Jen thought because she wanted Jen to see her as an equal, if not personally, then at least professionally. Whatever existed between them, she wanted to avoid creating a power dynamic. She'd been down that road and had paid the price for it. But being strong all the time also had its costs, and right now, it was a relief to have someone care enough to step in and help out.

Jen nodded toward the parking lot. "Shall we?"

Madison followed her. She'd dealt with her birth family before but not in recent years. Her birth father had drifted in and out of her birth mother's life, so he'd never really been all that parental before her removal. But he held on to their blood connection whenever he saw her, a sort of primal right. After the last "visit" with him, she'd finally cut all ties and left him in her past. Seeing him had shaken loose those memories filled with anger, hurt, and rejection. Feelings she wasn't ready to have around Jen but was having anyway.

All Jen's protective instincts had kicked in from the moment she'd seen the panicked look on Madison's face until she ushered her into the car. Now that it was over, she wasn't sure what to do.

Getting into the car, she looked over at Madison, and the last thing she wanted to do was leave her alone. Her own run-ins with her mother left her drained. She could only imagine what Madison was feeling right now with who knew what kind of history between her and that man. She felt terrible for brushing her off and had been hoping to find her alone but not like this. The least she could do was offer to listen. "How about a drink?"

Madison looked over and smiled, her color returning a bit. "That would be awesome."

The engine revved, and the radio blared. Turning it down, Jen stretched her hand behind Madison's headrest and backed out. She let the wheel spin in her hand and put it in gear.

Madison pulled her head up. "Thank you for stepping in. I kind of froze."

"Not a problem." She'd worried that she might have overstepped. Given their last few conversations, she wasn't sure where the boundaries were. Were they friends? Colleagues? Sleeping together had really fucked up her normal social script. "You don't have to tell me anything, but if you want to talk about it, I'll listen."

Madison shifted, and Jen was struck by her beauty full on. "Not much to tell. My birth mother lost custody of me when I was fourteen, and he was already out of the picture. He's pretty much the same person you met tonight. No layers to that onion."

Jen chuckled. "Yeah, well, my family has got plenty of onions. It's exhausting." Maybe if she shared a little of her own history, Madison would share hers.

"Like your mother?"

Jen glanced at her, momentarily confused. "Right, I forgot you met her. I'm so sorry."

Madison smiled. "She was something."

Jen flushed at the memory of Madison playing her date. Not many people stood up to her mother outright. Although Jen hated to admit it, it was a quality both she and her mother shared.

"How much do I owe you?"

Still thinking about the wedding, Jen didn't understand the question. "For what?"

"I saw you hand Travis some money. How much do I owe you?"

Offended that she'd even think that, Jen said, "Not a thing."

"Jen…"

Jen glanced over and gave her the look, the one that stopped Carter in his tracks.

Apparently immune, Madison frowned and crossed her arms.

Why wasn't she letting this go? Jen tried another tactic. "Besides, it's a business expense."

"How do you figure?" Madison asked. She wasn't buying it.

Committed to the ruse, Jen said, "I was going to set up another time to talk about your project anyway. This saves me the trouble."

"That's pretty flimsy."

Jen agreed but didn't say so. She shrugged and said the first thing that came to mind. "Well, if you must pay me back, you could owe me a favor." How ridiculous. She sounded like the godfather.

Madison shifted in the passenger seat, her expression unreadable. "What kind of favor?"

Jen's mouth went dry as several "favorable" ideas occurred to her in graphic detail, but then she really looked at Madison, and her heart wrenched. Social interactions were currency for Jen, but she could see Madison only lost in those types of transactions. As much as she wanted to change that for her, today was not the day.

"I gave him fifty dollars." A small price to get rid of him.

"I'll pay you back next week."

Jen didn't fight her anymore and shifted the topic. "Still no car?"

"No. It's at the shop." Madison's body posture relaxed slightly.

Jen took that as a good sign and kept the conversation going. "Why so long?" It had been a few weeks since she'd picked her up in the school parking lot.

"It needs a new alternator and some other expensive part. I can't afford it right now." She said it so nonchalantly, Jen assumed money was often an issue. Now she really didn't want the fifty dollars.

Despite telling Carter that Nat didn't fix cars like Madison's, Jen wondered if it was something she would be willing to fix. She tried not to take advantage of her friend's skills, but for Madison, she'd make an exception. Maybe she could bribe Nat with some new fishing gear. She'd been complaining about her current rod the last three times they'd fished together.

Jen racked her brain to come up with something more to say, but for once, came up empty.

Madison finally spoke up. "Where's Carter?"

Relieved to answer a question instead of asking one, she said, "He went home with a friend."

"Then what—"

"Am I doing at the school? Last-minute committee meeting." The conversation stopped again, but the silence felt less awkward, and Jen didn't want to fill it with small talk.

Jen took her to the Salted Slate off Wayland Avenue. It was a one-story brick building with a black slate bar that split the room into two separate seating areas. Jen directed them toward the bar and ordered Maker's Mark neat. She turned and smiled. "A Cosmo?"

Madison grinned and sat at the bar. "You remembered."

Jen held the Cosmo in contempt for both its popularity and the type of women—always women—who drank the pink concoction. Madison broke that mold for her, and she spoke without thinking. "Of course. How could I forget?"

Madison just laughed. "Yes, how could you. No Cosmo for me tonight." Madison glanced at the bar list and asked the bartender, "Do you have cider on tap?" The bartender shook her head but offered a couple bottle options. Madison picked one and put the menu down when their drinks arrived.

Jen held up her glass. "Here's to shitty families."

Madison smiled and clicked her bottle against the glass. "To shitty families."

Jen took a sip and cast a sidelong glance at Madison. She seemed more relaxed now that they were out of the car. She took another sip and grabbed the menu. Maybe she could get her to talk more if she fed her. "Are you hungry? I'm going to order something. Or do you need to be somewhere?"

Madison shook her head and leaned in. "Have you eaten here before?"

Jen smelled her perfume, the same scent that had lingered on her dress after Jess's wedding. Jen kept her head down, acutely aware of how close Madison was to her. Focus. She was here to be supportive, not hit on her again. "Yes. I like the raw bar."

Madison made a disgusted noise, and Jen looked up. Yep, too close. Madison's hazel eyes shone bright and clear. Jen slowly pulled back and pretended to scrutinize the menu. She was here as a friend. "So no raw bar for you."

"No, thanks."

She picked another shareable appetizer. "Charcuterie and cheese plate?"

"Charcuterie?"

"A meat board. Usually cured. Salami, ham, that kind of thing." Madison smiled. "That sounds good."

Jen got the bartender's attention. She ordered and turned back to Madison. She was sitting in profile, watching the bartender make a drink. Even though she'd seen her a handful of times since the wedding, she hadn't been able to look without being seen. The purple hair was gone, replaced by a sedate brown that fell past her shoulder blades. She had a gently upturned nose, lips, and eyes that gave her a contemplative look. Jen wanted to lean in and kiss those lips again. Stay focused. Friend. "Where's the purple hair?" Friends asked about hair, especially purple hair, purple hair that Jen found so hot.

Madison's grin widened. "Did you like it?"

There was an earnestness to the question that caught Jen completely off guard. She was expecting flirtation and got self-doubt. "Yeah, I did."

Madison nodded. "Me, too. I think I'll do it again."

"So you don't always color your hair?"

The bartender brought their food and a couple small plates. Since she'd have something in her stomach, Jen ordered another drink. They divvied out the food, and Jen took a bit of the soppressata. It was perfect—salty, slight spice, a little sweet.

"Oh, I do it every summer and sometimes over winter break. But the purple was something new. I really liked it. How about you?"

Jen tilted her head. "Do I dye my hair? My line of work doesn't lend itself to that kind of individuality. There's a certain decorum required to convince someone to hand over twenty-five million dollars."

"Then you always look this nice." Madison's eyes widened, and she bit her lower lip. The nervous gesture brought back a very specific memory of Madison sprawled across her bed while Jen slowly moved down her body. Desire pooled between her legs. What else did Madison think about her? Time to find out.

Emboldened, Jen teased her. "Apparently."

Madison blushed and looked away.

Jen leaned in; Madison did not pull back. "Can I ask you something personal?"

Madison made eye contact and nodded.

"Would you have slept with me if you'd known who I was?" Now it was out there, and they could talk about it instead of pretending it didn't exist.

Madison wrapped her hands around her bottle and turned it without looking up. "I don't know. Probably." Then she glanced up and gave Jen the same smile from the wedding. That cocky but underconfident smile. Fuck. She felt herself get wetter. "You were pretty irresistible."

Jen blushed this time, but she tried to hide it with a bit of bluster. She'd lost control of the conversation. "Naturally."

"This is new to me." Madison looked up and held her gaze.

"Sleeping with women?" Jen teased, grabbing hold of the conversation again.

Madison laughed. "No, I've been with women. I've never had a one-night stand."

Neither had Jen. She sipped her drink and moved closer. "Aw. You make it sound so tawdry when you call it that."

"What would you call it?" Madison's voice dropped an octave.

Jen leaned in and whispered, "A weekend affair."

Madison quirked her lips up, a tiny smirk that Jen desperately wanted to kiss. She was so close. "That implies more than one night. We only had the one."

"True." What were they talking about again? So much noise when all she wanted to do was lean in and capture those lips.

"What about you? Are you in the habit of picking up women at weddings?"

Stay focused, Winslow, she's still talking to you. Jen switched to conversational autopilot while she corralled her licentious thoughts.

"Weddings, no. Bars, sometimes, when an attractive woman offers to pay and sometimes when they don't." Okay, so that was a no-go on reining it in.

"Is that what's happening now?" Madison tilted her head and gave her a look that dared her to make the next move.

"Why? Is that what you want?" Her stomach fluttered, and she leaned closer.

Madison broke first. "Yes. And no." She exhaled. "It's just that I've been here before."

Jen deflated inside. Great. She reminded Madison of someone else, and it wasn't flattering. She took a guess. "Erika?"

"Yes."

She tamped down her natural aversion to that comparison and took the friend road instead. "What happened with her?"

Madison took a sip of her drink. "She wouldn't leave her wife. I don't blame her so much as myself for getting involved with her in the first place. It's my fault for not recognizing it earlier."

"You broke up with her?"

"Yes, and it was not good. She killed my academic career. I was working toward a PhD, and she moved my grants, essentially cutting my funding as well as my contacts. I'm lucky that I finished with a master's."

As if she wasn't already pissed at Erika for being a general asshole, Jen found herself holding on to a whole new level of disgust and anger. "I'm sorry. She's a dick. I know I told you this before, but you deserve better."

Like me. I'm better.

Madison laughed. "She is a dick."

Now that she knew the specifics, Jen could understand Madison's reticence about getting involved with her. Even though she resented being put in the same category as such an obvious asshole. She knew from their night together that Madison had been hurt before, but she didn't realize how deep the cuts had been. She needed to back off a little, both for her sake and Madison's.

"I spoke with a couple Johnson and Wales alums, and they're willing to donate the seed money to get the bagged lunch program up and running. I wanted to get your thoughts about how you wanted to disperse it."

"So soon?" Madison looked surprised. It had been less than three weeks since Jen had offered to help. "I can't believe you were able to do this so fast."

Jen laughed. "I did tell you I could make it rain money."

"I thought you were exaggerating."

It was a boast that should have embarrassed her, but it didn't. She was good at her job and didn't hide it. She shrugged. "It's not a big amount. I spend my entire work life raising millions of dollars."

Madison pinned her with a look and asked, "Why are you doing this?"

Jen avoided her usual glib, "Because I can" and answered honestly. "The work I do is to make more money for future generations. It's rewarding, but sometimes a little soulless. I want to build something that has immediate consequences."

As she spoke, the truth of her words resonated much deeper than she was expecting. This project had taken on a life of its own. What had started as a way to get closer to Madison had become so much more. She wanted to do this for Madison as much as for herself. She was tired of working for the Brians of the world. Sure, it wasn't a perfect solution. Hutchinson's was a private school with all the social barriers that came with private education. But it was trying to extend its community in new ways. She could help fund that for the future and for the student body right now.

"There's a company that a few of the parents use. Fresh from the Field. They deliver complete lunches. We could create an account for the year and get kids set up in the next few weeks or sooner if you have a place to store them."

Jen watched Madison do the numbers in her head. "There are twenty-two kids who qualify. Do they deliver the whole week? That would be over one hundred lunches we'd need to store."

Jen leaned over the counter to search for a pen. The bartender caught her looking and wordlessly handed her one. Grabbing a cocktail napkin from a nearby stack, she flipped it open and started writing her thoughts. "This would be so much easier to do if we actually had a kitchen and dedicated cafeteria staff. We'll need refrigeration at the school, or I bet I could get a few parents to store and transport them. Have you considered just having them donated to the students' houses?"

Madison nodded. "I want to keep them as a school benefit. I want to make sure their school needs are addressed first. If we need to address food for the whole family, we can do that but not as a first step."

"That makes sense. What we really need is that kitchen. We need more money."

"Can you do that? Get a kitchen?"

Even though her pride and sexual desire had gotten her into this project, she wasn't about to let it go, but this project was beginning to grow beyond her current capacity, and she needed to prioritize her endowment work. "Maybe. I don't know. I'll have to work further afield of my normal circle. I can't double dip from the same donors. But there's enough money in Providence—well, Rhode Island—for our endowment and this project."

"Really?"

Jen gave her a brief overview of the connections between business, money, and family in general and Rhode Island in particular. Surprised by Madison's interest and impressed by her intellect, she lost track of time as she spoke. Madison asked thoughtful questions and made intuitive leaps that her gift officers struggled to grasp.

"And where do you fit in?"

"I'm faded aristocracy."

Madison gave her a questioning look.

"It means I have the name but none of the money. I still belong socially not financially. It opens doors."

Madison shook her head. "There's so much about this I didn't know."

Jen spread her hands. "Anything you want to know, I'll share." Her watch chimed, and she glanced at the text. Carter's after-school date was over, and he was heading home. Disappointed, she held up her watch. "Except some other time. Carter's on the way back." She reached into her pocket and pulled out her wallet.

Madison grabbed her work bag and her own wallet.

"I've got it." Jen waved the bartender over and handed her the card.

"You helped me," Madison protested.

Jen leveled a look at her. "Because you can't afford to get your car out of the shop." She tapped her finger against her empty bourbon glass. "Besides, I had the heftier bill. And remember, business expense."

"We barely talked about the project."

Jen smiled. "Next time."

Madison relented, but Jen could tell the next time, she'd have to let her pay. Next time. Did she want a next time? Of course, she did. She needed it for the project. But she knew what she was really thinking. She liked Madison. She liked her at the wedding when she was a convenient diversion and then later when she was very pleasant company. That hum of sexual attraction and history buzzed a couple times during their talk, but there was something more to their interaction this time. Something deeper and Jen found herself wanting more of it.

As they headed back to her car, Madison thanked her again for the ride and the food. They drove in silence for the few minutes it took to get to Madison's place. Jen mulled over a few different ways to ask to see her again that didn't involve their work project, but without overt permission from Madison, she didn't think she could ask.

Madison unbuckled her seat belt and paused for half a second. "Well, thank you again."

Jen opened her mouth, but before she could say anything, Madison opened the door and got out. "Good night."

Shit. Feeling a mix of disappointment and frustration, Jen waited until Madison let herself into her apartment and then pulled away. She laughed at herself. What was she doing flirting anyway? She could read the signs, and Madison had said it herself. She wanted them to be a one-time deal. But not all the signs had said no. At least she knew why Madison was giving her mixed signals. Jen groaned. Why wasn't it ever simple?

CHAPTER EIGHT

Seeing Travis threw Madison off-balance for the next few weeks. Jen's kindness and support during and afterward messed with her resolution to keep a distance. Each time Jen's name showed up in her email, a thrill coursed through her along with a slight tinge of disappointment when they turned out to be highlights on the progress of their project. Only the first email had been personal.

I wanted to let you know I got the money. You know you didn't have to, but I understand why you did. I'm here if you need to talk. Jen.

She could hear her voice in those scant few lines, and it made her day better just hearing from her. She reread that email more than once, not sure what she should do or say, so she did nothing, and Jen's emails continued but with a work focus.

She left work late and had enough time to shower and change before heading to David and Eamon's party. She knew better than to show up empty-handed, so she grabbed a six-pack of cider and store-bought cookies. Her mother would be horrified. She spotted David in front of the fridge as she made her way through the people gathered in their kitchen.

David caught her eye as she put the cookies down. "Hey, there."

"I brought cookies and cider." She hefted the six-pack.

He smiled. "The essentials. Cooler's out back. So is Eamon." He leaned in and gave her a one-armed hug. He whispered, "If he's on that grill, move him off."

She smiled. "Understood." Eamon burned more chicken than he cooked.

She opened the back door and stepped out on the deck. Sure enough, Eamon was at the grill. She scanned the rest of the partygoers and spotted Ashley talking with a small group of people around the firepit. She hadn't seen her since their blind date and had forgotten she was a mutual friend of Eamon and David. Ashley waved. Too late to pretend she didn't notice. Wanting to avoid her but unable to be outright rude, Madison waved back and pointed to the grill, indicating she was going to be busy. Ashley smiled and nodded before she turned back to her group.

Eamon put down his tongs and gave her a hug. "Hey, you made it."

She handed him a bottle, and he opened it. She repeated the process until they both had something to drink. She took a pull and glanced at Ashley. She shouldn't look, that would just encourage her, but if she shifted a little, Ashley's view would be obscured, and then maybe she'd forget that Madison was there.

"What are you doing?"

"Hmm? Nothing." Embarrassed at being caught, she played it off.

He waved. "You're doing some sort of odd movement here."

Madison stopped moving and reluctantly said, "I'm hiding from Ashley."

He slathered the chicken with more barbecue sauce, and flames shot up. Madison cringed. He swung his tongs wide and almost hit her in the head. "Why? It wasn't that bad."

She snatched the tongs out of his hands while gently hip checking him off the grill. It was a practiced move. "Yes. Yes, it was."

He moved off, not looking the slightest bit annoyed. "Why? She seems like your type."

If by type, he meant a woman, then yes. But she'd had no chemistry with her, and they lacked the same interests. Nothing like that electric tingle she felt around Jen. "She's nowhere near my type."

He put his hands on his hips. "Well, what's your type?"

Jen's smiling face was still in her thoughts, and she spoke off the cuff. "Someone more like Jen Winslow." As soon as the words left her mouth, she regretted it. She could have said anyone's name, why Jen? Saying it aloud made it more real than it already was.

"Jen Winslow." His voice shot up a couple octaves.

She slapped his shoulder and looked around, hoping no one was in earshot. She didn't need her business spread about the neighborhood. There was no way she was telling Eamon about their summer tryst, especially now that Jen was working with her. "Shh."

He let out a low whistle and shook his head. "Shit. Really? You know she's on the board, right?"

"Yes. I do. As a matter of fact, I'm working with her on a food security project." She tried to be nonchalant, but her stomach roiled. Her boss already knew about it. She did not want any of her colleagues to know. She wasn't ashamed of having sex with her, but she didn't need her personal life crossing into her work life again. And he was the worst at keeping secrets.

"You know they're friends?" Eamon took a sip of his cider while David came out carrying a bowl and extra serving utensils. Madison flipped half the chicken thighs.

"Who?" David set the bowl on the table. He dropped a pair of tongs into the salad and stuck a spoon in the potato salad.

"Jen Winslow and Kathleen." Off David's look, Eamon clarified. "Principal Kathleen."

David finished his work on the buffet and turned. "And?"

Eamon waved him off. "Honey, you're not listening."

"I am listening. I know who Kathleen is. It was Jen Winslow that had me off guard. I didn't know she was on your board." He put his hands on his hips.

"I thought I told you," Eamon said.

Confused, Madison asked, "How do you know Jen?"

"She lives in the neighborhood. That arts and crafts bungalow over on Angell Street. Across from the park."

Eamon's face screwed up. "I thought that belonged to Rachel."

"It does. Rachel and Jen share the house."

Her stomach churned. Who was Rachel? Madison went over every conversation she'd had with Jen and came up with nothing. Jen had never mentioned that she lived with someone. A familiar feeling of betrayal clawed up her throat. "Rachel?"

"Her ex-wife." David smiled. "They have a kid."

"Carter," Madison breathed his name, and the lump in her throat shifted. At least she knew that much.

"Yeah, that's his name. Anyway, they split their time in the house together. Rachel lives with Carter while Jen stays somewhere else and vice versa. But I think she's on tour right now."

Her mind whirled with this new information. She hadn't given the details of Jen's life much thought since she'd relegated her to the work zone. But their last two conversations had been more than work related. They'd full-on flirted with each other. Knowing about Rachel, both her name and how she fit into Jen's life, made her a bit nauseous. It was too close to the way Erika had lived her life.

David handed Madison two plates. Still caught up in her thoughts, she stared at them for a moment before she realized what he wanted and started pulling chicken off the grill, then passed the full plate to David.

"Madison said Jen's more her type," Eamon said at bit too loud for Madison's taste. Now she regretted saying anything at all.

David gave her a delighted look. "Oh, honey, she's scrumptious." His approval reassured her; he was a far better judge of character than Eamon.

Eamon made a face. "She's a bit scary for me."

David put his hand on his husband's shoulder. "Honey, most lesbians are too scary for you. Jen's a sweetheart. Come on. I need you in the kitchen."

"What about the chicken?"

"Madi's got that covered. There's more in the bucket." David winked at her and pulled him away.

Madison opened the lid, and sure enough, David had prepared an entire bucket of marinated chicken. She adjusted the burners and pulled out more. What else did Jen hide? Worry gnawed at her, but before she could go much deeper, someone came up behind her, slung an arm over her shoulder, and kissed her cheek. Startled, she almost burned her hand.

"Hey, girl. I thought that was you." Ashley's breath smelled like a brewery, and her cologne was too strong.

Breathing through her mouth, Madison shifted away, but she was trapped in front of the grill with nowhere to go. She scanned the deck, looking for someone or something to interrupt them, but there was nothing. She was going to have to deal with this herself.

"We need to reschedule our date. Eamon said you were swamped."

"I still am." She should just say she wasn't interested and leave it at that.

Ashley moved to her. "Teacher, right?" Madison said no, but Ashley kept talking. "I could never do that. Babysitting all those kids every day."

Annoyed at this common misconception, she defended her colleagues. "There's a difference between babysitting and teaching."

Ashley waved. "Of course, but you've got to admit that a lot of your time is spent managing poorly parented kids."

Although she had a point, there was no way Madison was going to admit it. "No, I don't. And I'm not a teacher. I'm a social worker." Was this the second or third time she was telling her? The edges of the chicken were starting to burn. She needed to focus on the grill and not the woman next to her.

"Oh. Cool. What's that like? Getting kids jobs and shit?"

"Not exactly." Distracted by the meat, she didn't bother to elaborate.

"Well, what do you do when you're not doing that?"

"I have a gaming group." She answered automatically. This conversation felt familiar.

"Neat. I play Cards against Humanity."

"It's less board games and more like Dungeons and Dragons." Where was that plate David had given her?

Ashley leered and leaned in. "Do you dress up and shit? You're not one of those costume players, are you?"

Madison plucked the last of the chicken off the grill and grabbed more from the bucket. "It's called cosplay."

Ashley laughed. "That's what she said."

That was it. They'd had this entire conversation on their one and only date. Time to put an end to it. Madison put a hand on Ashley's shoulder. "Can you do me a favor? Watch the grill while I take this inside."

Not bothering to wait for an answer, she hoisted the plate and walked away. She didn't care if the rest of the chicken was burned or raw.

Once inside, she handed the chicken off to David and hid in the bathroom for a few minutes. She shouldn't have run away. She should have said that she just wasn't interested. But something held her back. Right now, Ashley was all she had. No one else was knocking down her door. Even Jen was only partially invested. The whole interaction with Ashley, especially on the heels of discussing Jen, brought the two up in full contrast. She could share a thousand details with Ashley, and she would never care about them in the same way that Jen had about the few details she knew. Her life, her intimacies, would always be a jumping off point to Ashley's interests and opinions. Jen saw her more clearly than Ashley ever would.

Knowing that depth already existed between Jen and her made the fact that Jen still lived with her ex so much harder to accept. She wanted to give her the benefit of the doubt. They'd never talked about where they lived or their past histories in detail. Still living with her ex felt kind of big, but she'd just have to trust her instincts, even if they'd been wrong before. And if not, she'd ignore this attraction and finish the project so she could quietly slip out of Jen's life before she got hurt.

CHAPTER NINE

Jen sat at her kitchen island with her laptop open, browsing her donor list. She was on the cusp of securing a six hundred-thousand-dollar gift to Hutchinson's endowment, the biggest one so far, but well under the million dollars range she worked with at Brown. The Hutchinson's gift had been a fluke recommendation from a friend of a friend that had required relatively little work on her part. Which was good considering that with Rachel on tour, she'd had no time for anything other than her work and Carter. Once this endowment gift was squared away, she could focus on her project with Madison and whatever else was happening between them.

Two weeks ago, Carter had brought home an envelope addressed to Jen with fifty dollars in it and a simple note thanking her for the help. She didn't know how to respond, so she'd deposited the money into Carter's college fund and had sent a quick email letting Madison know she'd gotten it. She'd opened the door to talk, but so far, Madison hadn't taken her up on it. She didn't want to let her drift away, and she had work to do with her, so she kept emailing.

"Are we still on for the Iron Pour tonight?" Carter asked as he walked into the kitchen.

"Always. Is that tonight?" Jen glanced at her calendar, and there it was.

His face lit up as he pulled out his phone and sat next to her. "Great. I'll tell Del that I'll meet him there."

She groaned on the inside. That meant one of Del's parents was going to be there, too. Neither option seemed particularly inviting.

Kim would be slightly aloof and socially awkward but not in an endearing way, and Shawn...who knew what Shawn would be. She did not want to face that alone.

The Iron Pour drew a wide range of people from the artist enclaves in Providence. People Jen knew at a distance but no one she could text beforehand. Her mind ran through her list of acquaintances, looking for someone to be her third wheel. Her closest friend there, Wilson Paige, was a master blacksmith and one of the event's cofounders. He was often busy working the forge or the crowd. She could pull him away with work talk. His money came from one of the founders of the silver industry in Providence, and he often contributed to charitable causes, like the scholarship money he'd put aside for art apprenticeships at Brown.

Madison. Jen could introduce her to Wilson. Madison could also be a charming and attractive buffer for Del's abrasive parents. This could be the perfect excuse to see her again.

She finished her breakfast and cleared her dishes. She kissed Carter's head and went upstairs. She checked the time to make sure it wasn't too early and grabbed her phone to text her only to realize she didn't have her cell. How did that happen? She felt certain she should have Madison's cell by now. She texted Kathleen instead. *I need Madison's cell.*

She took a shower and came back to her phone and two new texts. The first from Kathleen. *Can't give you her number, but I'll give her yours.* The second from an unknown number. *Hey, it's Madison. Kathleen said you wanted to get in touch.*

Do you have plans tonight?

No, what do you have in mind?

She smiled. That was easy. She wished she wasn't asking her for work purposes. *Iron Pour. Carter and I go every year. There are possible donors there I want you to meet.* Jen texted her a link and felt her excitement grow at the possibility of her saying yes.

Sounds cool. All three of us?

Jen paused. Was Madison hoping to be alone with her? Fuck, texts were so difficult to interpret. Best to go with the truth. *Yes. Hope you don't mind.*

Not at all.

Relieved, Jen texted back, *Great. I'll pick you up at seven. Wear something warm.* She facepalmed. "Could I sound any more like someone's mother?"

Jen spent the morning doing bills and the afternoon in the yard hacking back the English ivy growing up the side of her garage, reliving her cringeworthy warm comment and increasing anticipation of a fun night.

Carter headed over to Isaac's house across the street and came back close to dinner with Isaac and his father, Eli, in tow. Eli came bearing cookies, a product of his relaxation baking.

Jen stopped pulling ivy long enough to glance up and smile. "Are those what I think they are?"

He hefted the plate. "Chocolate chip."

Jen tossed the ivy in her mulch bucket. Putting her hands behind her back, she straightened and felt her vertebrae crack. She stripped off her gloves and plucked one from his plate. He had a gift. She could never get hers to be so gooey and crisp without burning them or serving them raw. "Tough week?"

He glanced at his son, who was disappearing into the house with Carter. "No video games!"

Carter looked at Jen, who nodded. She had no problem enforcing Eli's rules at her own house. They shared similar opinions on screen time.

Eli took a cookie and nodded. "Yeah. One of my clients lost their kids to their abuser."

Jen winced. She couldn't imagine doing his kind of work day in and day out without losing hope in humanity. She liked coaxing the better angels out of people through financial gifts. Everyone always felt better in the end. "That's rough."

He took another bite. "They have more money and access to the system." He frowned and then raised his cookie in a toast. "I made cookies."

Jen tapped hers against his. "Cookies."

They munched companionably for a bit before Eli said, "Carter invited Isaac to Iron Pour tonight. Are you okay with that?"

Jen nodded. They often shared child care with each other. It'd be easier tonight with Madison along. Carter would have someone his age. "Should be fine."

He grinned. "Great. Dani and I were thinking of going out to dinner and then stopping by to watch the show."

"You should." Jen chatted with him about possible restaurants and about the boys. He left after a few minutes but not without offering to leave the cookies in her kitchen. She wagged a finger at him. "Don't you dare."

He chuckled and walked back home. Eli and his family were one of the reasons she'd agreed to a nesting arrangement with Rachel. The neighborhood was just too good to leave.

She finished up and found the boys in Carter's room, looking through comic books.

"I'm hungry," Carter announced.

"We'll get food there. Go pee before we go." Jen entered her upstairs bathroom and paused at the reflection. "Definitely a shower." She was showered and dressed in fifteen minutes. A white button-down tucked into dark green jeans and a pair of smart wool socks. She checked herself in the mirror twice before she realized what she was doing, getting ready for a date. Obviously, her not-so-unconscious desires were making their wishes known. She laughed at herself. "It's not a date. Just two people getting together to raise money with my son and his friend along for the ride." Shaking off her nerves, she headed downstairs.

"Let's go." By the front door, she slipped into her black Blundstone's and her brown barn coat. She marshaled the boys into coats and boots and led them out the door.

Jen pulled out of their driveway with the kids tucked into the back seat. She zigzagged through the neighborhood and parked in front of Madison's house.

"Where are we going?" Carter craned his neck and looked around.

"Wait here. I'm picking up a friend." Jen got out and crossed the street just as Madison opened the door. Her breath caught as she took her in.

Madison wore a deep purple V-neck sweater that showed off her cleavage and formfitting jeans that defined her curves in just the right ways. She held a black leather jacket in her hands. "Is this warm enough?"

"You look great." Fuck, she looked stunning. Jen moved closer, just stopping herself from touching her. She had a feeling she was going to spend the rest of the evening fighting off that desire. Maybe this wasn't such a good idea.

Too late now.

Jen's appreciative smile made Madison feel like her outfit was the right choice. She'd debated longer than she normally did about what to wear. She wanted to look good when Jen introduced her, but she also wanted to impress Jen. She wasn't ready to let the pleasant hum of attraction between them die. She still wasn't sure how she felt about Jen living with her ex. But for the moment, she enjoyed Jen's attention and pushed her reservations aside.

Madison got in the car. Reaching for her seat belt, she said, "Hi, Carter." Another dark-haired boy sat next to him. "And you are?"

"That's Isaac," Carter answered.

Jen dropped into the driver's seat and started the car. "Isaac, this is Madison."

Madison turned back and smiled. She winked. "We've met. Carter just told me."

Jen nodded and held up her phone. "Any requests?"

"'Another Brick in the Wall,'" Isaac said, wiggling in his seat.

"Again?" Jen laughed and tapped her phone before putting the car in gear.

Madison stared at her. Jen's guard relaxed around Carter, and she liked this side of her.

Jen flashed her a grin. "Pink Floyd."

A shrill scream came out of the speakers, followed by a driving drum beat. The singing started, and the boys joined in. Jen sang with them as they shouted the lyrics, ending up in laughter when they started chanting toward the end. She liked car DJ Jen.

Jen adjusted the speakers to the back and switched on another station. An upbeat pop tune blared out the back, and the boys ignored it while they talked to each other.

Madison stopped laughing and shook her head. "That's so funny. Do they always do that?"

Jen smiled and shrugged. "Sometimes. We do a few songs. That one's in heavy rotation right now. Ten-year-old angst music."

"Where's that from?"

Jen grasped at her chest. "Oh no, please. Don't make me feel so old. It's from *The Wall*."

Madison didn't want Jen to think she was some kid, but she also sucked at music. "I'm sure I've heard it, but I don't remember."

Jen shook her head. "It's the classic anti-school song."

Kayla always knew songs. Her dad had played classic rock on Sunday mornings while he made breakfast for Kayla, her, and whoever else was staying over. Next time she saw her, she'd ask if he played Pink Floyd.

The flash of water was all the warning she got before she saw the bridge ahead and gripped the door handle in preparation. The road surface switched just a bit, but the car's suspension made it a much smoother ride than when she drove over it in her own car. She closed her eyes and held her breath.

Jen put a hand on her knee, and she opened her eyes. Jen squeezed and whispered, "Are you afraid of bridges?"

Comforted by her touch, Madison put a hand on top of hers and nodded. "A little. Can you use both hands please?"

Jen smiled. "Of course. Let me change lanes." She moved to the left lane and increased their speed.

The bridge wasn't very long, but Madison took a deep breath when they drove past the power station and onto solid ground.

"Why didn't you say anything? I could have taken another route."

Madison shrugged, self-conscious about her fear but putting up a brave front. "I didn't know where you were going, and you have to cross somewhere. Providence is built around lots of water."

"But there are less bridge-like crossings."

"It's okay. You don't need to take care of me." Madison smiled, feeling cared for even as she protested.

"I'm not taking care of you. I'm just…"

Jen had dealt with Travis. Madison didn't want her to cater to her every whim. And even though she was afraid of bridges, she handled that fear on her own without Jen just fine. She folded her arms. "Jen, seriously, you don't have to think of everything."

Jen exhaled. "I'm sorry, it's a knee-jerk reaction."

"I'm younger than you but not a kid."

Jen gave her a sidelong look that raked up and down her body. "Of that, I have no doubt."

Madison couldn't tell if she was serious or joking with that look so she smacked her in the shoulder and changed the subject. "What's your connection to Iron Pour?"

They got off the highway and drove along the river. The area was a mix of greenery and nondescript, single story industrial buildings. Traffic had tapered off.

"One of Rachel's bandmates dated the original organizers, and we've been coming on and off since it started. Rachel played occasionally, and then when Carter was born, we brought him pretty much every year."

Madison felt a nervous twitch in her stomach. It was the first time Jen had mentioned her ex since Madison had learned about their living arrangement. She wanted to know more, but first, she needed to be sure. "Rachel's your ex?"

Jen looked at her, confused. "We've talked about her."

"Not by name." Would she tell her that they still lived together? She was torn between wanting to know and asking herself why it mattered. They weren't dating.

"Oh." Jen frowned. "I forget what you know about me. Sorry. Yes, Rachel is my ex."

"Is she going to be there?" Even if they weren't dating, she'd rather not run into her.

"Not this year. She's on tour." Jen looked at her, then looked away.

She wasn't telling the whole truth. "What are you not saying?"

Jen glanced in the mirror before she shook her head. "I'll tell you when we get there."

"Tell her what?" Carter asked.

Somehow, that didn't comfort her at all. Even though the music was loud enough to give them the illusion of privacy, they were not alone. Which meant that Jen did not want Carter to know. She swallowed her worry and resolved to get the truth later. She already knew the big one, that Rachel still lived with her, so she hoped that it was just Jen coming clean without the kids listening. Although Carter already knew, so why wait? She didn't have much time to think about that as they turned into a crowded parking lot and climbed out of the car. Carter and Isaac started to run, and Jen called, "Watch for cars!"

The boys slowed and waited at the curb. They crossed the street with half a dozen people while cars waited to let them pass. Music poured from across the street. They walked through an open chain link fence with metal signs affixed to it. Most of the signs displayed artistic shapes, but three of them spelled out "The Steel Yard."

Once inside, Carter and Isaac took off. Jen and Madison strolled through the crowd. Food trucks lined the perimeter with a stage at the opposite end. In between sat all manner of metal and steel sculptures. Several people in welding masks were moving around with blowtorches, and sections of the yard were roped off around what looked like a large metal bird. As they moved through the crowd, her smile grew. It looked and felt like an industrial renaissance fair. These were her people. How had she never heard about this event? What else had she missed being away from home?

A shower of sparks erupted from the centerpiece. She tilted her head to the side and stared at the metal structure in surprise. Her mouth dropped open, and she turned toward Jen, clutching her arm. "Is that a dragon?"

Jen smiled and laughed. "Probably. There's usually some theme and story to go with the massive amounts of molten iron they pour." She tucked Madison's hand into her arm.

Jen's touch—so intimate and familiar—jarred with Madison's earlier thoughts. And as much as she'd like to pretend this was a date, there was still so little she knew about Jen. She pulled her hand back, reassured by the frown on Jen's face as she did it. Whatever else was going on, Jen wanted to touch her. "What did you want to tell me?"

Jen sighed and scratched the back of her neck.

She was nervous, and that added to Madison's anxiety. Surprised by how easy Jen was to read, Madison waited.

"Rachel's not the ex that'll be here tonight."

That was not what she was expecting. "Oh."

"Carter doesn't know about her, and I'd like to keep it that way. It was a mistake, but she's the mother of one of Carter's friends."

Madison's mind reeled with the implications. Jen had dated someone at school, and that someone was a parent, which meant Madison knew or knew of them. Great. She did not sign up for this. In fact, she didn't sign up for any of it. Jen had been a one-time deal that had bled over into her real life. "Who is she?"

"Shawn Jorgensen."

She had no idea who that was, but it didn't give her much comfort. The intersections between her work and personal life were getting too close for comfort. "Thanks for telling me."

Jen opened her mouth and then shook her head. When she finally spoke, she changed the subject. "We have about an hour before the show. Are you hungry?"

"What about the kids?" Jen's ease with the whole situation angered her. How could she drop a bomb like that and ask about food?

Jen shrugged. "They'll materialize when they're out of money."

Madison didn't know what else to do so they wandered up and down the food line, settling on a locavore truck with chimichurri cheesesteak for Madison and a fried chicken sandwich for Jen. Jen led them toward a low stone wall and sat.

Madison took a bite, and they ate in silence. The sun had already set, but the sky was still light. The yard was bounded by several low brick buildings that acted as a windbreak. People were beginning to fill up the open spaces. She tried not to feel trapped, but her instincts were telling her to get out. She'd let Jen introduce her to the donors, but after tonight, she was going to pull back.

Jen finished first and crumbled up her wrapper. "You're mad, aren't you? I should have been up front when I asked you."

Madison stopped eating and took the opening. "Yes, you should have."

Jen ran a hand through her hair. "I just wanted to see you again, and I thought this would be a good idea. For the project. For us. But obviously, I didn't think it through…"

Jen kept talking, but Madison stopped listening. Jen babbled when she was nervous. Madison made her nervous. And like their first night together, Madison took courage in it, but now it also gave her hope.

"Why didn't you tell me Rachel lives with you?"

"Rachel?" Jen laughed, a long, hearty laugh.

Madison stared at her, unsure what to do or say. Nothing was funny about this fact. "What?"

"I'm sorry. I shouldn't laugh. She doesn't live with me exactly. We share the house but not at the same time. We're nesting." Jen put the word nest in air quotes and glanced around before she leaned in and whispered, "It's a living hell."

Madison had heard the term before. Everything about this woman was so complicated.

"Aw, shit. We've been spotted." Jen nodded at a pair of women Jen's age walking toward them."

The pair stopped in front of them, and Madison stood, throwing her trash in a nearby can. The first woman extended her hand. "I'm Shawn."

"Madison." Her defenses went up.

Shawn barely touched her before pulling away. "This is my wife, Kim." Kim nodded and didn't reach out.

How unpleasant. She was beginning to see firsthand what Jen's life choices entailed, and she wasn't sure she wanted to be a part of it.

Shawn wrapped her hand around Kim's waist and leaned into her. Her eyes never left Madison while she spoke. "I'm so glad I found you in this mess. We ran into Carter and his friend. Delia's already gone with them." She paused and cut her eyes at Jen. "Is this her?"

Madison's senses went on red alert. Shawn knew about her?

"Jen said she was seeing someone."

Seeing someone? Madison felt a pang of jealousy, then everything became clear when Jen's arm circled her waist. "Yes, it is."

What the hell was going on? Jen's arm tightened around her waist, an almost desperate pull, and suddenly, Madison didn't care. Jen was asking her to help, and she couldn't say no. She squeezed Jen's hand to let her know she was game.

Shawn looked Madison up and down. "How did you meet? Are you a student?"

Do I look like a high school student to you? Madison didn't take the bait and bit back her first reply.

Jen laughed. "No, we met at a wedding."

Shawn eyed her with disbelief. "You look familiar. You don't have kids at the school, do you?"

Madison recognized that look. Many of Erika's friends had it whenever they talked to her. It said, you're too young for this. She beamed. Relentless cheerfulness often won them over or tired them out. She didn't care either way. "Not yet."

"But I'm sure we've met."

Great. She was fake dating a parent while talking with another parent. "I'm the social worker at Hutchinson's."

Shawn's demeanor soured. "Oh, right." Her focus shifted to Jen. "You should come in next time you drop Carter off at the house. It's been so long since we hung out. Well, we should check out the work."

"Nice meeting you," Madison called. She'd kill her with kindness if she had to. Only Kim looked back. Madison stared after them until the crowd closed around them, then she moved out of Jen's arms. "Whoa. What was that about?"

With a groan, Jen rubbed her forehead. "Sorry, I panicked. I didn't expect her to find us so soon."

"Instead, you let her think you were dating the school's social worker." She should be pissed, but seeing Jen so off her game softened her anger.

"I'm sorry. I ran into her a few weeks ago and told her I was seeing someone. I fucked up. I wasn't thinking. I'll go talk to her. Tell her it was a mistake." She looked so dejected that Madison took pity on her.

"What kind of damage could she do?"

Jen squinted, a hint of her calculating persona coming back. "Minimal. Nothing I couldn't rein in."

And if Jen couldn't, well, Madison had been through that before and had come out the other side. Jen had needed her tonight. Maybe she'd been too hard on her. She wasn't perfect, and beneath that confident personality was a human being capable of making mistakes with real consequences. Given that detail, she could at least empathize with Jen. "How long did it last?"

"A few months. After Rachel and I split up."

How could Madison share the same sex tree with Shawn?

Jen met her look. "What? It was the end of my marriage, and I was lonely."

Madison shook her head. "I'm not judging."

Jen lifted an eyebrow as if to say, "Really?"

"Not exactly. I'm just trying to figure out what you saw in her." And what she saw in Madison, but there was no way she was asking that question now.

"She wasn't always so brittle." Jen opened her mouth to say more, but then Carter, Isaac, and Del showed up.

The next half hour was spent getting everyone fed, and then Isaac's parents arrived. As they all gathered to watch the show, Shawn and Kim came back. Still cool and standoffish, they took up a place on the opposite side with the kids between them. Standing near one of Jen's exes while they pretended to get along highlighted the differences in their lives. While Madison had run from her problems, Jen had stayed and dealt with them on a daily basis. That took a different kind of courage. A courage she didn't have but wanted to.

The lights went down, and along the yard, the red glow of the forge mixed with a low hum that started on the sidelines and grew into the pounding beat of drums. The music coursed through Madison, and the swell of excitement built up inside her. The kids started to jump up and down. Isaac's parents beside her were wrapped in each other's arms, laughing and smiling, in stark contrast to Shawn and Kim, who stared ahead stone-faced, the very picture of unhappy.

She now understood how Jen could have been with Shawn; her unhappiness was so palpable that Jen would want to fix it. Madison didn't care if Jen had a past as long as she was here in the present. Jen had already admitted that tonight had been an excuse to see her, and that was what mattered right here, right now.

She reached out and captured Jen's hand in her own.

Jen turned toward her with a questioning look before interlacing their fingers together and squeezing.

A brass band stepped into the light, and a quartet of trumpets played an accompaniment. Fire dancers emerged, their bright red flames casting shadows across the gathering. Her body swayed with the tempo, and Jen pulled her into her arms. The heat and the sound wrapped around them and held them tight.

A woman spoke across the darkness, invoking ancient rhythms and telling a tale of dragons and knights while molten metal poured across the structures.

Jen leaned in and spoke next to her ear, her breath hot against Madison's neck. "Pretty fucking cool, right?"

Still riding the high of the fiery display, she turned, inches away from Jen's face. She caught her scent amid the food and molten metal smells. "Yes."

In front of her, brass and bass crashed together, and a wave of heat erupted as the dragon burst into flames. But she barely noticed, her eyes locked on Jen. Jen's hand moved up her back, and the crowd roared around them.

The kids jostled into them, and Jen lost her grip. Madison stumbled, and someone steadied her. The show was over, and the crowd was pushing in on all sides.

Madison wanted to pull her back in, but the moment was gone.

Carter announced, "I'm thirsty."

And Madison looked at him and then over at his mother. Thirsty? Yeah, she was definitely thirsty.

Chapter Ten

Jen collected everyone's drink order, and Eli volunteered to go with her. She waved Madison off. "I've got it." She didn't trust herself to be alone with her just yet after their almost kiss. She couldn't believe she'd almost kissed her in the middle of Iron Pour. They moved through the crowd and toward a white food truck with the words South County Distillery painted on the side. Harry's truck. She doubted the craft distiller would be staffing it. Too bad. Jen always liked talking with her.

Eli fell into step beside her and said, "She seems nice. How long have you been dating?"

Jen smiled and looked back at Madison, wishing her answer was different. She still thrummed at the way Madison felt in her arms. "We're not."

"Oh." He looked confused. "Well, you could do worse."

Jen got into line and looked back. Madison was laughing with Carter and pointing at the remains of the show. She looked relaxed and happy. Jen smiled. Not too far away, Shawn and Kim stood stiff and rigid with no smiles or anything to indicate they were having a good time. Seeing them so close together, the differences were obvious. She could do worse, and she had.

On their way back, she spotted Wilson leaning near the forge, sipping beer with a couple teenagers and pointing toward the smoldering sculptures. "Eli, can you keep an eye out for Carter?"

They'd been to enough events together with the kids that he was used to her needing someone to run interference while she worked. "Sure."

After handing out drinks, Jen leaned toward Madison and pointed toward a cluster of people working the forge. "Are you ready to work? There's someone I want you to meet. Wilson Paige. He's old money, family of silversmiths and costume jewelers. Strictly arts-giving but lower income arts-focus. I think he can help us with additional funding."

She waited until the crowd thinned around Wilson and then stepped in.

Their conversation took a half hour, and by the time they were done, he had pledged five thousand dollars and given Jen two additional people to talk to for Madison's project.

When they were far enough away, Madison leaned into her. "I can't believe you just did that. Five thousand dollars."

"Not me. You." Jen deflected her praise, even as she basked in the attention. She knew the moment by Wilson's eyes when he'd made up his mind, and Madison had been the one to do it. Wilson's calculated net worth was close to five hundred million dollars. Five thousand was like asking for a twenty. However, Madison's project didn't need big donations but several small ones. Most wealthy people had a budget for big donations so smaller asks were easier.

"Thank you for bringing me tonight."

Jen smiled. "We're not done yet."

By the time they returned to their group in front of the stage, Jen had secured another seven thousand dollars from three other people. Madison's enthusiasm for the project really sold it. There was an idealism and an obligation to her pitch that grabbed them and left no room to refuse. She was a fucking natural. It was a side of her that Jen hadn't seen yet. It was infectious, and Jen was charmed.

The music turned off, and the lights came up. One of the event organizers walked onstage. "Tonight, I want to introduce a special guest. She's been a regular here at Iron Pour since we started. She's currently on tour right now, but she's back home for one night. Give it up for our hometown girl, Rachel Clarke."

Carter started jumping up and down and grabbed Jen's arm. "Did you know? Did you know?"

She hid her anger and gave him an enthusiastic reply. "No, honey, I didn't. What a nice surprise." She was going to kill her. Twice in September, she'd broken promises to Carter, citing tour commitments, and to have her show up at Iron Pour without telling Jen in advance pissed her off. No doubt she'd disrupt whatever plans Jen had for the weekend.

Once the applause died down, Rachel stepped up to the microphone. "Thank you. Thank you. I wasn't sure I was going to make it tonight." She started playing a riff that the crowd recognized. Jen remembered her writing it between midnight feedings. Beside her, Madison started swaying with the beat, and when Rachel started to sing, so did she. Carter and his friends, Isaac's parents, even Shawn were all dancing and singing. She couldn't blame them; it was one of Rachel's catchier tunes. She was the only one with baggage around that song.

Madison moved closer and started to dance with her. She stiffened. It was too weird to have all three of these women in close proximity and even weirder to dance with one while the others sang. Rachel was oblivious, Shawn jealous, and Madison...well, she didn't even know what Madison felt because they weren't talking about what had happened at the wedding and were playing a game of fake dating that felt less fake as the evening wore on.

Madison leaned in and shouted, "Are you all right?"

Jen nodded and lied. "Fine."

"You look upset. What's wrong?"

The song ended, and the crowd roared with applause. Rachel quieted them. "I've got a new one to share. I wrote this for my wife when we were going through a rough patch. I call it 'Never Enough.'"

Jen's pulse began to pound in her head. Wife?

And then Rachel started to sing, "Just the other day, I caught you walking away." With each line, Jen's anger multiplied. Her hands clenched, and her jaw tensed. "All the nights and days and it was never enough."

Eli touched her. A little bit of the anger left her as he whispered in her ear, "I can take the boys home if you want to take off."

Jen pulled back. "Really?"

He nodded. "Yeah. Go be with your fake date."

"Thanks." She got Carter's attention and told him she was heading out. He nodded and said, "You're mad at Mama."

"No. I'm just tired." She lied to him and hated Rachel a little more for that. "I love you. Eli's going to bring you home tonight."

She tried not to read too much into his disappointed look as he turned back to his other mother onstage. The separation had been hard on him. She shoved her parental guilt down and turned to Madison, who'd stopped dancing and was staring at her. "What's going on? Are you two leaving?"

Jen leaned in and said, "I am. He's not. Do you want to get out of here?"

Madison looked at her, confusion and concern on her face. "Are you okay?"

No, I'm not okay. There're too many people here who want a piece of me, and I'm suffocating. And you're the only one opening a window. "I'll be fine. Shall we?"

She held out her hand, and Madison took it. Jen led them through the crowd and away from the stage, past the smoldering remains of the main event and toward the parking lot.

"Hold up. You're walking too fast." Madison tugged on her arm, and Jen slowed.

"Sorry."

Madison squeezed her hand. "It's okay. That was Rachel, wasn't it?"

Jen took a deep breath. "Yes. Surprise."

Madison waved her arm and said, "Can I buy you a drink?"

Jen smiled, and some of the tension left her body. "That would be lovely."

They drove to the Scofflaw on Wickenden Street. She liked its Prohibition style—red bricks, gilt mirrors, and brass accents—but it also was one of the best whiskey bars in town. She grabbed a table with bench seating, tucked in the corner.

Madison sat and looked around. "This is nice. Do you come here often?"

Jen laughed at the inadvertent bad pick-up line, and Madison rolled her eyes. "Sometimes. When I want a good whiskey."

Madison grimaced.

"That's right. Only sweet drinks for you." Jen winked and grabbed the cocktail menu.

"Oh, I get it. You're a drink snob."

Jen shrugged. She had her there. "Maybe just a little."

Madison leaned her arms on the table and pulled the menu from her hands. "Fine. You pick the drink, and I'll try it."

Jen plucked it back and flipped it open. The thrill of a challenge bubbled inside her. If Madison wanted to play, she could play. "Okay. They do spirit flights. Let's see where your palate lands, and we'll go from there."

The waiter came over, and Jen ordered two flights of bourbon. "Let's start with Bulleit, Four Roses Single Barrel, Hudson Baby Bourbon. Then Buffalo Trace, Basil Hayden's, Weller twelve year. Neat. And glasses of water. And can you bring out two orders of the chocolate plate?"

"Chocolate?" Madison asked.

Jen leaned in, warming to her subject. "It pairs really well with bourbon. Corn and cacao are both native to the Americas. There's something to be said about pairing foods regionally."

"Where'd you pick up a love of bourbon?"

She smiled, remembering the big bear of a man who'd introduced her to the world of whiskey and in particular, bourbon. "James Cowles, one of my favorite donors, owned a sizable interest in the Beam company, Maker's Mark. I gained an appreciation and a palate from him."

"You must meet very interesting people."

She nodded, thinking about all her donors. "Sometimes I do. Mostly, I spend a lot of time talking to people. Figuring out what they like, what they don't."

"Is that what you're doing with me? Figuring out what I like, what I don't?"

Jen was seeing a pattern with Madison, bars, and flirting. Not that she minded. In fact, she planned to enjoy it. "Maybe I already know."

Madison blushed, and Jen smiled. *Gotcha.*

The waiter came back with the flights. Jen scooted closer and walked Madison through the taste profiles, savoring the feel of their thighs pressed together.

Madison listened intently, asking questions about which ones she liked and why. When the waiter came back with the chocolate—tiny truffles dusted with cocoa powder—and two glasses of water, Madison asked for a paper and pen. "To take notes."

Delighted by her interest, Jen still teased her. "You know there won't be a test."

Madison leaned forward, a slight lift to her chin. "I'm not so sure about that. Now which one do I start with?"

Deciding she liked this cocky side, Jen embraced the role of tutor. "If you start with the sweetest, it will make everything harsher, so let's start here." She picked up the Basil Hayden's and handed it over.

"Do I sniff it?"

Jen waggled her hand. "There's some debate over that. If you do, breathe—"

Madison sniffed and coughed.

"—through your mouth so you don't burn your taste buds."

She gave Jen a look that said "thanks for nothing" and then took a sip. She gagged and squeezed her leg before she passed it back. "How can you stand this?"

Jen almost missed her question, Madison clutching her thigh completely short-circuited her brain. Her proximity had Jen's senses on high alert, and the touch overloaded her. She handed her the Four Roses, spilling a little in her haste. "Here. Try this."

Madison picked it up and took a cautious sip. "That's better."

"Do you mind?" Jen picked up the Basil, knocking it back and relishing the heat as it slipped into her chest. If Madison knew what she did to Jen, she didn't let on, nor did she move her hand. "Try the chocolate."

Madison reached over, abandoning Jen's thigh, and popped one of the truffles in her mouth. Her moan stoked the growing fire in Jen's body. "Oh wow, that's really good. The chocolate tastes sweeter."

Jen finished off the Four Roses, too. An altogether different warmth settled into her stomach, and she grabbed a chocolate. "Try the next."

Madison progressed through each glass, passing them along for Jen to finish before finally settling on the Hudson. A slow smile appeared. "Okay, this is the one."

Jen lifted the Weller and gently clinked the glass to hers. "I'm glad we found a winner."

Madison smiled. "I'm not sure I would order it, but in a pinch, I know what to get."

Jen pulled another glass closer, a pleasant buzz suffusing her body. "A stunning endorsement. I have an idea." She waved the waiter over. "What cocktails do you make that could use the Hudson?" He listed two, and Madison picked the one with habanero and maple syrup.

"And for you?"

"I'll be finishing this." She gestured at the array of glasses on the table. She wrapped her hand around the glass in front of her. She was no longer sure which one it was; her palate had been saturated with too many flavors at once. "Thank you for this. I needed to get out of there."

"I didn't realize Rachel was Rachel Clarke."

"Yeah. She's fairly famous in the lesbian folk world. I think it's only a matter of time before she moves beyond the Americana niche and into the larger scene."

"How did you meet?"

Jen finished the Bulleit or maybe the Weller. She wasn't sure, her body infused with the warm tingle bourbon gave her. If she was going to talk about Rachel, she was going to need another drink. "We met at a local bar where she was playing with a cover band. I was in grad school."

"How long were you together?"

"Seventeen years." If they were going to go down this rugged road, she wanted a little something better. When the waiter came back with Madison's drink, she said, "Do you have any Pappy Van Winkle back there?"

He smiled. "The Family Reserve? Yes. We just got an order in this week."

"I'll take a glass. Neat." She turned to Madison. "You're not buying this drink. It's one hundred and seventy-five dollars."

Madison coughed. "What?"

The waiter returned and set the drink in front of her. "Enjoy."

"Oh, I will." Closing her eyes, Jen hummed her appreciation as the first drops slid down her throat. It was really extravagant to buy such an expensive drink on a whim, especially when drinking with someone who couldn't even afford to fix her own car. But oh, the taste. She opened her eyes and caught Madison staring.

All the bullshit in her life just stopped at that look. Rachel and her denial, Shawn and her drama seemed so small. Even Carter and his needs, while always on her mind, felt so much lighter in Madison's presence. "I wished we'd exchanged phone numbers at the wedding."

"Would you have called?" Madison asked.

"Yeah," Jen said without thinking. Then added, "Maybe. I don't know."

"I wasn't that hard to look up."

"Neither was I. I left my number." She let that sink in. She had an idea why Madison hadn't called.

"I know. I chickened out. I thought you were married."

"You're not wrong. She won't sign the papers." The words spilled out with ease. She could blame the bourbon for her honesty or simply admit that it was easy to talk to her.

"Why?"

Jen sipped her exquisite bourbon and shook her head. "You saw her tonight. She still wants to be married."

Madison shook her head and sipped her cocktail. "What's the deal with her? She called you her wife."

Jen frowned, annoyed that Madison witnessed Rachel's active denial. "Caught that, did you? Yeah, she thinks we're on a break. Won't leave the house."

Jen caught a flicker of fear in Madison's eyes and rushed to answer before Madison could close up on her. "Before she was on tour, we split our time between the house and our apartment so Carter had a stable place to stay. We were never there at the same time."

"That's what you said."

Jen almost forgot that Madison had confronted her about it this evening before Shawn showed up.

"It sounds terrible. For you. And maybe for Carter, maybe not."

"It was. Is. Whatever. The last six months before the wedding, I'd been couch surfing at a friend's house. Sharing an apartment and a house with her was too much. I needed my own space, even if it was in someone else's guest room. And as disruptive as the tour has been for Carter, it's a relief that she's out of town most of the time."

"Is Carter close to her?"

"Yeah. When she's around." Jen felt bad immediately. "I'm sorry. That's not fair. When he was born, she rearranged her entire tour and recording schedule to allow us to travel with her. Then she put her career on hold to stay in Providence when Carter went to school."

"How long did you tour with her?"

"For the first three years of Carter's life. Then again after he went to school, we did three summer tours." She smiled. Those had been the good years. Rachel's band was tight-knit, and Carter wasn't the first kid in that group. Having kids changed the way the band toured. There were still late nights, but there were museums and parks. All these places she'd seen before, but now she saw through her son's eyes.

Madison's hand settled on her forearm. "It looks like you miss it."

Jen groaned. While she valued the mellowing effects bourbon had on her mood, she forgot that it also tended to make her a bit more sentimental and worse, maudlin. She tapped her glass. "That's the bourbon talking. I've made some bad choices with my libido."

That felt a bit unfair to Rachel, but she didn't care because all this talk of her had effectively killed any sexual tension.

Madison clucked. "I slept with my adviser, and she tanked my professional career when we broke up."

Jen lifted her glass. "Here's to bad choices involving sex."

Madison raised her glass. "Cheers."

Jen finished off her drink and looked down at it, surprised and disappointed by how quickly it had disappeared.

"Are you okay?"

Jen sighed. "I really wanted more of that."

"You look so sad."

Jen leaned her head on Madison's shoulder. "I am. It's really good bourbon."

Her laugh shook their joined bodies. "I don't know what your finances are, but I suspect that three hundred dollars for two drinks is a little out of your budget." Slinging an arm around her shoulders, Madison nudged her. "Come on. Let me take you home."

Jen looked up, and their eyes met. Madison's hazel eyes were dark in the dim lighting of the bar. Jen felt the mood shift. She knew that look. She'd seen it at the wedding and in her fantasies over the past three months and a few hours ago. They'd been dancing around this physical intimacy all night. Playing at dating, touching and staring a little too long, probing each other's secrets. She wanted to lean in and kiss those lips that had pulled so much information from her. She wanted to fill her melancholy with the passion she knew lived inside Madison. The part of her brain enjoying the slight disconnect between reality and consequences took over, and she leaned in.

Madison closed her eyes, and her lips parted.

Jen inched closer, her hands braced on both sides of Madison's body and just before she moved in, her rational mind returned. What the fuck was she doing? She jerked back so quickly, she knocked into the table. Covering her intention with a cough, she said, "We should go."

Madison opened her eyes, not sure if she was disappointed or relieved that Jen hadn't kissed her. Either way, it was time to go. She called the waiter and handed him her credit card. Jen interceded and said, "Put it on my card."

Madison frowned as the waiter hesitated. "I did offer to buy you a drink."

Jen waved him away and looked at her. "Not a two hundred dollar one."

"Okay, but next time, it's on me." The words came out before she could take them back.

Jen grinned. "I'd like that."

Giddy relief ballooned in her chest. "Me, too." She followed Jen out the door. There was a slight sway in her walk that was both attractive and concerning.

Stopping beside her car, Jen dropped her keys pulling them out of her pocket. She leaned down to scoop them up, and her phone clattered to the pavement. "Damn it."

Madison picked up her phone and read a text from Rachel. *Can I stay at the house? With you guys?*

Relief overtook disappointment about the kiss when she saw that message. Even though she'd delighted in their flirtation, she'd gained a better understanding of Jen's life tonight, and she wasn't sure how ready she was to get back into bed with her.

She handed her the phone, and Jen glanced at the display. She made a disgusted sound. "Really? She can't find a fucking hotel room in all of Providence?" Jen stuffed the phone in her pocket and fumbled with her keys again.

Madison did a mental count of how much alcohol she'd consumed and how much Jen had. "I think I should drive."

Putting her hand on the roof, Jen finally unlocked the car and looked over. She glanced at the car, stepped back, and nodded. "Yeah, you should."

They switched places. Surprised at how easy it was to convince her, Madison sank into the driver's seat. She rested her hands on the leather steering wheel and did a quick look at all the dials before turning it on. The car purred to life...it actually purred. She could feel the power coursing through her hands. It was the nicest car she'd ever sat in and probably the fastest.

"Do you know how to drive stick?"

Madison glanced over at her and lied. "A little."

"Define little."

"My high school girlfriend taught me."

Jen covered her face with her hands. "Okay. Well, that's not as far back as my high school, and we're going to be on the flats anyway, so you should be good with just the basics."

Jen gave her the ten-second overview, then Madison popped the clutch and put it in gear. She switched her foot to the gas pedal, and the car lurched forward. "Use both feet. One on the clutch, the other on the gas and brake."

She arranged her feet quickly and maneuvered through the tiny parking lot.

"When you start to accelerate, watch the RPMs. When it's hits three or four, you shift. You can hear in the engine that it's time."

The Scofflaw's parking lot was tucked behind the back of the building. She glanced down to make sure the lights were on and flipped on the turn signal. Muscle memory kicked in, and she made it all the way back to Jen's house, only stalling once at a red light. She was so flustered she barely noticed Jen's hand over hers when she started the car again, and Jen silently helped her shift. Her hand was still resting on top when Madison pulled into Jen's driveway and cut the engine.

Jen's phone rang, and she clenched Madison's hand before answering it. "Yes? Yeah, I got it." Judging from her posture and the tightness of her grip, Madison figured it was Rachel.

Trapped under Jen's hand and in her car, Madison sat quietly while Jen spoke. The more she listened, the angrier she got at how Rachel treated her. "You really can't find a hotel…Was it his idea or yours?" She sighed. "Never mind, just put him on."

Jen's whole demeanor changed. "Hey, bud…Yeah I heard. Is that what you want?"

Madison heard his faint voice, and then Jen's grip on her lessened. "Okay, she can stay…No, baby, she's your mama, too. See you soon."

Jen hung up and rested her head against the headrest. "Ugh. I don't want to go in."

Aware of their hands still together, Madison spoke without thinking. "You don't have to."

"What are you saying?"

Not sure how to answer, the offer hung between them. What was she saying? She wanted to give Jen a sanctuary from all this drama, but Jen was not some random hookup. She was intimately involved with Madison's work life. And they were sitting here in Jen's driveway waiting for her ex-wife and son to show up. The risk was too great. She couldn't afford another Erika.

Jen extracted her hand and opened her door. "When you figure it out, let me know." Jen got all the way to her front door before Madison realized she had the keys and was still sitting in the car.

Switching off the ignition, she hopped out and jogged up the walkway. Handing her the keys, she said, "Here."

Jen unlocked the door and handed them back. "I'll pick it up in the morning."

"Are you sure? I'm only a couple blocks away."

"It's late. Take the car."

Madison was halfway down the walk before Jen called out, "For what it's worth, I had a good time tonight."

Turning around, Madison's insides got mushy, and she felt a silly grin pull at the corners of her mouth. All the mixed emotions solidified into warm affection. "Me, too."

Chapter Eleven

D id you really say rain money?"
Jen grimaced and cast back into the river. Nat had texted her in the predawn hours for some early morning fishing. Thankfully, her metabolism had left her without a hangover after last night's bourbon tasting. The whole event had left her needing some alone time with a reel and one of her oldest friends. On the walk through the salt marshes, she had filled Nat in on her current project at the school. "Yes."

Nat chuckled and reeled in her line. "Can you deliver?"

Jen flipped the lock and spun the handle. "Of course." She considered her current situation. "Well, probably."

Nat pulled her arm back and snapped her line out again. "I see. Now tell me why you want to do this on top of your other work."

Nat's normal directness irked her, probably because she was perfectly happy not thinking about her motivation. Why did she want to do this? She could have just given Madison a few names and a couple donors, then been on her way. But no, she proposed a whole new construction project instead. Ego? Sure. But it was more than that. She'd liked Madison from the moment they'd met and wanted to keep that connection alive. Without the project, she was worried Madison would fade into the background of her life, and she didn't want that.

"Because I like her." Jen's lure got fouled in her rod, and in her attempt to fix it, one of the barbs cut her hand. "Fuck."

Nat shook her head. "Careful. You got a Band-Aid?" She reeled her line in and hooked her lure into the rings before leaning it against their cooler. Nat pulled a couple wrinkled Band-Aids and a small tube of antibacterial lotion out of her fishing vest. "Here."

Jen bandaged her hand and resumed untangling her line. She finally had to cut it and knot the hook again. Nat continued casting a little farther upriver. Pole fixed, Jen followed, grateful that she'd worn thermal underwear beneath her waders as she sloshed through the marshy waters.

Nat glanced at her as she settled in beside her. "Do you want to talk about it?"

"No, I'm good." Whatever Madison was, Jen most definitely didn't want to talk about it. Nat cut through her bullshit with almost no effort. She didn't want to look too closely at what was going on with Madison. She wanted to nurture and protect it for a little bit longer.

Nat's line tightened and the conversation paused while Nat reeled in a minnow, then tossed it back. "I got a '56 Thunderbird in the shop. You should come see it. It needs a lot of work, but the bones are there."

Nat specialized in classic car restoration. Before Jen bought her Porsche, they'd spent weeks looking at cars, discussing the pros and cons. Nat would never say anything, but Jen thought she was disappointed that Jen didn't buy something she could fix up. She wondered if that instinct to tinker would translate into helping Madison with her car.

She reeled in her line. "You can say no."

Nat smiled and rolled her hand. "Go on."

"I was hoping you could take a look at a friend's car and maybe fix it."

"What kind?"

"Just a friend." Count on Nat to get right to the heart. That was why she didn't want to talk about Madison.

Nat smiled. "No, what car?"

"Oh, right. A Honda Fit." Whoops. Well, that was a dead giveaway.

Nat made a face. "That's not really a car."

"I know, but I don't think she can afford a better one." Well, now that it was out there, she planned to make her best case.

"Is she a teacher?"

"Social worker."

Nat threw her line back out and stared across the water, slowly reeling it back in. "Does she do good work?"

Jen paused. She couldn't say really. She'd never seen her at work, but last night, she'd seen her passion and enthusiasm while she talked up her project. That kind of advocacy only came from someone who cared. She smiled. "Yeah, she does."

"Where is it now?"

"I think it's at her mechanic's."

Nat cast again. "Do you know what's wrong with it?"

"Alternator. And something else. She didn't say." She knew Nat would say yes. They had too much history between them, and this was the first time she'd ever asked her for something like this.

"Find out and get back to me."

"Thanks. Let me know how much I owe you."

Nat shrugged. "Don't bother. If I can fix it, get it towed to my place, and I'll do it. I can work it into my schedule this week."

She already had a thank-you pole in mind for Nat. She just had to figure out a way to break it to Madison so that she'd accept the gift. Considering Madison paid her back for chasing off her birth father, she'd have a lot of work to do. Maybe a little white lie, perhaps convince Madison she was doing Jen or even Nat a favor. She churned through a few scenarios, each one getting more elaborate until she finally settled on the truth. She'd just tell her and ask her to accept it for what it was, a gift between friends. Right, friends. Friends that almost kissed twice last night. Friends that had slept together. Standing next to Nat in water up to her knees, she couldn't lie to herself any longer. She wanted something more than friends, but she wasn't sure how to get there from here.

On the drive back to the city, one of Rachel's new songs came on, and Jen reached over to mute it. "Do you mind?"

Nat shrugged. "I like it, but I get it." Her relationship with Nat had always been slightly apart from her relationship with Rachel.

That was the way it had always been. Their history went back to boarding school in their teens, and their closeness predated most of their relationships.

Jen's mood shifted as she got closer to her house, and the prospect of dealing with Rachel loomed.

Nat pulled up and parked on the curb. "Where's the Porsche?"

Jen flushed and rubbed the back of her neck. "At Madison's house."

"The project person?"

"She drove me home." There was no way Nat was going to let that lie there. But lying about it felt wrong.

"She drove the Porsche?" Nat's right eyebrow rose.

"I was probably beyond the legal limit." Jen squirmed under her look. Maybe a little white lie would have been okay.

"You never let Rachel drive it."

"Have you seen Rachel drive?" She could hear the defensiveness in her tone, but that wasn't Nat's point and she knew it. Jen never let anyone drive her car. It was the one luxury she'd bought herself just before their breakup.

"Let me guess, she owns the Honda."

Jen said, "Yes?" Well, shit. Guess she was having this conversation after all.

Nat shook her head with a smile. "That wasn't a question. Where'd you meet?"

Jen rubbed the back of her neck and mumbled, "Do you remember my wedding hookup?"

Nat whistled. "Oh, Jen. Why is it never simple with you?"

She opened her mouth to object, but Nat knew where all the bodies were buried. She crossed her arms, a little surly. "I don't do it on purpose."

"No, trouble finds you. Wasn't she, like, twenty?"

Jen scoffed. "No. She's twenty-eight." That sounded much better in her head.

Nat's look echoed her thoughts. "Hmm. How'd she find you?" She didn't know that Jen had left her number. When Madison hadn't called, Jen's pride had hurt just enough that she had packaged the story into a funny anecdote, minus the detail about leaving a note.

Now she had to walk that story back a bit. "She's the social worker at Hutchinson's."

Nat frowned, but before she could say anything, Jen raised her hand. "I know, I know. Don't shit where you eat."

"Last time didn't work out so well."

Jen rolled her eyes. "Shawn was a fucking train wreck. Madison's different."

"How so?"

"She's not desperate. She's not tied to anyone or anything. She's her own person." All of that was true, but she was so much more. She was intelligent and empathic. She was easy to talk to and understood nuance. She was guarded and open, sometimes at the same time. She had layers to her that Jen wanted to peel back and figure out. Madison clicked with something deep inside Jen. But she was sending her mixed signals, which tantalized and frustrated her to no end.

She sighed. "It doesn't matter. She's kind of damaged by this other relationship. She's not buying what I'm selling." And the truth of that hurt more than she was expecting.

"Jen." Nat's tone softened.

"She doesn't have a lot of money." She didn't want Nat to pull her offer because she hadn't been forthcoming with their quasi-relationship.

Nat remained quiet, her stare steady and calm.

"Say what you're thinking." Jen knew she sounded defensive. Nat often led the conversation where she wanted, using thoughtful questions and gentle prodding, like the way she diagnosed a car. Jen was in the mood for neither.

If Nat was surprised by her directness, she didn't show it. "Just don't spend so much time taking care of her that you forget your needs."

Jen paused, somewhat surprised. Was she taking care of Madison? Had it become so second nature that she didn't even think about it? When had her life become about serving other people's needs before her own? Sure, Carter started it, but then it spread to Rachel, Shawn. Was it her go-to romantic template? Fuck.

Jen sighed and shook her head. She'd let her life with Rachel exist in limbo for so long that a conversation about their future—or lack thereof—was overdue. She felt such guilt at the way she'd ended their relationship that she'd avoided talking about it. But last night's intro really reinforced that Rachel still nursed hope for them. Hope that Jen had done little to discourage.

Finally, Nat took a deep breath. "You're pissed."

Jen glanced over. "No." Nat just looked at her, so she put a little more effort into it. "I'm not. I'm just surprised by what you said. When I met Rachel, she was everything my mother wanted for me. I grabbed hold of her with two hands, and that was it. And life moved on. We changed, and I'm now the woman my mother always wanted me to be. Settled and established. Minus the pedigree. There's only so many eligible debutantes per generation."

Nat laughed.

Jen watched the early morning sunlight play along the crabapple's branches in her yard for a few minutes, gathering her thoughts. "When did I get so stuck?"

Nat drummed her fingers on the steering wheel before she said, "You're not stuck. Your priorities changed. You spent the last ten years raising a child, maintaining a relationship, and working full-time."

She snorted. "I'm still doing that."

Nat shook her head. "No, you're not. Despite physical evidence to the contrary, Rachel occupies less space in your life. It's given you clarity."

She laughed. Nat's definition of clarity must have been pretty murky if it matched up to Jen's reality. "I don't feel very clear."

Nat shrugged. "That'll come."

The front door opened, and Rachel sauntered out with a cup of coffee in hand. She nodded at Nat and gave a half wave.

Nat just shook her head. "I didn't know she was back in town."

"She showed up at Iron Pour last night."

"Couldn't find a hotel?" Nat's delivery was so dry and matter-of-fact that only the words revealed her sarcasm.

"That's exactly what I said." At least she had outside validation for that one.

Nat shook her head. "Good luck with that."

Jen groaned. "Thanks. See you later." She steeled herself for the conversation ahead. She just wanted to crawl back into the truck and drive away. Well, not really. She wanted Rachel to get in a truck and drive away.

Rachel held the door for her. "How's Nat?"

"Good. She says hi. Is that fresh?" She squeezed past her and nodded at the cup.

Rachel shook her head. "No, sorry."

She didn't bother to hide her irritation. She'd made a pot this morning and had left a little in the carafe. The least Rachel could have done was make more. She set her thermos in the sink and washed her hands.

"Are you mad at me? About the coffee?" Rachel walked over and leaned against the sink. Just a little too close.

Jen dried her hands, using that act to keep her annoyance at bay. "No. Yes. It's not the coffee. What are you doing here?"

Rachel pulled back. "I live here."

Irritation became frustration, and she slapped the towel on the counter. "No, you don't."

"Well, I pay the mortgage."

"We both pay the mortgage. And it's not about that. You can't just breeze in and out of our lives. We negotiated a schedule." Anger bubbled up inside her. Why did she have to be the one to enforce it? She was done rehashing this.

Rachel threw up her hands. "Is that what you think? I'm on the road twenty-four-seven for this family. For us."

Jen erupted. "For us? Get your head out of your ass. There's no more us. There's you and Carter, me and Carter. There's no more family."

"Mom?" Carter poked his head downstairs.

Fuck. She put aside her anger and frustration and pulled up a smile. "Morning, honey. Did we wake you?"

He walked down the stairs and shrugged. "Kind of. I heard you fighting."

She gave Rachel a look that she hoped conveyed her annoyance at being heard by their son. "Why don't you get dressed, and Mama and I can take you out to Darcy's for breakfast?"

"Okay." He grinned and ran halfway up the stairs, then turned. "But no more fighting."

Before she could respond, Rachel said, "No more fighting."

She worried that he might have heard her declare that they weren't a family, especially since she'd promised that they would always be one after the initial separation. They'd worked so hard to create a unified front after the separation. But the unified front had always benefited Rachel and not Jen. When she was sure she heard him in his room, she whispered, "This has to stop."

Rachel grabbed her hands. The full force of her personality—her onstage presence—poured out in her words. "I want it to stop. I want to come back."

Jen swallowed her own feelings and sighed. It always came down to this. Rachel wasn't ready to let go, and Jen didn't know how to make her. Her guilt always got in the way.

"I still love you. Don't you still love me?" Her voice broke.

Jen reached up and held her face. Some of her old love surfaced and took the edge off her frustration. She needed her to hear her so she spoke softly. "Yes. But I'm not in love with you."

Rachel covered her hands. "I can live with that."

"But I can't." She removed her hands and stepped back. "I think we should—"

A quiet knock at the side door interrupted her mid-thought, and she didn't bother to finish it. Answering the door was more productive than convincing Rachel to let go. Jen looked up, but no one was there. Curious, she opened the door and saw Madison at the edge of the driveway, her hands tucked in her back pockets as she looked toward the street.

A burst of joy surprised Jen with its intensity, and she stepped outside and closed the door behind her. She wanted to keep as much distance between Rachel and Madison. "Hey."

"Hi." Madison gave her an adorable half-smile and held out her keys. "I brought your car back."

Jen glanced over Madison's shoulder at her Porsche. She couldn't resist a slight tease. "In one piece?"

Madison gave her a look. "You're two blocks away."

"True, but a lot can happen in two blocks."

Madison rolled her eyes and stepped back. She pointed toward the door. "I'll let you get back to it."

Jen turned and saw Rachel staring out the door looking like some weird stalker. She exhaled and ushered Madison away. "Don't mind her."

Madison shrugged. "I didn't mean to interrupt. It looked pretty serious in there."

Jen considered the previous conversation. "It was. It is."

"Oh, okay." Madison started backing off.

Something felt off. Did Jen do something to offend her? Was it the almost kiss? Shit, she hoped not. Maybe Rachel did something through the window. Jen wouldn't put it past her. She could be a bit possessive, even though she had no right to be. Not wanting to let Madison go, she said, "Hey, what are you doing this Friday?"

"Uh. I'm not sure."

"We're heading to the Jack-O'-Lantern Spooktacular. Do you want to come?" Like Iron Pour, the jack-o'-lantern festival at the zoo was a family tradition, but Carter had started to distance himself the last two years. He was at that age where jack-o'-lanterns weren't as cool anymore.

Madison glanced over her shoulder.

If Rachel was still standing there, Jen was going to rip her a new asshole. "Don't worry, she'll be gone by then."

"I don't want to intrude."

Jen shook her head. "She's intruding, and you won't. He usually runs off with one of his friends. It'll be nice to have adult company." Having spent the better part of ten years with the parents of Carter's peer group, she was done making small talk. She wanted to go with someone interesting. And Madison was the most interesting person in her life right now.

"Will you dress up?" Madison's smile left no doubt in Jen's mind that this was a test of some kind.

Shit, she hadn't planned on that. Did Madison want to dress up? How far was Jen willing to go to spend time with her? "Like what?"

"How do you feel about *Harry Potter*?"

She paused. She'd read the books to Carter, and he was a big fan. But did Madison mean robes and wands? "Let me get back to you on that."

Madison smiled, and Jen knew she was in trouble. "I won't go unless you dress up."

Damn it. She'd been outmaneuvered. "Okay."

Madison's smile turned into a grin. "I look forward to it."

Shaking her head—she had no idea what dressing up meant, but she could imagine all sorts of things—she watched Madison walk away. Maybe she could convince her to move away from *Harry Potter* and into other more risqué costumes. *Wait, Carter's coming, so no.*

"Who's that?"

Jen jumped. She hadn't heard Rachel come up behind her.

Not wanting Rachel to get the wrong idea or rather, the right idea, Jen brushed past her. "A friend."

"What was she doing with your keys?"

"Returning them." If she was going out to breakfast, she should probably change. Her fishing pants kept her quite dry, but just the same, an odor of fish was something she'd prefer not to dine with. Fuck, she'd totally been wearing them when Madison showed up.

"She drove your car?"

"I had too much to drink." She started upstairs just as Carter came down. "Are you ready?"

He nodded.

"I never get to drive your car," Rachel called.

"Not the way you drive," she called back as she walked into her bedroom and closed the door. While she might have let herself be coerced into cosplay, she wasn't averse to it. If she was going to wear a costume, she was going to go all in. Time to figure out what house she was. Two could play this game, and she liked to win.

Chapter Twelve

Madison walked home from Jen's house with mixed feelings. Watching Jen with Rachel had her on edge. She'd seen them through the window, and they looked as if they were about to kiss. She almost didn't knock, but she couldn't just leave the keys on the porch. It was an expensive car. What if they'd had heard her pull up? She didn't want to pull back out and draw attention to herself. And then Jen had opened the door and acted as if her ex-wife wasn't hanging out in her kitchen as if she lived there. Which she kind of did, according to what Jen had said last night.

She didn't know how to take that, and Erika had lied to her for so long about leaving her wife that Madison didn't always trust her own instincts. But her instincts had drawn her to Jen and her natural charm, and so she'd said yes to another outing. Something about it felt more personal. In fact, she hadn't considered it might be another networking event like Iron Pour. But Iron Pour hadn't felt like a business event, either. Not really. And the way they'd flirted, the almost kiss, that was very personal. Her body still hummed with unspent arousal.

What the hell was she doing? Getting involved with the parent of a student, said her rational voice. She should avoid being alone with Jen. That was when things had changed last night. Jen had been so open. Madison had responded to her presence at a gut level, the way her eyes had darkened with intent and the way her perfume had enveloped her.

Madison groaned, aroused all over again. She just needed to get the lunch proposal funded, and then she could pull back gracefully. That was the professional choice, but it didn't feel like the right decision.

Standing in her mother's yard a few hours later, she got a text from Jen.

Forgot to tell you. I talked to a friend of mine. and she wants to look at your car.

Madison cradled the rake in her arms and texted back. Jen's generosity made her suspicious. *Why?*

She's willing to fix it as a favor to me.

Madison tucked the phone back into her jacket and looked across her parents' backyard. She wasn't sure what to say. She didn't have the money to get it fixed right away. It would be so easy to let herself be seduced by Jen and everything she offered.

"What's her name?" Her mother took a sip from her water bottle.

"Who?"

Her mom pointed. "The woman you're texting with."

Madison bent over and scooped up a pile of leaves. "What makes you think it's a woman?"

Her mom set her water down and grabbed her own handful of leaves. She waited for Madison to drop hers into the wheelbarrow. "I've seen that look before."

Madison brushed an arm across her forehead. She grabbed her rake and scraped it across the lawn. What look? She didn't have a look, did she? And what kind of look? A dreamy, starry-eyed look or a distracted hot and bothered look. She hoped it was neither, but if it was, let it be the dreamy one in front of her mother. "Yeah, well, it is, and it isn't."

"What's going on?"

Madison shrugged. "I don't know. She says she has a friend who can fix my car." Her parents had already offered to pay, and she'd declined. "For free."

"Free? Honey, that's fantastic. Why don't you look happy?"

Madison scooped up more leaves and dumped them in the wheelbarrow. "I don't know what it means."

Her mom picked up her own pile and followed suit. "Why does it have to mean anything?"

Madison took a deep breath. She had no idea how to explain this to her mother without going into detail, and the last thing she wanted to say was, "I had sex with this woman I just met, and it turns out her son goes to my school." But there was no way to end this conversation without coming clean. "She's not just a friend. I slept with her at Jessie's wedding."

Her mom stopped raking and leaned against the handle. "Oh. Well, I've had less romantic gestures."

Madison laughed. "Romantic?"

She stopped. Was it romantic? She didn't get the sense that Jen acted from that kind of place. Her reputation and Madison's own interactions bolstered that opinion. Jen did things for a reason, but she was always up front about them. If it was romantic, Madison would know about it.

Her mom chuckled. "Well, you think about that. But let me ask you. Is she paying to have it towed?"

Madison cocked her head. "I don't know."

"A friend helps you out. A lover pays for things." Her mom winked and went back to raking the yard.

She stepped back. Her mother continued raking, ignoring or unaware of her surprise. Lover? Jen wasn't her lover. But she wasn't exactly a friend, either. She didn't have a lot of comparisons.

Erika was the only other girlfriend Madison had ever had, and she'd never offered to do things like that. She certainly paid for stuff but not the things that mattered. And her purchases were always write-offs and cash, things that couldn't be traced. Her gifts had always felt like an afterthought. Jen wasn't like that. She took care of people. That included Madison. But she didn't want to be just another person in Jen's life. Did Jen even see the difference?

She finished the yard work before her mom drove her home. In the car, she got another text from Jen that swept aside her doubts.

Tell me where it is, and I'll get it towed for you.

She groaned. Her mother was right.

Her mom patted her arm. "Your woman again?"

"She wants to tow the car."

Her mother chuckled.

"Stop." But she said it without any real intent behind it. "What's so wrong with having a relationship with this woman?" her mom asked.

"She's married, well, separated, but her ex is still in her life, she has a kid, and she's on the board of my school." Not to mention she'd just decided that she didn't want to get involved.

"Well, when you put them all together like that, it sounds like a bad idea." But her tone disagreed.

"It does, doesn't it?" But the fight had left her. Her heart wasn't listening. Jen wanted to pay, and a lover paid. Madison threw out her decision to cut off contact after the project. She wanted to be special to Jen. But there was no way she'd let her fix her car. She didn't want to be a checkbox that Jen ticked off. She didn't want to be taken care of, at least not like that.

Before she got out, her mother stopped her and offered again. "Listen, honey, if you need money to get your car on the road again, we can help."

"I know." She thanked her and promised to be there for next week's Sunday dinner.

That night, she laid in bed unable to sleep, weighing the pros and cons of accepting Jen's help or her parents' money. Now that the possibility existed, Madison wanted her relationship with Jen to have as few strings as possible. Decision made, she grabbed her phone and tried three different sentences before she came up with simple and short.

Thanks. I'm all set.

Not expecting a reply, she put it down and rolled over. Her breath caught at the immediate response, and she picked it up, dreading the acknowledgement but not willing to ignore it.

Are you sure?

She stared at those words, trying to decipher what they meant. A gentle question asking her to reconsider or the opening to another push? She'd have to text back to find out.

I'm sure.

Okay. Three little dots appeared again. *I ordered my robes.*

And just like that, Jen let it go. The tension drained out of Madison's body, and she relaxed. *Already?*

She grinned, remembering how reluctant Jen had been to dress up, but within eight hours, she'd already bought something to wear. She shifted around and typed back, her excitement creating typos that she quickly fixed before sending. *Which house?*

You'll have to wait and see. A winking emoji.

Madison groaned and flopped back on the bed. Was Jen trying to kill her? Madison's desire turned up a few notches. Between their near kisses last night, her mother's comment about lovers, and this last text, Madison was beginning to think that maybe, just maybe, Jen wanted more. Knowing that made her anticipation for Friday and the Spooktacular sweeter, even and especially if it was a date.

CHAPTER THIRTEEN

Friday arrived with no more texts from Jen, and Madison's insecurities surfaced. Erika would disappear for days, make plans, and then cancel at the last minute. She covered her nerves by inviting Kayla over to get ready, but by the time she arrived, Jen had already texted her with a time and another damn emoji. And a Hogwarts gif that made her laugh. She immediately felt foolish for dragging Kayla over and said so.

Kayla hugged her, and she relaxed for the first time in a few days. "It's okay. Erika really did a number on you. I'll take off after she gets here."

Madison shrugged into her yellow and black Hufflepuff robe. Kayla pulled on a similar robe in deep burgundy with a lion crest on her left breast. She wore a white dress shirt tucked into dark jeans and held a matching tie in her left hand and asked, "Can you tie this?"

"You could come with us." Madison waved her over. Hanging the tie over her own neck, Madison made quick work of it and handed it back.

Kayla raised an eyebrow. "Not in the back of a Porsche. No, thank you. I'll just pull the big sister routine on her and leave."

Her stomach plummeted. "No. Please don't."

A mischievous grin on her face, Kayla cinched the tie up to her neck, then readjusted it. "What time is your date showing up?"

"It's not really a date. Her son's coming along." She kept telling herself that it didn't matter if Carter came. Jen wanted to spend time with her, and sometimes her son was a part of that deal.

"Don't sell yourself short."

The doorbell rang, and she hurried downstairs. Rubbing the sweat off her palms, she straightened her own tie and opened the door.

Wearing Madison's Hufflepuff colors, Jen stood behind Carter in his Gryffindor robes with a half-smile on her face that said "Hey, we match," and all Madison's worries faded away.

She grinned. "You two look fantastic." She crouched to talk to Carter. "Where's your wand?"

He grinned and tapped the inside of his robe.

"Excellent."

Jen spread her arms and spun in place. "Carter made me take one of those quizzes. Apparently, I belong in Hufflepuff."

Kayla walked up behind Madison and said, "No shame in that."

Jen shook her hand. "It's good to see you again. Kayla, right?"

Kayla gave Madison the, did she really just remember my name, look.

"Are you coming with us?" Jen asked.

"Nah. I just wanted to get ready with this one." Kayla slung an arm around her shoulder, and Madison knew the "talk" was imminent.

Jen shifted her focus to Madison. "Then are you ready?"

Madison nodded and quickly grabbed her keys. Just before she walked out, Kayla nudged her and whispered, "She dressed up."

Madison shrugged. Although inside, she was totally impressed. "And?"

"That's fucking cool." Kayla gave her a look that said, "And you know it."

Madison grinned and nodded. "Yeah, she did. In Hufflepuff." Even though she'd had a vision of Jen as a Slytherin, the fact that their robes matched was more significant than she was expecting. How else were they compatible?

In the car, Jen asked, "Is the College Street Bridge okay? I could also go farther north and avoid the bridges."

Even more important than their house match, Jen remembered her fear. Touched by her thoughtfulness, Madison said, "You don't have to drive out of your way for me. I95 is the fastest route."

Jen shrugged. "We'll take the scenic route. Besides, I can make up for any lost time with this beauty." She tapped the steering wheel.

Madison chuckled, and they drove toward the setting sun. She asked Carter about his wand, and they talked Potter until they pulled up to Roger Williams Zoo. The sun had set, and the park was lit up with tiny orange lights leading toward the entrance. A crowd had gathered in a line. Someone called Carter's name, and he ran over to greet a boy dressed in a Captain America costume. They followed and met up with a man and a woman, presumably Cap's parents, who greeted Jen.

Jen introduced Madison, placing a hand on the small of her back as she spoke. It was so unexpected and yet natural that she completely missed the couple's names in return.

"Nice costumes," the dad said. They were dressed in jeans and sweaters, and she couldn't tell if he was teasing or approving.

Either way, Jen left him no room for criticism and spread her arms. "It is, isn't it?"

It made Madison happy to know that Jen embraced it. So many people in her life dismissed her hobbies and interests as silly. Jen respected them and participated without condition. While Jen did most of the talking, Madison picked up a slight tone and cadence to her voice that felt familiar. She tried to place it but came up with nothing. It bothered her because there was a warning in that tone that she couldn't place until the husband asked about Rachel. That was it. She used the same tone when talking about her ex. Nothing else in her mannerisms gave it away, but Madison knew she didn't like them. That tone changed as soon as she spoke with Cap himself. Her dislike did not extend to their kid.

Having figured that out, Madison tuned out the small talk and focused on the music as they moved closer. The ethereal sounds invoked a fairyland, and that was when she observed the plethora of fairy princesses in line and a smattering of other fairytale creatures.

Confirming Madison's earlier assumptions, Jen leaned in and whispered in her ear. "We'll ditch them as soon as we're in."

And they did. Cap and his family moved off. Carter stayed with Jen and Madison, and they wandered the trails filled with hundreds of glowing pumpkins. Not sure of her place with them, Madison stood slightly apart, watching his enthusiasm and Jen's encouragement among the exhibits; her silly faces matched his goofing off. Jen caught her looking and pulled her into their play. Madison joined in willingly, and soon, they were all laughing and riffing on each other's comments, completely at ease. All her anxiety disappeared, and she finally relaxed.

Eventually, Carter moved past them, and Jen linked arms with her. "Thank you for coming with me."

Madison leaned into the touch. She'd always appreciated the artistry behind the pumpkin carvings, but seeing it through Carter's and Jen's eyes, she experienced a joy and wonder she didn't know she'd been missing. "Thank you for inviting me. I love your robes, by the way."

Jen did a twirl, a move reminiscent of their dance together. "I look good, don't I? I wanted the green one. I feel so much more Slytherin, but Carter insisted that I follow the sorting quiz."

Madison was fairly certain that how someone felt about their house was as much an indicator as some random quiz on the internet. Her inner geek couldn't believe she was actually talking with a "date" about Hogwarts's houses. Even with Carter along for the ride, there was no question in her mind that this was a date, complete with hand-holding.

Carter ran back with another kid in tow. Madison recognized him from Hutchinson's. "Hey, Mom, can Matt and I do the zipline?"

"Zipline?" Madison asked. When did the zoo get a zipline? Fear trickled through her.

"Of course." Jen grinned and tugged on her hand. They weaved through more jack-o'-lanterns and cut through a side trail.

It wasn't really a traditional zipline. Two people were loaded into a chair lift at the bottom of the line and slowly pulled backward over the lake toward a tower on the far shore before the cart sped back down to the loading zone. A lump formed in her throat.

Madison looked at the water, the tower, and swallowed her fear. "How tall is that?"

Jen looked up. "About a hundred feet." Her face changed. "Oh, right. I feel like such an asshole. We don't have to do this." She started to pull them out of line.

"Wait." Jen's empathy gave her courage. Madison felt safe with her. She could do this. It wasn't a bridge…no, it was worse, said her scared half. She shoved that fear aside. She could manage for the length of the time it took to get up there and back. Besides, it looked really fun.

Jen held both her hands. "Are you sure?"

The line moved again, and they shifted with it. No, she wasn't sure, but she didn't want fear holding her back from sharing this experience. She squeezed Jen's hands and straightened her shoulders. "I'm okay. I can do this. I want to do this."

Carter touched her forearm. "It's not really that bad. I was scared at first, but now it's easy."

"I bet." She doubted it would ever be easy but nodded anyway. Jen stared at her with a soft expression. She couldn't read it, but it made her feel warm and seen. It wasn't desire but something deeper. It was nothing she'd ever seen before, but she wanted Jen to look that way at her again and again.

Jen's smile lit a part of her that she didn't realize was dark. A deeper darkness much older than her adult relationships. A place where her fears thrived on insecurities and preyed on her daily life. Marveling at the way Jen's presence cleared a path, she lost a bit of her fear and embraced her newfound bravery.

Carter went first with his friend and came off the chair laughing and smiling. Jen whispered something to him as she handed him her cell phone. Jen climbed up into the chair and held out her hand. "Shall we?"

Madison took her hand and settled next to her. The ride attendant strapped them in and checked their harnesses. Then the chair began to pull up and away. Still holding her hand, Jen leaned in and said, "You okay?"

Madison realized she was squeezing Jen's hand and forced herself to relax. Beneath them, the lake turned black as they lifted into the air. All around them, the flickering lights of hundreds of pumpkins dotted the shoreline and beyond. The noise of the crowd disappeared, and the crickets' chirping took over. The wind picked up, and their robes flapped in the breeze as they moved above the trees. At the top, they paused, and she could see the downtown skyline off to her right. She could almost forget that they were hanging from a chair one hundred feet up in the air. "It's beautiful."

"It is." Jen's face was in shadow, with just a hint of a smile, but she wasn't looking at the view. She was looking at Madison, who now didn't care that her feet were dangling in the wind. A light fluttering feeling moved from her stomach to her lungs, and her breath caught in her throat. Was she going to kiss her? No, this was something more, a deeper bond growing between them, fueled by her desire, and yes, she wanted Jen, right there, right then. Out here above the ground and away from everyone, this was distinct from her body's yearnings.

The moment hung between them, and then the chair accelerated.

Madison screamed, then laughed as they rushed toward the dark water and glowing pumpkins below. Almost immediately, they leveled off and came to a smooth stop at the landing site.

Madison helped Jen get out then pulled her hand away as Carter ran up to them. Jen glanced at her with a questioning look, and Madison wondered if she'd felt that moment above the lake the same way Madison had.

Carter handed Jen her cell, and she laughed before tilting the phone toward her and showing her a pic of the two of them coming back, smiling, laughing and holding hands, their black and yellow robes flapping. She almost didn't recognize herself, she looked so happy.

Jen tucked her phone away, and they headed back into the jack-o'-lantern display. She linked arms with Madison and said, "Are you glad you did it?"

Exhilarated and proud, Madison leaned close. "Absolutely."

They wandered through the rest of the pumpkins, pausing now and then to admire the work and detail. Carter and Matt walked ahead, which gave them space to talk privately.

She wanted to get back to that moment above the lake, but she didn't know how. Instead, she brought up something else that she wanted to make sure Jen understood. "I wanted to thank you for offering to fix my car."

Jen tilted her head. "But you're still going to say no, aren't you?"

Madison took a deep breath before she opened up. "I never really set out on my own. I went straight from college to grad school and during that time, Erika took care of things. I let her, thinking she did it because she loved me. But really, she needed control."

"That's not what this is about. I'm not trying to control you. I just want to help."

"I know. But there is a power imbalance between us, and I can't ignore that."

Jen frowned. "A slight one. And I'd never abuse it."

At least she acknowledged it. She'd been afraid that she'd deny it or worse, not even recognize it. She didn't want to always owe Jen something, and although the promises helped, she didn't really believe them. "I'll hold you to that."

"You should." Jen pulled her to a stop and faced her. "I mean it."

The tension that had lodged itself inside her body disappeared for the first time since Jen brought up fixing her car. "It's still no."

She saw Jen's smile in the half light of a pumpkin. "Of course."

Even though Madison was telling her no, Jen could hear the yes that hadn't been said. Yes to something more. Madison's concern about the power between them was a relationship issue, not a friend one, and she couldn't hide the smile or suppress the giddy surge through her body.

Carter came bounding back without Matt. "I'm hungry."

"Me, too," Jen said. "Let's finish up and grab something to eat. Sound good?" With so much still unsaid, she didn't want the evening to end just yet.

She took them to a hipster burger place with hand cut french fries and a huge list of burger toppings. Dinner came fast, and Madison was surprised.

Jen chuckled. "Yes, it's what first attracted me to this place when Carter was little. We could eat fast and get out quick. Now it's a staple."

They talked about their favorite pumpkins while they ate. It moved quickly to other interests, and Jen enjoyed listening to Madison and her son talk video games. Madison's knowledge seemed vast, and she shared Carter's enthusiasm. At first, Jen thought it was because of her work at the school, but her interest was genuine and personal. She actually cared about his hobbies because they were her own. For once, Jen didn't have to keep the conversation going, and she could relax.

The car conversation had bothered her but not for the reasons Madison brought up. She'd just assumed that Madison would want her help. Hearing her say no made Jen realize that the offer was part and parcel of her romantic pattern, taking care of her romantic or soon to be romantic partner either emotionally or physically. And that gave her pause.

After dinner, Carter asked if he could play a few games. There was an old style arcade across the dining room with *Skee-ball*, *Centipede*, and *Pac-Man*. Jen dug out a token card and handed it to Carter. "Go. There's ten bucks on that. Let me know if you need more."

Alone at last, she turned to Madison and said what had been on her mind for the past hour. "I'm sorry about the car."

"It's not your fault it's not working."

"No, I mean for assuming you'd want my help. Nat, the one who can fix your car, said something that made me think: I sometimes take care of things without thinking." Now that she knew, she didn't want to recreate that pattern with Madison.

Madison smiled. "Why am I not surprised?"

Jen laughed. She found the transparency between them refreshing and freeing. "Subtlety is not my strong suit."

Madison leaned forward. "You don't have to take care of me."

She let Madison's answer soak in before she changed the subject. "What are your plans for Halloween?"

"Kayla and I always do this ghost tour if I'm in town. We dress up. Of course."

"Of course." Jen smiled. She could see Madison decked out in black and Victorian lace. An urge to see her in more intimate lace popped into her mind. Heat rose to her cheeks.

Madison grinned, a smug look on her face. "You should come."

Was her desire that obvious? If it was, she didn't care. Unfortunately, she had to say no. "I can't. I want to, but I always host a party for the neighborhood kids. It's a tradition." That she would totally miss this year to see Madison in a corset or a fitted vest.

Was that disappointment under her smile? "That's sweet."

Carter plopped back in his seat.

Jen was a bit disappointed he was back so soon. She admonished herself. If she really wanted alone time with Madison, she could get a sitter. In fact, next time she would. "All done?"

He shrugged. "I got tired of losing."

Madison laughed. "Come on. Let me try."

Jen watched as Madison took him back to the arcade. She was torn between going with them or leaving them alone. The waiter came with the check, and she paid while they played. Madison's ease with Carter and their gentle competitiveness stirred feelings she wasn't expecting. She could love a woman who loved her kid. She held her breath for a second too long before she exhaled. What the fuck was she saying? Love? They hadn't even gone on a real date. *Slow down there, Jen.*

Pushing away from the table and those thoughts, she came up behind them and cheered them both as they played skee-ball together. Carter lost but not by much. He grinned. "I want a rematch. Go again?"

Madison looked at her and said, "Only if your mom plays, too."

Unable to resist her, Jen stepped forward. "Oh, it's on." They played two more games, with Carter taking the second game and Jen intentionally losing the last one in Madison's favor. She couldn't remember the last time she'd felt so light.

On the way to the car, Madison looped her hand through Jen's elbow.

Wrapped up in the feeling of being close to her, Jen didn't expect Madison to chide her. "I told you I didn't need you taking care of me."

Jen looked at her for a second, and then it dawned on her. Madison knew she'd lost on purpose. She shrugged, unrepentant. "My mother always taught me to be a gracious host."

Madison made a noise. "I've met your mother. I have my doubts."

Jen choked on a laugh.

"Don't do it again." The warning tone brooked no arguments, and Jen knew she'd comply. Jen might have more money and status, but Madison had the ability to see right through her. Something no one had ever been able to do; it made her nervous and excited.

"Never again. I promise." And she actually meant it.

In the car, Madison asked Carter what he was going to be for Halloween, and he went on and on about his plans, finally adding, "You should come to our party."

"She might have plans." Jen didn't need Carter putting Madison in the position of letting him down easy.

Madison turned to face him in the back seat. "I do." She looked over at Jen and raised an eyebrow. "But maybe after?"

Surprised but pleased, Jen said, "It's usually a pretty late affair. But if you're game, I am."

"I'll text you if I can make it." Madison put her hand on the door and said, "I had a good time tonight. Thank you for inviting me."

"My pleasure." Jen smoothed down her robes. "And now I have a Halloween costume."

Madison grinned. "Well, the colors suit you."

Jen knew those words had a deeper meaning to Madison. She might have to brush up on her *Harry Potter*.

She didn't walk her to her door, even though she wanted to. Carter was in the back seat, and this wasn't exactly a date. She waited for Madison to walk into her apartment before she pulled out.

Carter kept talking, but her mind was on autopilot, playing that moment on the zipline when everything had stopped, and it had been just the two of them. Such a perfect blend of place and person that she'd never capture again. But she knew she would try.

Carter brought her thoughts to a halt. "She's nice. I like her."

Jen sighed and couldn't help but agree. "Yeah, me, too." She just hoped the feeling was mutual.

Chapter Fourteen

Madison almost let it go to voice mail, but a Saturday afternoon phone call from Jen proved too much of a temptation. She barely got in a hello before Jen asked, "Do you want to shop for refrigerators?"

"What's wrong with your old one?"

Jen laughed. "Nothing. Well, it's for my garage. For the lunches. Are you in?" Jen had rounded up a group of parents to house the bagged lunches while they worked on funding the kitchen.

"Well, when you put it that way, yes."

"Great. I'll pick you up in five."

Madison hung up and glanced at her clothes. Was this going to be another one of their non-date dates? Shit, she wasn't even showered, and she didn't have time. She brushed her teeth, changed her clothes, and stuffed her hair into a baseball cap. A huge black truck pulled up at the curb just as her phone dinged.

Here.

Madison stared at the cab, and sure enough, Jen was at the wheel. Climbing up into it, she said, "Is this your truck?"

Jen grinned and patted the dashboard. "I know it looks good on me." Madison stared at her outfit—heavy sweater, black jeans, and hiking boots, rural Jen—and decided she liked the look. Catching Madison's appreciative gaze, she winked. "I dressed down for you."

Madison laughed. "I see." Apparently, it was going to be another non-date date, but she didn't mind. This easy banter felt right.

"It's actually Nat's. I do have an ulterior motive for inviting you." She leaned over, and Madison leaned in. For one second, she felt like Jen might kiss her, but then she bypassed her lips and whispered in her ear. "I need someone to do the heavy lifting."

Madison's brain tripped on her words, and she pulled back. Jen's playfulness was new and it knocked her off-balance. "What?"

Putting the truck in gear, Jen navigated the first few streets while she explained. "I don't want to wait to have it delivered. We're bringing it home today."

Something about that felt flimsy—she couldn't wait a few days?—but Madison didn't call her on it. She'd go pretty much anywhere to spend time with Jen.

In the appliance store, one of the sales reps greeted them, and Jen asked, "Is Diane working?"

"Not today. Is there something I can help with?" He stepped forward, and Jen did the talking. They wandered down aisles of washers, dryers, dishwashers, ranges, and ovens, finally coming to a stop in front of the refrigerators.

Madison only paid half-attention, opening and closing doors while he talked. As he showed them the features, something about Jen's tone alerted Madison to her growing annoyance just before he asked, "Now, are you two sisters?"

Uh-oh. Madison popped her head back out and glanced at Jen. Her ability to see through Jen's facade was working overtime. The question here was, did she want to stop Jen or join in the blowup?

Jen's lips pursed, and she said, "No."

He looked at them for a moment and then smiled, "But you're related, right?"

Madison cut another look at Jen, her expression tight. He was a second away from getting his ass handed to him. Even though he deserved it, she chose to sidestep the blowup with another tactic that she knew Jen would enjoy. "Honey, take a look at this." She wrapped her hand around Jen's bicep and pulled her toward a stainless steel fridge. "Wouldn't this look lovely in our beach house?"

He faltered for a moment and then adjusted his pitch to their relationship status. Madison clung to Jen for the rest of the visit. Without acknowledging what was going on, they kept up the ruse for the next two stores, with Jen grabbing her hand in the next one and Madison picking hers up on the third one. Halfway through the second store, it stopped being a game, and Madison let herself sink into the fantasy of being Jen's girlfriend. The more she played, the more she wanted it to be real. This project between them made it hard to discern Jen's true feelings. These non-date dates were killing her. Did Jen even see her as a dating partner? It was hard to tell. And if she did, how did they start dating when they'd already slept together? That was the real question.

Once outside, she let go of Jen's hand, tired of the ruse, but Jen pulled Madison against her. Madison put her hands on Jen's shoulders to stop herself from falling into her.

Jen steadied her and said, "You're getting very good at playing my girlfriend."

Distracted by Jen's closeness, Madison ignored her uncertainty and demurred. "I've had practice."

Jen raised her eyebrows. "So you fake date other women."

"Only you." She wanted the words to mean so much more.

"I feel special."

You are. Jen's smile did things to her that made her want to show her. But she had no idea how Jen felt, so Madison slipped away and called over her shoulder, "You should."

Jen sagged against the truck, trying to control her desire to chase Madison. Fuck. What was she doing? Shopping together had turned out to be the most domestic and erotic thing she'd ever done. All those little touches, overt and furtive, in front of the salespeople. After a particularly teasing touch, Jen had almost dragged her out behind the garden section. The only thing holding her back was the on-again off-again signals she was getting. Like now. They kept coming up to this line only to step back. It was frustrating and exciting and had her totally aroused.

Taking a deep breath, she clambered into the truck. It was almost noon, and she was getting hungry. "Can I buy you lunch?"

Maybe they'd talk about what was going on. She suggested Sugar Magnolia off Thayer Street. Madison seemed a little ambivalent, but Jen couldn't figure out why. Was she frustrated, too? Maybe this had been a bad idea.

When they arrived, the place was loud and packed with a mix of locals and college students. The young woman who greeted them at the door shrieked and hugged Madison. An unexpected stab of jealousy rushed through Jen. Was this woman the reason for Madison's reluctance? "Oh my God, Kayla said you were back in town."

Madison pulled back and grabbed Jen's hand. "Jen, this is my cousin, Deanna."

Oh, cousin. Deanna gave Jen a quick hug, and Jen's pettiness disappeared with Deanna's warm smile. "Welcome." She then whispered something in Madison's ear. Madison blushed and shook her head. Judging from the way Deanna looked at her, Jen figured she was being checked out. What she couldn't decide was if it was favorable or not, and for once, that mattered to her.

Deanna ducked behind the podium, checked something, then fished a couple of menus out from the stand. "I've got you covered. Follow me."

One of the waiting college kids said, "I thought they didn't take reservations." Jen just smiled at him and waved.

Deanna led them through the cramped dining room toward a tiny table in the back. She grabbed some silverware and deposited it at the table while they sat. "It's not the best in the house." She mock glared at Madison as she handed them their menus. "If you'd let us known, we could have set aside something nicer. I'm going to let Aunt Evelyn know you're here. She'll want to see you." She hurried past and walked toward the kitchen.

Jen turned her attention to Madison and smiled. Her early reticence made sense now. "I didn't know your family owned this place. What did she whisper to you?"

Madison blushed. She grabbed her napkin and fiddled with the knot. "She asked if this was a date."

Jen found her slight awkwardness charming, and her heart melted a little bit more. Taking a risk, she asked, "And is it?"

Madison held eye contact while fidgeting with her utensils. "I don't know. Is it?"

Jen wanted to laugh. Of course Madison threw it back. They really needed to talk, but the idea that this thing between them would dissipate in the harsh light of reality kept her quiet. She skirted the truth instead. "Well, if it is, I'm not sure I want to own up to it. I mean, really, who takes a date appliance shopping?" She looked for clues to what Madison was thinking, seeing her face falter, then change to a smile at the joke about appliances. Both reactions made Jen feel better. It wasn't just one-sided.

"I've had worse dates."

Jen leaned in. "Do tell."

A reed thin woman came to their table with her arms open and swept Madison into a hug. "Your mother said you were back for good." She was probably ten years Jen's senior. "I'm Evelyn."

Jen stood and shook her hand. "Jen Winslow."

Evelyn gave her a quick up and down, not checking her out, per se but more like sizing her up. Jen took it in stride and put on her best donor face, asking about the restaurant and the best dishes on the menu. That broke the ice, and soon Evelyn was bringing out drinks and giving suggestions.

After she left with their order, Madison shook her head and laughed.

Jen leaned in. "Something funny?"

Madison rubbed her forehead. "I don't know what I was thinking bringing you here."

Jen glanced over her shoulder to where Evelyn had disappeared. "Technically, I brought you. But I thought that went well."

Madison shook her head. "Maybe. I don't know. She's hard to read."

Apparently, Jen had missed the subtext of the situation. She touched Madison's hand. "Well, I didn't notice. She seems nice. And she obviously cares for you...they both do."

Madison squeezed her hand. "Yeah, they do. I'm just not used to them having opinions about who I'm dating."

Jen grinned at the slip. "Dating?"

Madison groaned. "That's not what I meant…I'm mean, yes. No. It's been a long time since I've been home, and I didn't date much in high school. It's just weird."

Jen let her ramble a bit before she let her off the hook. But they'd get back to that later. "How did you end up with your family?"

The subject change worked, and Madison's shoulders relaxed. "What? They don't look like my birth parents?"

She chuckled and played along. "It's the eyes. There's a difference in your bone structure that says you're adopted."

Madison swatted her shoulder. "That's such bullshit."

She shrugged. "Well, actually no. It's not. But there's also the fact that you're white, and they're not."

Madison took a drink before answering, "After my fourth removal, my mother relinquished custody of me, and they adopted me."

Fourth removal? Angry for her, Jen finally understood Madison's need for independence.

Madison nodded. "Yes. I was fostered by them three out of the four times. They always kept tabs on me, so when I came up a fourth time, they adopted me." She laughed with a slight edge. "My birth parents are total racists. It kills them that I ended up with a black family."

Her brief interaction with Travis only confirmed that. "How old were you when they adopted you?"

"Sixteen."

Jen imagined Carter going through those life experiences, and her heart hurt for Madison. So much uncertainty going from house to house at such a young age. No wonder she'd insisted on taking care of herself. "I'm sorry you had to go through that so young."

Madison straightened her silverware. "It was hard. I was angry all the time, and then it got better."

Jen held her hand, and they sat in silence until Madison shifted and pulled away as Evelyn arrived with a huge tray and tons of food. There was no way they were going to eat all of it.

After the first bites, Jen offered her own history. "I was thirteen when my dad came out."

From then on, the conversation flowed between them. She talked about her father's coming out and her parents' divorce. She shared stories of her own early dating experiences, people and places she hadn't thought about in years.

She offered to pay, and Madison brushed her off. Madison and Evelyn argued briefly about the check before Madison whispered something in her ear. Evelyn glanced at Jen, then took Madison's credit card.

Curious, she asked, "What did you say?"

Madison gave her that awkward but slightly cocky smile that she was finding it harder and harder to resist. "I told her the truth."

Jen's heart skipped a beat. "And that was?"

Madison looked down and then up. "Its's a date."

Jen tucked her hand into Madison's elbow and acknowledged the truth. "Yes, yes, it is."

They slipped outside, and she only pulled away when she helped Madison up into the truck. She climbed in on the other side and caught Madison staring. Heat swelled inside her at the intense look. "What?"

"Does this answer your question?"

Madison leaned across the console and captured Jen's lips.

Surprised, Jen recovered quickly and breathed the word yes against Madison's lips. She let Madison dictate the heat of the kiss, delighting in the feather soft touches but longing to pour all of her pent-up passion into the kiss. She'd waited this long; she could wait some more. And when Madison pulled back, Jen didn't follow.

Seconds passed as Jen tried to figure out what to say or do. The woman who could read any room and navigate social situations with ease didn't have a sense of her next move or Madison's.

Madison broke the silence before it got awkward. "Where do we go from here?"

"I was kind of following your lead."

"I've never done this before."

Jen smiled, certain her sarcastic quip was written on her face.

"You know what I mean."

"Well, we can pretend we didn't share a night of fabulous sex. Which we already did and look where it got us."

Madison laughed. "You thought it was fabulous?"

"And you didn't?" Jen joked, but part of her was afraid she'd read her wrong.

But then Madison gave her that smile that felt so dangerously addictive. "I did."

Unimaginably relieved, Jen continued, "Or we could see where this could take us."

"And if it doesn't work out, then what?"

Jen suppressed her urge to laugh. She'd had plenty of experience dealing with her exes on a daily basis. If it didn't work out, she'd just add another to the group. But this was the crux of the matter with Madison, and she knew it. Madison had been burned by Erika, and she needed to address that if she wanted to move beyond her shadow. She wasn't going to sugarcoat the truth, but she could promise her one thing. "I can't give you guarantees, but I'm not Erika."

Her point made, Jen put the truck in drive. The silence felt less awkward after she caught Madison glancing her way more than once, and her mind circled back to the original purpose of their day together. In hindsight, finding a refrigerator had just been a pretense to spend time with her. "I don't suppose you'd still be interested in another round of appliance shopping."

Madison's chuckle filled the cab, and Jen smiled at the warmth it gave her to hear it. "I could be convinced to spend another hour."

"I promise I won't make you carry it." And she didn't. Her urgency to have it delivered that day disappeared in favor of spending more time with Madison.

An hour later, she pulled into Madison's driveway and hesitated. Should she get out and open the door or lean in for another kiss? For all their talk, nothing was settled. Madison took that uncertainty away by giving her a kiss on the cheek. She pulled back before Jen could respond and said, "Next time, you need to up your game." Jen's smile mirrored her heart. Next time she would. Especially now that she knew it was a date.

CHAPTER FIFTEEN

U p my game." Jen had lost count the number of times she'd muttered that phrase. Sometimes with a smile, sometimes with a chuckle, and sometimes with a groan. This last time was with a confident smile as she put the finishing touches on her outfit. She had changed shirts three times, her pants twice, and she had almost switched her underwear before settling on the current pair. A mix of casual and chic: light blue pants, black boots, cream-colored sweater, black lace underwear.

Her babysitter arrived just as she was rubbing perfume on her wrists. She walked Parker through the last-minute details more as a way to settle her nerves than out of any real necessity. Parker had watched Carter several times before.

Leaning over the couch, she kissed Carter good night. "Are you all set?"

"Yeah," he answered without looking up, and then he wrinkled his nose. "What's that smell?"

She rolled her eyes. "Me."

"What is it?"

"It's perfume."

He turned toward her. "Is this a date?"

"I told you I was going out."

"Not on a date. Does Mama know?"

She kept her irritation and amusement hidden. No need to advertise her feelings about Carter's other parent in front of him. "No."

He smiled. "Don't worry, your secret is safe with me."

Time to nip that one in the bud. "You don't need to keep secrets for me. You are welcome to share whatever you want about me with your other mother." A part of her wished he'd keep quiet. She could already hear Rachel's voice now, but it wasn't safe to teach him to keep secrets. Carter was very protective of his parents, and the conversation made her wonder if Rachel had asked him to keep stuff from her. That one was going to need sorting out later.

She pulled up to Madison's apartment and got out of the car as Madison opened the door. Jen's smile grew as she took in Madison's low-slung jeans and light red shirt.

Putting her puffer jacket on, Madison paused at the edge of the sidewalk and gave Jen a once-over. She pointed. "You said casual." She waved at her. "That's not casual."

Jen opened the passenger door. "You said to up my game. This is my game upped." Madison gave her a side-eye and brushed past. Jen traced the curve of her ass in those "casual" jeans and caught her eye. Leaning in, Jen said, "You look fucking hot. I like your jeans."

She got a blush for her compliment, and she practically skipped around the front of the car, giddy at the prospect of taking Madison out on the town. But her nerves kicked into gear as soon as they were on the road again and heading toward their destination.

She hadn't dated in a long time. She was worried that her ability to impress a date was gone. Shawn had been catch-as-catch-can, furtive and compressed. Planning a date was almost impossible. And Rachel had been so long ago, and she'd been the one who'd chased Jen. Because that was what Jen was doing, chasing Madison.

With all this going on in her head, Jen fell back on a safe topic. "I spoke with Kathleen and…" She picked up on Madison's folded arms and slightly hunched form. "What?"

"How much does she know about us?"

"Kathleen? Just the broad strokes. We met at the wedding, we connected."

Madison gave her a look. "Had sex."

"Okay, in my defense, I didn't think I'd see you again." She paused. Well, that sounded terrible. Maybe another tactic. "If you're worried about conflict of interest, I could go on record with our relationship."

"Oh hell, no."

"Okay." That was not the answer she was expecting, but maybe she should have, given the way Madison's relationship with Erika ended. But right now, Jen needed to know what the fuck Madison was thinking. Didn't she have enough trouble with Rachel? Madison was almost a decade younger, without the same life experiences that could make a relationship harder. If Madison was going to bail, Jen wanted to know now. She could go through the dance tonight and then gently distance herself enough to finish the project, giving her desire a chance to cool and either work itself out or fade away.

Madison sighed. "It's just weird for me, being so close to work again. I had a blueprint for how I wanted this to go, and it failed spectacularly."

Jen reached out. "I know. I don't have a blueprint for this, either. There's a trail of failed relationships behind me."

Madison shook her head and smiled. "Is that supposed to comfort me?"

"No, I guess not. If it helps, Kathleen has some of the best personal professional boundaries I've ever met. What I share with my friend does not show up with the principal."

She was met with silence before Madison said, "Maybe this is a mistake."

Oh no, not the mixed signals again. She'd gotten serious back-off signs before, but this was not what she was expecting tonight. What she hadn't told Madison was that she didn't really do one-night stands. She didn't have the emotional stamina for it. Ironic, considering a relationship carried just as much emotional work, but somehow, she felt it was more worth the time. She guessed that said something about her. Suppressing her disappointment, she ordered her thoughts and opened her mouth.

Madison beat her to it. "I'm sorry. I thought I was ready, and I'm not. I feel like an ass. I really like you."

Oh, great. Here it comes. It's not you, it's me. Why the fuck did she get her hopes up? And that was really the issue. She'd wanted this more than she realized. From the beginning, Madison had been a breath of fresh air in her very stale life. And now it had fallen flat. Fuck that. She was not giving up without a fight.

Jen eyed a parking spot and pulled in to it. Putting the car in neutral and setting the brake, she turned in her seat. "Talk to me. Tell me what's going on inside that head. I'll take you home right now if you want, but this is not the same woman who told me to up my game."

"Erika called me."

Well, that was not where she thought it was going. "When?"

"Yesterday."

Fuck. "Why?"

"I don't know. I didn't talk to her. She didn't leave a voice mail. It doesn't matter."

Oh yes, it does. She's fucking up my date. "Are you still in love with her?"

Madison choked on a laugh. "No."

"Good." She sensed the unspoken half and said it aloud. "But she still loves you."

Madison groaned and put her hands in her head. "I don't know. Maybe."

Somehow, this revelation felt better. Knowing that Erika had recently cropped up and stirred shit felt easier than some fundamental flaw in their own dynamic or unwillingness on Madison's part to pursue a relationship. This was something they could deal with together if they wanted to, and Jen wanted that. She just had to remind Madison that she felt the same way.

"Look, I think we're putting too much pressure on ourselves. Fuck Erika, fuck Kathleen, fuck everyone. Let's go out and have a good time. See where that leads. Okay?"

Madison took a deep breath and nodded. "Okay."

Jen groaned. "You could say that with a little more enthusiasm. Just to make sure my ego recovers."

Madison smiled and, pulling Jen's hand to her, kissed her knuckles. The gesture charmed her and made all her misgivings subside. "Thank you. I mean it."

Jen deflected her comment more to switch the subject than to ignore it. "You're not the only one with baggage. I've just had longer to pack it up." She extricated her hand and merged back into traffic.

"Where are you taking me?"

Jen smiled. "You'll see."

❖

Madison took a deep breath. Jen's flirty smile made her feel better about her little freak out. Erika always screwed with her head, even when she wasn't trying. It made her angry and put her on edge. She wanted to make up for it. She'd teased Jen about her look because she'd felt self-conscious in her own clothes. Jen obviously put her money into her wardrobe. "You look incredible tonight."

Jen dipped her head and gave her a small smile. "Thank you."

It was too dark, but she thought Jen might have blushed. She debated where to take the conversation next, now that they had reset the evening. She had put aside her anxiety about the work connections and the age difference, but then Erika's mysterious phone call had put her slightly on edge. She'd been thrilled that Jen had asked her out and had looked forward to it all week. Every day she'd find a new memory of the way they'd danced together, the way they'd moved together, the way they'd talked together. Their connection pulled her in. Iron Pour, Spooktacular, even and especially during the refrigerator shopping. Who knew that doing something so domestic could also be so charged with sexual tension? She tried not to take too much meaning from it, but it was hard not to.

By the time Jen parked next to a massive, red-brick factory, Madison was feeling much better and more engaged in what was to come. She got out as Jen appeared at her side.

"Ready?" Jen held out her elbow, and Madison hooked her hand in its crook.

Inside, the building opened up into a glass atrium and an interior courtyard with several shops and restaurants along its sides.

"One of my friends' firms does historic renovations. This used to be a textile mill."

She looked around. "It's huge."

"Yes. They don't build them like this anymore. It's about six acres. It used to be bigger." Jen led her toward the far corner and said, "Wait until you see this."

Madison followed her into a room with white brick walls and warm wood floors, but what stood out were the six vintage bowling lanes in front of a long bar. It was so kitschy and cool that Madison grabbed her arm and said, "Bowling. Yes."

Jen smiled and spread her arms. "So have I upped my game?"

Madison turned back to the room and walked toward the reception. "You're definitely improving."

They ordered boozy shakes, lobster mac and cheese, and tater tot nachos while Jen walked her through the rules of duckpin bowling, which involved a smaller ball.

She felt a twinge of jealousy. "Have you been here before?"

Jen shook her head. "No, but I looked up the rules before I came." How sweet. Jen cared enough to do research.

They laughed and touched all evening, sharing drinks and food while they played a competitive but good-natured game. By the time they left—Madison had won one set and lost the second—her sides were tender and her cheeks sore from laughing and smiling.

Jen parked at the curb and let the engine idle. The gentle hum reminded Madison of her first time behind its wheel and how much she'd wanted Jen that night.

She unbuckled her belt and shifted in her seat. "This was fun. Thank you."

"It was." Jen leaned in and kissed her lips. A quick peck good night.

But Madison had waited too long for that kind of kiss. She wanted more. She curled her fingers behind Jen's neck and pulled her closer. Jen moved with her, and her tongue brushed Madison's lips, asking and receiving permission to enter. Madison warmed at the feel of Jen's tongue inside her. It touched off nerves throughout her body and curled down to her toes. Nothing like their kisses from the wedding, this one carried the weight of expectation rather than the haphazard passion of two people attracted to each other. She gave herself over to that feeling of expectation, building kiss after kiss until Jen moved back.

Her hair was mussed in back, and she had a sloppy smile on her face. "I should go."

Madison came back to reality, too aroused to make sense of what Jen was saying. Go where?

Jen leaned in and kissed her again. This time, she didn't let go. Jen's hands slid down her shoulders and wrapped around her waist, pulling Madison toward her as best she could with the gearshift between them. Far too quickly, the knob pushing into Madison's belly overtook her more pleasurable senses, and she gasped as it hit a particularly tender spot. She rubbed her lower abdomen.

Jen glanced down and covered her hand. "Are you okay?"

She grimaced. "Yeah. Making out in a car is not as much fun as they say it is."

Jen laughed. "Yes. Ironic, considering this kind of car sells sex." She looked over her shoulder. "Even the back seat sucks."

Madison spoke without thought. "Do you want to come in?"

Jen tilted Madison's face toward her. "Yes. But I'm not going to."

Anticipation and disappointment crashed into each other, and Madison asked, "Why?"

Jen moved a hand between them. "This. This is good. But it's still too new. And just two hours ago, you told me this was a mistake."

Madison grinned and grabbed Jen's hand. She brought it to her lips and nipped a knuckle.

Jen sucked in a breath.

"Not that new. And I was wrong." Her need had overtaken her early fears, and she struggled to understand why she'd had doubts in the first place.

Wrapping her hands around Madison's, Jen leaned in. "Let me be clear. I want to go upstairs and fuck your brains out."

Madison's arousal flared. Images she was already familiar with flashed through her mind, and she could almost feel Jen moving inside her. She groaned and whispered, "Don't say that."

Jen kissed their joined hands. "Shh. Don't worry. We'll get there. But I think we have something different here. Am I the only one seeing that?"

No, she wasn't. Tamping down her desire, she swallowed the last of her fear and sighed. "No, you're not."

"And I really like it. I want to see where it takes us, so I don't want to fuck it up with more sex too soon."

Madison had imagined this particular scenario several times after the wedding. But then Jen had shown up, not in a bar or a restaurant, but at her work and with her son. Everything was so much more complicated. Jen wasn't Erika, and Madison's wariness about getting involved with people in her professional circle did not apply. Jen's relationships showed a woman who did not destroy people after a breakup. In Rachel's case, Madison could argue that Jen went out of her way to make sure her ex had a soft landing wherever she went. If she said no now, she'd let her fear win. It was time to take a risk.

"Then next time it's my turn to take you out."

Jen grinned. "Deal."

Chapter Sixteen

Jen checked the clock, surprised she was going out at a time when she'd normally be getting ready for bed. She and Carter had dinner before she'd packed him for a sleepover at Eli's. She'd distracted herself with a random cooking show while she'd waited. When her phone chirped, she got up and opened the door. Madison walked up her stone walkway wearing a lacy black blouse and blue washed jeans reminiscent of an outfit Jen had owned in college, down to the pair of Doc Martens that were still tucked in the back of her closet. She felt out of place in her casual sweater, black cords, and Oxfords.

Madison paused at the edge of her stoop and tucked her hands into her back pockets. Her eyes raked up and down Jen's figure. "You look great."

She smiled and kicked herself for not saying the same thing first. She'd been so distracted by the Doc Martens. "So do you."

Madison leaned in and kissed her cheek. A hint of citrus and mint lingered in her wake. Jen chuckled at the gesture and nodded toward her car.

Madison winked. "Ready?"

Jen nodded and locked up. She walked toward the car, but Madison hooked an arm around her waist, steering her toward the Honda Fit. "It's my date. I drive."

Jen opened her mouth to protest.

Madison flashed a grin that said she knew she was making her uncomfortable. "Jen, do you have control issues?"

"No. I just prefer to drive."

Determined not to show her discomfort, Jen discreetly braced her hand against the door as Madison backed up. "Where are we going?"

"The Boat House." She said it as if Jen would know what she was talking about. "Bridge Street. 90s night."

"90s night?" She cut Madison a sidelong look. "You do know that I was in college during the 90s?"

"I did. I thought it would be fun."

Jen wasn't so sure. She was a far cry from her college persona, and she liked that. For her, maturity brought a level of confidence that, in her youth, had been bolstered by anger and arrogance. Past Jen was an asshole.

"How are you doing over there?"

Jen followed her look and realized she was gripping the door handle. She shook her head and released it. She had to admit, Madison's driving was fine and that thinking about her past had resulted in the death grip. She smiled. "I'm fine."

Madison stopped at a red light and raised her eyebrows.

"I'm good. I let you drive my car. That should say something." She could still hear Nat's voice teasing her. Only Nat and Jen's mechanic drove her car. She managed her low-grade anxiety while Madison drove toward South Water Street and the set of ultra-trendy restaurants and bars.

She checked out the clientele and figured she was about ten years above the average age. Even Madison was a little bit older than most of the crowd. Madison showed her ID and paid their cover. The bouncer didn't card her; she wasn't sure if she should feel insulted or not. The dance floor was packed, the bar was starting to pile up two deep, and the chorus of "What is Love" hit her on the way in, a song that she linked to SNL skits and cheesy movies but which the entire bar seemed to enjoy.

"I love this song," Madison shouted and tugged her toward the dance floor.

Suppressing her inner grump, Jen surrendered to the scene and started dancing. By the fifth song, she was laughing at the music and Madison's moves. She'd heard at least two songs from her club days and another she didn't remember at all. Her more formative music came from the 1980s, but as the words "Tik Tok" morphed into "I Wanna Sex You Up," Madison slipped into her arms, and she had a newfound appreciation for the songs of this decade. The tempo gave her an excuse to run her hands along Madison's body and move against her in ways the ballroom dance at the wedding didn't allow.

She twisted and turned, rubbing her front and back against Madison as the sound wound its way into another slinky, sexy beat. She twirled away only to be pulled back in, closer than before. She held Madison's gaze and watched every move she made register on Madison's face. It was more intoxicating than alcohol.

The music faded and turned down as the DJ announced, "It's 8:30. There's flashlights by the door or grab your phone. It's time to say good-night."

Confused at the abrupt shift, Jen stopped moving. Madison handed her a flashlight on their way out the side door. She followed her toward the railing that looked over the water. The outdoor lights switched off, and tiny flickers of lights shined through the windows of a large building across the water. What the fuck? Around her people, flicked their lights, aiming at that building.

Madison held up her flashlight and switched it on and off. Leaning in, she said, "It's the children's hospital. They do this every night before bed."

Jen had read about it in the paper. Several businesses along the waterfront flashed lights back and forth, both to say hi and to let the kids know they weren't alone. A lump formed in her throat. Ever since Carter, certain events, usually around kids, made her cry. It didn't matter if it was joyous or tragic; it could be a commercial, a parade, really anything, and she'd start weeping. And now, as she joined a bar full of people reaching out in the middle of their drunken revelry to those kids, she felt tears prick her eyes.

It was over in ten minutes, and when the last lights switched off at the hospital, the music came back up, and people returned to the bar. Jen tucked the flashlight under her armpit and wiped at the corners of her eyes, hoping Madison hadn't seen. She didn't want to explain. It would only make her cry more.

If Madison noticed, she didn't say a word, just took the flashlight and said, "I'll be back."

The Boat House had a glassed-in area for winter waterfront views, and a bunch of tables sat around the edges. Jen snagged one while she waited. By the time Madison returned with two glasses of water, Jen could talk about it without tearing up. "Does that happen every night?"

Madison scooted closer so they could talk over the music. "I think so. My sister told me about it. She's heard the kids talk about it. They love it. Did you like it?"

Jen swallowed down the sudden lump. "Does your sister work at the hospital?"

She shook her head. "Paramedic."

The tears returned, and Jen choked out, "It's sweet." She blotted a stray tear with her fingers.

Madison reached out. "Are you okay?"

"It's nothing. It's silly really. These things get to me. I don't know why." Except she did.

"I know. Me, too. When I think about those kids up there..."

When Jen looked into Madison's eyes, she saw her own tears mirrored back at her. Rachel, for all her sensitivity, would have made a joke, but Madison just let them sit with it. It was what she needed but not what she expected. They finished their water, and Jen finally said, "I'm going to the bathroom. I'll be right back."

Standing in front of the mirror washing her hands, she considered her next moves. Madison was more than just a fuck. She'd suspected it from the beginning. There'd been an instant understanding between them that went beyond the physical. While it surprised her, it didn't scare her. She'd had connections before with other people, but something about Madison was different. Her lack of pretense, perhaps. Something was building between them, and she liked it. Not wanting to dwell on it too much lest it dissipate, she left the bathroom and threaded through the crowd with renewed determination as Lita Ford started singing "Kiss Me Deadly."

Joy bubbled up at the music, and she wanted to dance. Madison stood and walked over.

"This is not a 90s song," Jen shouted even as she laughed and pulled Madison into the crowd.

Madison shrugged and smiled. "I like it anyway."

Jen grinned. "Me, too." And she knew all the words.

Chapter Seventeen

Madison's apartment was an open floor plan, with a tiny kitchen along the back wall and a table demarcating the line between it and the living room. Jen could see the bathroom and the bedroom through two open doors at the far end of the room.

Madison took off her coat and tossed it over the back of a chair. "You thirsty?"

"Yeah." Jen hung her jacket on a nearby chair. She should be exhausted. It was late, and she'd danced for hours. But all those lingering touches and longing looks had left every nerve in her body pulsating with need.

"Water?" Madison opened the fridge and pulled out a pitcher.

"Sure." She leaned against the kitchen sink and watched Madison reach into the cabinets for a set of glasses. The hem of her sweater pulled up and exposed her back. Jen traced the swell of her ass to the little dip in her lower back. That was all it took. Desire moved Jen forward, and she pressed up against her from behind.

"I love the way you look in these jeans." She slid her hands into Madison's back pockets and caressed her ass.

Madison sucked in a breath and closed the cabinet. She leaned her head against Jen's shoulder, and Jen kissed along her ear. "I keep thinking about that night. At the wedding."

"What about it?" Jen kissed a line down her neck.

Madison moaned. "How you tasted. How you moved. The sounds you made."

She traced the line back up, alternating nips with a kiss. "What else?"

"The way you looked when you came. The way you held me and touched me."

She ground her hips into Madison's ass, slipping her hands up to cup her breasts. "Like this?"

"Yes." Madison reached back and grabbed her hair.

The slight point of pain turned her on, and her desire exploded. She spun Madison in place and pinned her against the kitchen counter. She tried to get her hand down Madison's pants, but they were too tight. With a twist and a turn, she yanked them down and pushed her legs apart once they were off. No more languid touches or gentle exploration, just raw need punctuated with gasps and moans. She moved with a franticness unknown to her. She'd waited long enough; she needed to fuck Madison right now.

Dropping to her knees, she hooked one of Madison's legs over her shoulder and pulled her straight to her lips. Jen closed her eyes at the first taste. Madison was as exquisite as she remembered and so very wet. Her tongue slid easily through Madison's folds, tasting and teasing with quick strokes, then moving toward her center and sucking.

"Oh yes. Like that."

Using the short gasps and sudden jerks as a guide, Jen focused her efforts. Madison clutched her head, again pulling on her hair, and again igniting her desire. The more Madison pulled, the harder Jen sucked.

Madison came almost too quickly, but rather than ease off, Jen intensified her touch, slipping a finger inside her. Madison responded by bucking her hips and moaning.

"Oh yes. More."

Jen added another finger and pushed inside. She twisted and turned. Madison's heel dug into her back, holding her in place. When she came a second time, Madison teetered off-balance. Jen stood and caught her.

"That was...You were..."

Jen chuckled and kissed her cheek. "I know there's a sentence in there somewhere."

"Come here." Madison pulled her into a light kiss that slowly grew more passionate. Her kisses were deep and intense, demanding Jen's full attention. She'd never had anyone kiss her like that. She'd always been dominant in the bedroom, leading while her lover followed, but something was shifting, and Madison was taking control. Surprised but not scared, Jen let it happen.

Madison ended their kiss and pulled her toward the bedroom. "Come with me."

Jen chuckled at the double meaning and followed her to her nightstand.

Madison opened the top drawer and waved at the modest but not insignificant sex paraphernalia. "Take your pick."

Jen eyed the leather cuffs. Good to know. Anal plug, surprising but not unwelcome. Remote control vibrator. The exhibitionist in her came up with a few scenarios before passing it by. Neoprene harness and bright blue dildo...imagining the feel of that inside her.

She must have taken too long to decide because Madison reached out. "I'm sorry, I didn't ask. Are toys okay?"

"Yes." She pointed to the harness. "This."

Madison hefted it. "Good. Take off your clothes and get on the bed. I'll be right back."

Amused by the command, Jen stood in the middle of Madison's bedroom, taking in the collection of Funko figures on the dresser and framed propaganda posters from several different science fiction franchises on her wall. She smiled at the clothes strewn along another chair and the half-open closet door with a pile of shoes spilling out. She heard a bang in the bathroom and shouted, "You okay in there?"

Figuring compliance was mandatory, she shed her clothes quickly—leaving them on the chair—and sat on the edge of the bed, waiting. Another bang and then Madison strolled into the room, fully naked and wearing the harness.

Jen met Madison's eyes before she stared at the harness. "Are you okay? I heard some noise."

Madison rolled her eyes and waved at her waist. "No, just a little trouble with this."

She raised her eyebrows. "I would have helped you."

"I'm sure you would have." Madison moved toward her, the dildo at eye level. She paused at the nightstand and pulled out the lube. Pouring some into her hand, she gradually worked it up and down the length. "Any requests?"

Mesmerized by the slow hand job, Jen missed the question. "What?"

Madison's crooked smile brought a new flood of wetness. "Positions you prefer? Slow and deep? Fast and hard? Ways you like to be fucked?"

She swallowed around a very dry throat. She'd never heard Madison use that word before, and it definitely worked for her. "Yes."

Chuckling, Madison climbed on the bed and lay down in the middle, her laugh so deep and throaty it promised so much more. She reached out, and Jen scooted over. "Closer."

She crawled across Madison's body and settled on her lap.

"That's better."

Madison stroked up and down her sides, the feel of skin on skin delicious. Sitting slightly higher on her lap, Jen ducked her head and kissed her. Not as feverish as the kisses before, they built one upon the other until Jen pulled away, panting. Leaning back on her heels, she stared at Madison's swollen lips and flushed face.

"Ready?"

Jen nodded and gasped when Madison's hand dipped between them, touching her folds and revealing her wetness. She shuddered as two fingers slipped inside and moaned as they slipped out.

Madison leaned forward and whispered, "Do you want more?"

"Yes."

"Then come and get it."

Jen shifted her weight back and helped Madison guide the dildo to her opening. Taking a deep breath, she slowly let her body sink down its length. It was a bit longer than the one at home but a nice fit. She exhaled and stopped short of taking it all.

Madison's hand held hers. "Too much?"

"A little"—she gasped as more of it slid home—"longer." She moaned long and loud as it went all the way in. She steadied herself on Madison's thighs, adjusting to the fullness inside her.

"You look so hot." Madison's open admiration was a total turn on. She pulled her up for a searing kiss. The shift in position caused another jolt inside her, and she moaned against her lips.

"Can I fuck you? I want to fuck you."

"Yes. Do it." The use of the word fuck was putting her over the edge.

The first thrust knocked her back, and Madison quickly gathered her in her arms. "Sorry. Got a little excited."

Jen grabbed her face. "Stop apologizing and start fucking."

"Yes, ma'am." She slammed her hips up without warning, and Jen clutched her shoulders.

Arms wrapped tightly to Madison's, Jen matched each upward thrust with a downward one until they blurred together. Her need grew, but it was too much. Too deep, too close, fuck, she needed to come. She dug her hands into Madison's back and flipped them over. The dildo popped out, but before she could mourn its loss, Madison leaned over her and slid it back inside. The fullness returned, but the ache remained.

She grabbed Madison's wrist and said, "Touch me."

The thrusts paused, and Madison shifted again.

Even expecting the touch, the first brush across her clit made her jump. The featherlight touch that followed had her panting for more. "That's it." Madison increased the pressure on her clit and Jen hissed with pleasure. "Yes."

Jen arched toward her, drawing the dildo in and urging her faster and harder. Jen drove her hips up, and Madison met her on the downstroke, again and again. Flickers of light danced at the edge of Jen's vision, and her nerve endings crackled on overload, her arms and legs going cold as the blood rushed toward her center. She wrapped her entire body around Madison and locked her in a fierce grip as the edges of her orgasm burned through her and then crashed down.

Jen hunkered down under Madison's weight, cocooned in her scent and sheltered in her arms. Her thoughts drifted by, and she let them spool out of her head. In the morning, she'd probably wake up sore and groggy from too much sex and too little sleep, but it was worth it. So fucking worth it. The late hour caught up with her, and she fell asleep almost instantly.

❖

Madison woke up to Jen padding around her bedroom. She yawned and stretched. "What time is it?"

Jen's head shot up. "Almost five."

"So early." She yawned again, then realized Jen was mostly dressed. "Are you sneaking out?"

Jen had a slightly guilty look on her face. "Yes?"

Madison sat up and tossed the covers aside. "Seriously. Why?" Her sleepiness faded away, all her insecurities alert and ready for rejection.

"To go fishing."

She stared for a second and then started laughing. "You're joking."

Jen grinned and shook her head. "I'm not." She sat on the edge of the bed and slipped her arm around Madison's waist. "I have a standing date with Nat, and I almost slept through it. I'm already late." She smiled and pointed between them. "I wasn't expecting this. Not that I mind."

Madison started to stand. "Do you need a ride? I can take you."

Jen held her down and brushed her hair back before capturing her lips in a tender kiss. "I'm good. I'm better than good."

Madison slipped her hands into Jen's hair and leaned back, pulling her down on top of her. She slid her bare leg between Jen's and rubbed along the seam of her pants.

Jen groaned and pulled away. "Temptress. I've got to go."

Madison flung her arms to the side and smiled. "And leave me here, alone and naked."

Closing her eyes, Jen threw her head back and said, "Yes. I'm sorry."

She looked so genuinely guilty that Madison took pity on her and said, "Go. I release you."

Jen smiled. "Thanks. I'll call you." She got up and glanced down at her sweater. "Do you have something else I could borrow? Something that could get fishy."

Madison threw off the covers and got up. Something about the whole domesticity of it charmed her. Sure, she was disappointed that there would be no continuation of last night this morning. She'd hoped for a morning of breakfast and sex. She rummaged in her dresser and heard a soft ping that sounded like a cell phone text. Pulling out a T-shirt and a faded blue sweatshirt with a Captain America logo on it, she held them out for Jen's inspection.

Jen changed quickly. Madison enjoyed the tattoos and the sinewy muscles of her back while she dressed. That little ping went off again, and Jen glanced at her watch. "Shit, I gotta go." She leaned in and gave Madison a quick peck on the cheek. "I'll call you, I promise."

Madison watched her walk away and wanted one more kiss. "Wait." She pulled her into one last, lingering kiss.

With one final nip, Jen groaned and shook her head. "I can't believe I'm leaving you here."

Madison smoothed down her lapels and winked. "Neither can I."

But as she watched Jen leave, she knew that she'd be back.

Chapter Eighteen

Madison lounged on her parents' sofa and watched football with her mother and her sister. She half listened to them provide their own commentary on the plays and tried not to yawn.

"We're not putting you to sleep there, are we?" Kayla nudged her, and Madison shifted away.

"It's not the most thrilling matchup." In fact, the yelling was mostly rote because the Providence Friars were winning.

"What's Jen up to this weekend?"

"I don't know. Her ex is in town." And despite Jen's assurances, it made her very nervous. Rachel's fame intimidated her. She'd heard one of her songs on the radio last week. Jen had promised her that with Rachel around, they could actually spend the day together. She still hadn't heard from her yet.

Kayla gave her a look. "And how's that going?"

"Oh, come on," her mother shouted. Then she muted the television. "Is this the woman you were talking about? The one Evelyn saw you with? You should bring her to Thanksgiving."

Her stomach flip-flopped at the thought of bringing Jen to that raucous get-together. The questions, the teasing, she would be the center of attention, and that always felt uncomfortable, even if they were her family and loved her unconditionally. "It's too soon." As soon as she said it, she regretted it.

Both Kayla and her mom turned, and she knew there was no way to avoid this conversation. "What do you mean too soon?"

"How serious is this?" Kayla followed up.

Trapped by her own words and unsure of her feelings, she finally said, "I care enough about her that I'm not sure I want to subject her to the whole family."

Kayla laughed. "You totally ducked that question."

"Not really." Madison had said just enough that they would back off.

"I've met her. She's not going to wilt under pressure." Kayla glanced at the TV and said, "Oh, that's terrible. Mom, turn the volume back on."

Her mother hit the switch, and Madison quietly left the room. She found her father in the kitchen singing to Bob Seger and grating carrots. He smiled. "Got tired of that?"

They shared an ambivalence toward football. He had played in college before an injury had sidelined him and had some real ethical objections to college football. She preferred to watch women's sports if she watched any at all. But they both respected Kayla and their mom's passions.

"Evelyn says you brought a date to the restaurant."

She laughed. She'd left one room to avoid a conversation about Jen, and she walked right into another. "You, too. I see the Hewitt network is up and running."

"Always. Was that what you were talking about in there?" He dumped the carrots in the salad bowl and threw in a handful of cherry tomatoes.

"Kind of. Mom wants me to bring her to Thanksgiving."

He picked up a spoon and stirred a pot on the stove. "And?"

She plucked a cherry tomato and popped it in her mouth. "And what?"

"What's stopping you?"

"They can be a little much."

"Do you think they'll scare her off?"

Madison laughed. Kayla was right about one thing. Jen didn't scare easily. "Not at all. It's just, it's early stages, and I don't want to ruin it."

Her dad put his spoon down. "Do you think we'd ruin it for you?"

"No, no. You're great, all of you. Loud. Opinionated. But she's got a kid and an ex-wife. I just don't want to pressure her." So many people put demands on Jen's life, and she didn't want to add to the list. She wanted to be her refuge and not her obligation.

"Sounds like you care about her."

She thought about the time they'd spent together and smiled. "I do."

He nodded toward the living room. "Go tell them they have five minutes until dinner."

❖

She was brushing her teeth when her phone dinged in her bedroom. Walking out with toothbrush in hand, she read Jen's text. *Would you bail me out if I murdered my ex?*

Madison chuckled. *Depends. Would this be a one-time deal or a pattern of homicides?* She walked back to the bathroom and finished brushing.

Crawling into bed, she flipped on her TV and picked up her phone. *Lol. One time. Good question, though.*

She picked out a western sci-fi and texted back. *I have self-interest in the answer.*

I don't see you as an ex anytime soon.

Does that make me current?

What do you think?

She knew Jen was teasing, so she tossed it back. *I think I need physical verification.*

Do you?

She could almost hear the sex in her voice and clenched her thighs together in anticipation. *I'm already in bed.*

Turning off the TV, she slipped out of her underwear and ran her hand down her body.

Really?

Don't you want to come over? Tossing the phone aside, she slipped her fingers between her legs. She closed her eyes and touched herself. Just the possibility of having sex with Jen had made her so wet.

I shouldn't leave.

She wanted to remind Jen that she said it would be easier to schedule with Rachel in town. Instead, she said, *But that's not a no.* She didn't wait for an answer. *I'm so wet.*

Her phone dinged, and she ignored it. If Jen wasn't going to come over, let her wait.

It dinged again, and when she read it, her anticipation turned to expectation.

Fuck. I'm coming over.

Madison met her at the door, wearing only her robe. She barely got it closed before Jen was kissing her so hard, she lost her balance and bumped into the wall. Jen pulled off her robe, and slipped her arms around Madison's waist. Jen brushed her clit on the way toward her opening. Madison gasped and arched toward her as Jen's finger slipped inside and then pulled out.

Jen's voice was rich and playful and sent shivers down her spine. "Is this what you want? A quick fuck right here, right now?"

She moaned, and Jen laid her out on the stairs. Jen kissed her with a thoroughness that brought all of her attention to her mouth until Jen's hand moved inside her, and Madison forgot how to kiss. Her focus dropped between her legs as Jen's fingers moved through her folds, sliding and rubbing, back and forth, up and over her clit before plunging inside. She arched, drawing Jen in and urging her faster and harder.

Jen bit her earlobe and said, "Like this?"

Madison struggled with words. "Yes…like…this."

Jen's smile turned ferocious. and she pumped harder and harder. Each thrust hit her deeper and deeper but left her wanting more. Opening her eyes, she sought Jen's face and said, "Touch me."

Jen brushed her clit, moving up one side and down another. And the thing that was missing, that was holding Madison back, fell into place, and she came with a rush.

Reaching out, she pulled Jen toward her. Jen rested on her chest, rising and falling with each breath, trailing little kisses up and down her neck. The stairs were starting to cut into her back, but she didn't care. If she moved, Jen might leave, and she really didn't want that. But she knew their time was short.

"How long can you stay?"

Jen kissed her neck. "All night."

Sitting there with Jen in her arms, she admitted how afraid she'd been that Rachel's presence would derail their growing relationship. Apparently, she shouldn't have worried.

Chapter Nineteen

The Diamond Guard corsairs drop out of FTL and surround your ship. The Diamond Guard leader appears on your viewscreen. She looks like Angela Bassett circa 1995 with those awesome dreads from *Strange Days* and says, 'Lower your shields and prepare to be boarded.'" Kayla paused and looked at Celia, Beck, and Madison seated around the table. "I need you to roll initiative."

A chorus of groans accompanied her statement. They were going to see who reacted first in their upcoming battle.

"Oh no, hold up," Celia said. "I want see if there's a peaceful way out of this."

Kayla smiled. "What would you like to do?"

Celia described her approach, and Madison added her own idea. Beck agreed and then Kayla said, "Okay, then, I'm going to need you to roll."

Madison's phone dinged as she reached for her dice. Kayla gave her a look when she pulled it out and read it.

It was Jen. *Where are you?*

She rolled and told Kayla the number. She listened with half an ear as Kayla narrated the actions that everyone's dice rolls created.

Gaming. She hadn't expected to hear from Jen. They had settled into a weekend night together and then a week off. Not that she wasn't happy to hear from her, but this was her off week.

Oh. She got a frowning emoji. A pit formed in her stomach. Was Jen angry?

"Instead of smoothing out the situation, you've made her even angrier. Your sensors pick up several target locks. Roll for initiative."

"I tried," Celia said. Several sets of dice clacked against the table, and everyone read out their number.

Kayla nodded at Madison. "You go first. What do you want to do?"

Distracted by the text, Madison concentrated on her character sheet, trying to figure out what she wanted to do and where the encounter was going.

Her phone dinged again. *I'm home alone.*

Did she want her to come over? Erika had thought gaming was frivolous and had constantly sabotaged her schedule. And Madison had let her. She didn't want another repeat of that. She'd wrap up her conversation and finish playing, no matter what Jen said. Decision made, she told Kayla what she wanted to do and rolled. After Kayla told her the results, she texted back. *Where's Carter?*

With Rachel. Gone for the weekend. Want to come over? This time, a smiley face.

Of course, she did. She missed her on their weeks off, but she also wanted to finish her game. It had taken them a month to schedule it and even longer to get so close to their objective. If she said no, would Jen be mad?

"Do you need to go?" Celia nodded toward the phone. Kayla held her hands up, saying in gesture the same thing Celia had said in words.

Holding up her hand, Madison said, "Give me a minute."

"Go. We'll get some more snacks."

She stood and moved into the downstairs bathroom. Pulling the door closed behind her, she screwed up her resolve and texted back. *Can I swing by later?*

Yes. I'll be waiting.

Relief poured through her. Now she could play without that fear of reprisal hanging over her.

Three hours later, she parked in front of Jen's house and knocked on the front door. No answer. She pulled out her phone and texted, *I'm here.*

She waited for a few minutes and wondered if maybe Jen had changed her mind. Maybe she'd been wrong, and she should have come over when Jen texted. But nothing about their conversation had indicated such a move, and she pushed it away as nonsense. She tried the door. Locked. Then she remembered the side door near the garage.

It opened on a dimly lit but spacious kitchen bounded by the door and windows on one side and a set of stairs leading up to the second floor on the opposite side. Two archways on either side led to the rest of the house. Closing the door behind her, she called, "Hello? Jen?"

She heard familiar voices and the blue glow of a television through the left archway. *Farscape*. Jen had picked up her boxed set and asked about it. She'd gushed for an embarrassingly long time and told Jen she should watch it. Jen had said she would, but Madison thought she was just humoring her. Seeing proof of her commitment to share the things that mattered to Madison opened her heart a little bit more.

She walked into the living room and spotted Jen wrapped up in a blanket and asleep on the couch. Madison picked up the remote and hit pause. Jen didn't move. Madison just stood and watched her sleep. She looked remote and unapproachable. Her sharp features softened so often around Madison that she forgot how intimidating Jen could be.

Madison debated waking her up, then thought better of it. She'd let her wake up on her own, and they'd go from there. She wanted to cuddle up and hold on to this moment. For once, they had time, and she could wait.

She locked the door and rummaged through the downstairs, finding another blanket for herself. She sat on the opposite end of the couch, resting her hand on Jen's ankle before she hit play.

Chapter Twenty

Jen woke up shortly before dawn, disorientated and with a vague memory of inviting Madison over. She'd fallen asleep on the couch. Not the first time. Usually, she got too cold and headed upstairs, but this time, something was warming her feet. She sat up and saw Madison curled up on her couch. Normally a light sleeper, Jen hadn't heard her come in. Apparently, Madison's presence didn't raise any alarms. A warm fuzzy feeling spread through her body and settled in her chest. Leaning forward, Jen touched her shoulder.

Madison started and opened her eyes. "Wh…are you okay?"

"Shh." Jen held out her hand. "Come to bed." She took Madison's hand and led her upstairs. She crawled into bed, waving toward her dresser. "If you want sleep clothes, help yourself."

Madison opened and closed drawers, and Jen was mostly asleep by the time the bed dipped with her weight. "I've never been in your bed."

Jen's surprise quickly gave way to guilt. Consciously or not, she'd been keeping Madison at arm's length. She rolled over and pulled Madison close, wrapping their bare legs together. "We should change that."

She woke up several hours later, drawn downstairs by the smell of coffee and sausage. Was Madison making breakfast? She couldn't remember the last time someone other than her son had cooked for her. Looking through the bannister, she paused and watched Madison move in her kitchen, opening and closing the cabinets until she found what she was looking for. The kitchen had always been her domain.

She didn't like trespassers. But Madison was different. She liked seeing her move in her space. It felt right.

"Who puts the glasses over the sink?" Madison said.

Jen got a good glimpse of her ass as Madison pulled down a glass. She smiled. "That's where the old cups go."

Madison squeaked and jumped, clutching the cup to her chest.

"Oh, I'm sorry. I didn't mean to startle you." Jen's voice was froggy and deeper than normal. She walked into the kitchen and brushed past Madison to open a cabinet under the island. She heard a quick intake of breath. "Most of the cups are down here. For Carter. When he was little. I just haven't bothered to move them higher."

"Thanks." Madison put the other glass away.

Jen plucked a pair out and put them on the counter. "Why didn't you wake me last night?"

Madison moved closer. "You looked tired."

Jen swatted her. "What a terrible thing to say to an older woman."

"I didn't mean," Madison said, looking horrified. "That's not what I meant. I just didn't want to wake you."

Even though Jen was teasing, a part of her worried that she did look tired, especially to someone a decade younger than her. But Madison looked genuinely flustered, so she took pity on her and let her off the hook. "What are you making? Looks good." She moved closer to get a better look. Scrambled eggs and sausage. Did she have sausage in the freezer? She didn't remember buying it. Maybe Rachel had bought it and left it behind. That idea disturbed her. Not controlling her own space was getting old.

Madison turned back to the stove and stirred the eggs. Jen took in the low-cut shorts and generous ass. Suddenly, sausages and Rachel didn't matter.

Coming up behind her, Jen wrapped her arms around Madison and breathed in her scent. She started kissing the back of her neck. "Good morning."

Madison leaned into her, and she could hear the smile in Madison's voice as she said, "Good morning."

Jen nipped her ear and whispered, "Come back to bed."

"And let the eggs get cold?"

She couldn't tell if Madison was serious or not, so Jen reached across and shut off the burner. "We can make more."

Upstairs, she moved her toward the bed and quickly stripped Madison out of her clothes. Then she slowly pushed her backward on the bed until Madison was spread out before her. Stepping back, Jen traced her curves, noting each dip and dimple she wanted to touch and kiss. She had nowhere to be and no one to take care of. She was going to take her time.

She stared so long that Madison started to curl in on herself. "Oh no, you don't. No hiding here. You're fucking gorgeous." She waited until Madison relaxed again and met her eyes without hiding.

How did she get this woman into her bed? Before she'd settled down, Jen had had her share of lovers. If she wanted someone, she rarely got turned down. But she'd come out of her marriage in her forties, and women looked at her differently. She had to work a bit harder and after a few tries, she'd finally given up. And then Madison had shown up at the wedding. So captivating and so fearless, hinting at so much more underneath. She held her own against Jen. Not many people did. She wanted more, hoped for more…hell, she'd left her number. Then Madison had come back into her life, and she'd taken a chance. She'd been so lucky to find her again.

"Jen?"

Snapping herself out of her thoughts, Jen slipped out of her robe and stalked forward naked. "I can't believe you came back."

"To your house?" Madison stared, her forehead doing that cute little crinkle when she was confused.

Jen leaned down and brushed a kiss just above her center. "No, to my bed."

Madison gasped at the touch and lifted her hips. Jen gradually kissed her way from waist to stomach to breasts. Madison's breasts proved too tempting to simply move beyond, and she lavished extra attention to them, earning her an, "Oh yes."

She mapped a path with her hands and lips down Madison's lower body and then back up, slowly kissing her inner thigh before reaching her dark curls. She knelt on the floor and moved Madison to the edge of the bed.

"Oh, that feels so good." Madison moaned and spread her legs farther.

Leaning in, Jen licked along the length of her and swirled up along her clit. She kept a slow pace, bringing Madison to the edge and then pulling back. She could feel her knees complaining about the length of time they'd been on the floor. But she stayed the course, slow and steady, revving up and pulling back.

Finally, Madison's hands clenched in her hair, and she felt that tingle that brought her straight to the edge. She redoubled her efforts as Madison rocked against her mouth. Madison's hands clenched in Jen's hair and along her shoulders as Jen sucked and nipped her toward release. Jen savored the taste of her as Madison arched into her and stayed with her as she came down.

Madison tugged her hand, dragging her away from her center and making eye contact. "Come here. You're too far away."

Jen got off the floor and winced as her knees popped. Fucking bamboo, so pretty and so hard. She really needed to get a rug in here.

"You okay?"

"I'm fine." Jen climbed up and laid beside her. That question made her feel so old. Even though her knees hurt, she didn't want Madison to feel like she couldn't keep up. But she was going to have to build her stamina if she wanted to keep up this pace. More gym time for her. She traced Madison's ribcage, marveling at the lack of stretch marks and relatively unmarked skin.

"That tickles." Madison wiggled.

Jen stilled her hand and burrowed closer. "Sorry." Although she wasn't. "I just like the way you feel."

Madison squeezed her. "Me, too."

Smiling, Jen leaned into her and said, "Do you have any plans this weekend?" She wanted her to stay but she didn't want to pressure her. She didn't want to move too fast, but she only had these pockets of time, and she wanted to spend them with Madison.

Madison shook her head. "Nope. How about you?"

Suddenly shy, she avoided eye contact but still asked, "Would you like to cuddle on my couch and watch movies all day?"

Madison glanced down, a huge grin on her face. "Do I have to get dressed?"

Inside, Jen was doing happy cartwheels, but what came out was a dry remark. "Clothing optional."

Madison shifted, and then Jen was looking up at her instead of down. That smile stoked her arousal, and her body grew hot again.

Madison leaned in and whispered, "Good because I'm not done yet."

❖

They eventually got out of bed and went downstairs for breakfast, which had become brunch. Madison was slightly disappointed at the microwaved eggs. She'd planned a nice breakfast for Jen that would have tasted better fresh. But the chance to explore Jen's body without a time limit was too good to pass up.

By the time they made it to the couch, they were fed and still completely naked. Jen snuggled up to Madison and sighed.

Madison smiled and tucked her closer. She wondered how often Jen curled up in someone else's arms. Had she done this with Rachel on this very couch? Probably. Madison knew Jen had a past that wasn't completely gone from her present, but she was beginning to see her place in Jen's future. She let the warm feeling from holding her take over and kissed Jen's forehead. "Comfy?"

"Very. I miss this."

"Lying naked on a couch?" Madison joked, trying to make light of the fact that Jen had, in fact, done this with other people.

Jen playfully punched her arm. "No. Just being at home. Alone. Well, without Carter. I keep thinking he's upstairs doing his homework or reading."

"Is this the first time he's been away from you?" She had a hard time believing that Jen had never gone anywhere without him.

"He's been at friends' houses before. After the separation, Rachel and I split our time here with him. Whoever had the house had him."

Madison couldn't imagine how much effort that took. Having to constantly share space with someone she was no longer with. It was half-time living. She didn't think she could do that. She'd have nothing left to give. Jen's strength amazed her. "That must have been tough for you."

Jen snorted. "You don't know the half of it. We also shared an apartment. All this negotiation. I couldn't do it. It was too much. When she gets done with her tour, it's going to stop."

Madison felt hope for their future, but Rachel's role in Jen's life worried her. "But you're still married to her?"

"Not by choice. She won't sign the papers."

And that was the real issue. Jen was still wrapped up in Rachel, and it was an undercurrent that kept coming up. Did she think Jen would go back to Rachel? No, but Erika had been with someone— she'd been married—the entire time they were together. And Rachel wasn't going anywhere.

Jen sat up and turned toward her. "What?"

Even though she wanted to be this obligation-free space, Madison struggled with her own doubts and insecurities. Jen had this whole life without her. "Where do I fit in?"

Jen touched her face. "Where do you want to fit in?"

She had known Jen would pick this route, always accommodating someone else's needs. She held her hands and didn't break eye contact. "I'm asking you."

Jen looked away and stood. "I need some tea. Do you want any?"

She covered her hurt. She'd pushed too hard, and now Jen was avoiding the question. "Sure."

But she wasn't about to give up. She followed Jen into the kitchen and leaned against the island while Jen switched on an electric kettle. Grabbing a ceramic pot from an open shelf, Jen opened another cabinet above her head and said, "Anything in particular?"

She wanted Jen to own her feelings. She'd used up her vulnerability with Erika. But she'd give Jen a moment to sort through her emotions. "Something decaffeinated."

Jen nodded and pulled down a rosewood box, intricate and beautiful. Jen tilted it toward her. "A gift from a friend."

"Nice friend." Madison didn't care about the tea box.

"She travels back and forth from Hong Kong and is notoriously hard to pin down. Guilt gift. But totally worth it."

She could almost see Jen sifting through her thoughts as she pinched two portions and dropped them into a strainer seated in the pot. Pulling down two mugs, Jen pushed the tea pot across the island and tilted her head. She spoke in an almost wistful tone. "She's getting married."

Whatever Jen was trying to work out had something to do with this friend. Was she another of Jen's exes? A friend of Rachel? Just how many people did Jen have ties to? The room suddenly felt very crowded. "The tea person?"

Jen checked the tea and put the lid back on. "Yes. It's kind of sweet, actually. Not something she expected. Lindsey's like my alter ego, the person I would have been without Rachel and Carter. And now she's getting married, ceremony and all."

Suddenly, Madison saw her beneath all that bluster and confidence. She'd known that a deeper, more vulnerable part of Jen existed. She'd seen glimpses of it before, but this was Jen's essence laid bare. Madison had inadvertently exposed a fear, and she felt both bad and incredibly lucky to have seen it. "Is that something you want?" As soon as she said it, she realized that Jen had already had that. "I mean, again?"

Jen folded her arms and shook her head, avoiding eye contact. "My track record's a little damaged."

Madison moved closer and tilted her head up. "But you're not."

Jen bit her lip and locked eyes with her. "You think so?"

She opened her arms. "Yes. I do." She held Jen close, and the background noise of her doubts faded. It didn't matter where she fit in. She was already here. Jen would figure things out with Rachel soon enough.

Madison held her while Jen rested her head on her shoulder. She sniffled in Madison's ear and clutched her shoulders for a brief moment before she pulled back and wiped the corners of her eyes.

"I think the tea's ready." Jen avoided eye contact and handed Madison her tea.

Madison gave Jen space, and they shuffled back into the living room, cradling their cups. Jen pulled a blanket off the couch and wrapped it around her before sitting down on the couch.

Madison felt more naked than before until Jen swung one side of the blanket open. "Coming?"

Jen might not want to talk about it, but she wasn't ignoring it. With a smile, Madison settled in next to her, letting the blanket drape over her shoulder and snuggling up to Jen's warm body.

Jen scooped up one of the remotes and said, "What do you want to watch?"

They scrolled through their choices and picked the latest wizarding world movie. As the movie progressed, Jen slowly sank farther and farther until she was lying with her head on Madison's lap. Something about her stretched out felt very homey. Even more so than the appliance shopping. Madison had always felt at ease with her, but this quiet time in her home felt different. There was a sense of possibility. They weren't just playing house for the weekend. They were seeing if they could be together without their daily lives interfering. It felt real, and now that she had a taste for it, she knew she'd want it again.

CHAPTER TWENTY-ONE

Rachel blew back into town the day before Thanksgiving and disrupted any plans Jen had to spend time with Madison. She insisted on staying at the house, citing the holiday season, and rather than argue, Jen put her in the guest room. She regretted it almost immediately, but part of her knew this was going to be the last holiday they spent together at the house, and she wanted to give that to Carter. She chose to keep it just the three of them because of that. But by the next day, she was ready to throw her out again or leave altogether.

Everything Rachel did now stood in stark contrast to Madison's time at the house. Rachel hogged the remote, got in the way in the kitchen, and did all the easy work. Madison had stayed at her house for two days. Two wonderful days where they'd talked and laughed, cooked and fucked, slept and hung out in front of the TV. Two days where she got a taste of what life would be like with someone else, and she had been happy. If she wanted that happy feeling to stay, she needed to bring the two sides of her life together. Now that she'd decided to go all in, she needed to talk with Carter first. She'd rehearsed it a couple times in her head, but the time hadn't presented itself yet.

After dinner, Rachel fell asleep on the couch, leaving Carter to help out and put the dishes in the dishwasher. Jen's phone dinged, and she smiled at the *Happy Thanksgiving* from Madison.

"Who is that?" Carter pointed at her phone.

Jen tucked the phone away quickly and almost said no one. But her immediate guilty response was a clue that she needed to come clean with him. The times he had spent with Madison had been communal events: Iron Pour, Spooktacular. He'd been preoccupied with his own friends, and she'd still been dancing around the role Madison was playing in her life, friend or lover. Even though he knew about her date a few weeks ago, they hadn't talked about it. Things had changed, and he needed to hear it from her. She put the last dish in and closed the dishwasher. No time like the present. She took a deep breath. "How would you feel if I started dating someone else?"

He shrugged.

She sighed. She needed him to engage with her on this. Falling back on their old standby, she bumped shoulders with him. "Use your words, honey. I need to know how you'd feel."

"I don't have any words."

Well, at least he was honest. "Do you feel happy, sad, excited, blah?"

Another shrug. "Blah."

Great. Well, she asked, didn't she? She could so clearly see how the teenage years were going to go.

He looked at the door. "Does Mama know?"

She sighed. "Not yet."

"She's going to be sad." At least he could recognize someone else's feelings.

She should get a gold star parenting award for instilling empathy. She nodded. "I know. But you know I love you. That's not going to change."

He rolled his eyes. "Yes. I know. So does Mama." He sighed. They'd had this conversation multiple times since the separation. "Can I play my game now?"

She smiled and wiped her hands on the dish cloth. "After a hug."

He gave her a halfhearted one, and she squeezed him before he could get away. He squirmed and giggled. "Mom…"

She chuckled and let him head into the living room where Rachel would probably sleep through *Mario Kart*.

❖

Kayla stood as the credits stopped, and the lights came up. Madison pulled out her phone and checked the time and her texts. Nothing from Jen. Not that she expected anything.

"Did she text?" Kayla nodded at her phone.

Madison shook her head. She didn't need to say who. Kayla knew what was going on in her life at all times. "No."

Kayla hauled her to her feet, and they left the theater. "I'm sorry."

"Her ex is in town. Again." She hated that she sounded petulant.

Kayla didn't call her on it, which was a small kindness, but she did school her a bit. "She has a kid. If she's the kind of person you describe, you're going to come second to that. And if you didn't, she's not the person you'd want to be with."

"I know. I'm just..." She wasn't worried so much as disappointed. Kayla was right; Jen did put Carter first. She just wished Rachel wasn't a part of that first.

Kayla looped an arm around her shoulders. "Don't overthink it." Kayla dropped her off at her apartment, and she almost went inside before she decided that the night was too nice to be indoors just yet.

She wandered the neighborhood, ending up in front of Jen's two-story bungalow with the black Porsche in the driveway. A single light shone upstairs, but the front was totally dark. She stopped and stared from across the street. It looked so ordinary, and yet its significance loomed large. She imagined what it would be like to call a place like that home and to come and go with the woman she loved. Loved? She didn't love Jen, at least, not yet. But the potential was there, and that was what had her unsettled. She'd loved someone before, and the fallout had been awful.

"Madison?" Shit. Jen emerged from the shadows of her house and stood at the edge of the road. "Are you okay?"

Madison groaned internally. For a half second, she wondered if she could pretend it wasn't her. She surrendered to the embarrassment and said, "I was in the neighborhood." Then she realized how lame that sounded and tried for the truth. "I missed you."

Jen stepped into the streetlight and shaded her eyes against the glare. She wore gray yoga pants and a fitted black T-shirt. Madison's heart rate picked up as Jen walked over and hugged her. "I missed you, too. You should come in."

Madison pulled back and nodded toward the house. "Isn't Rachel still here?"

Jen rolled her eyes. "She took Carter to her parents for the night."

Madison glanced at Jen's house, half expecting Rachel to open the door but the idea of spending the night with her squashed any indecision. She wanted to be with her. "Okay."

Jen took her hand. "Come on. I'll make us some tea." Inside, Jen washed her hands, switched on an electric kettle, and pulled down the lacquered box.

Madison had no intention of drinking tea and moved closer. She leaned forward, and Jen's perfume enveloped her. Jen met her halfway in a heated kiss, pushing her back against the counter. The intensity of their kisses drove a deeper need.

Jen pulled back enough to whisper, "I've wanted to do this for days." She peppered kisses along her neck.

"Me, too." Madison pushed against her and kissed harder.

Warm steam enveloped them, getting hotter and hotter until Jen stepped back and tugged on her hand. "Let's do this somewhere else." Jen led her into the living room and toward the couch.

Jen spun Madison around and pulled her into her lap, Madison dipped her head and nipped at her lips. "I like this."

Jen slipped her hands up Madison's back, enjoying the weight of her. "Being on top or in my arms?"

Madison chuckled. "Both."

"Good." Jen smiled, and their kisses returned to their original intensity.

Madison maneuvered Jen onto her back and sat back, hands skimming the bottom of Jen's shirt. "Is this something you want?"

"You have to ask?"

"Well, it wasn't on the original menu this evening." Madison grinned, and Jen's heart flip-flopped. Fuck. She'd felt that before. That frisson of affection blooming into something akin to love.

It took her a second to respond with her emotions ping-ponging all over the place. Madison started to pull away, disappointment evident all over her. Wrapping her hands in Madison's shirt, Jen yanked her down and said, "Yes. So very yes."

Later, in bed, Jen spooned Madison and rested her head on Madison's shoulder. "I spoke to Carter this morning. About you."

"About me?" Madison's voice squeaked in a cute way.

"Not you, but about dating. Is that okay?" She couldn't quite tell what Madison was thinking, and she worried she'd moved too fast by bringing up Carter.

Madison turned in her arms. "No, it's fine."

Relief went through her.

Madison cupped her cheek. "What does that mean?"

Jen turned her head and kissed her open palm. "It means I bring you home and introduce you as my girlfriend." Madison laughed. Not the reaction she was expecting. She pulled back. "Is that nervous laughter?"

"No, well, maybe. My mother wants me to bring you to Sunday dinner. They want to meet you." Madison moved closer.

Jen tried not to read too much into the fact that Madison's family wanted to meet her. Of course, they were curious. "What did you tell them about me?"

Madison smiled. "Well, Kayla's already met you."

"Right. Okay, so I'm the woman you hooked up with." Her stomach dropped.

Madison kissed her, hard. "Nothing wrong with that."

Jen wasn't so sure that was how she wanted her girlfriend's parents to think of her. Between kisses, she said, "I'd prefer that your parents not know me as only your booty call."

Madison shifted a leg between hers. "Again. I'm having a hard time finding fault with this."

Now she knew Madison was teasing. She slapped her shoulder. "Stop."

Madison held up her hands. "Okay, okay. They know we're dating and that I…care about you."

Jen heard her stutter between the words and suspected another word felt more natural there. She'd begun to feel that word, too, as she spent more time with Madison, but she didn't want to say it. So much of her life was not hers to give.

"So you'll come?"

That word made Jen smile. "Of course. What do you want me to bring?"

"Well, Carter, perhaps?"

Jen thought about that. "Let's see how he reacts first." She tried not to think about how devastating it would be if Carter reacted negatively. It wouldn't change the way she felt, but it would make everything so much harder. One step at a time.

CHAPTER TWENTY-TWO

Jen parked in front of a nondescript ranch house with its Christmas lights already on. It sat among similar homes built around the same time period and with varying degrees of holiday decorations. Last week's snow still covered the yards and lined the sidewalks. "Ready?"

"Why did I have to come again?" Carter sounded more confused than petulant. Her conversation about Madison had gone rather well. He'd shrugged and told her, "I kind of guessed."

"Because we were invited. It's just this once, and I won't make you do it again. Okay?" Jen reached behind him and grabbed the bottle of gin. Madison had said that her parents didn't drink wine, but she couldn't show up empty-handed.

Madison opened the front door as they came up the walkway. She caught Jen's eye before turning all her attention to Carter. "Welcome. I'm glad you could come. Let me show you where to put your coat."

He flushed under the attention and cleaved to Jen's side when they entered the living room.

Brushing a light kiss against her cheek, Madison wrapped her arm around Jen's waist and whispered in her ear. "Be forewarned, there are more people here than usual. Kayla's birthday is next week. We're celebrating early. Are you nervous?"

Jen squeezed her hand. "No."

"Liar. You'll do fine."

She wasn't lying, exactly. She wasn't nervous, more apprehensive. The last time she'd met someone's parents had been over twenty years ago. A lifetime.

Madison led the way with Carter and Jen behind her. An older but fit woman in her late fifties walked across the room. People automatically made way for her as she came closer. She extended her hand to Jen and smiled. "Welcome, I'm Tisha."

Jen shook hands with her and said, "This is Carter."

Tisha shook his hand. "Hi, Carter." She focused her attention on him. Jen liked her instantly. She asked him a couple questions about school, and then she hit on one of his favorite subjects. "Do you like video games?"

He smiled. "I have a Switch at home. I have *Minecraft, Mario Kart 8 Deluxe...*" He rattled off a whole list before launching into a description of his newest *Minecraft* creation.

Jen could tell Tisha had no idea what he meant. "Well, okay, then. You should check out our basement. There's a whole bunch downstairs."

He hesitated, and Jen asked, "Do you want me to go with you?"

Madison tapped her, and her expression said, *I've got this.* "You like *Minecraft*? Wait until you see what my sister has been building."

Jen watched them walk away. Her instinct was to go with him, but Madison had already engaged him. Jen had forgotten how much nerd culture the two of them shared.

"He's sweet."

"Thanks." Well, shit. Jen had been so grateful at how welcoming Madison was toward Carter, she didn't realize that meant she was left alone. Time to kick into gear. "Madison says you don't care for wine. But that you like a gin and tonic." She handed over the gin.

Tisha pulled it out of the gift bag and eyed the label. A slow smile spread, and Jen knew she'd done the right thing. "Carriage House. I've heard of this. Thank you."

Tisha led her past the living room and straight into the kitchen where the bulk of the family were sitting around playing cards, watching TV, and cooking. A broad shouldered, muscular man was standing at the stove, stirring a pot as she walked in.

Tisha came up to him. "This is my husband, Xavier."

He put the spoon down and walked over to greet her. "Welcome, welcome."

Jen extended her hand, but Xavier swept her into an unexpected hug. Jen stiffened and then relaxed, wrapping her arms around his bulk. They were about the same height, but he was much broader in the shoulders.

"I'm glad you came."

Tisha handed over the gin. "She comes bearing gifts."

Xavier *tsked*. "Now, you didn't need to bring anything."

"Like hell, she did." Tisha winked at Jen, but she wasn't completely sure it was a joke. "She's dating our youngest. She needs to make an impression."

Tisha introduced her to a whole plethora of people. Family and friends of all ages had squeezed into their house. It was good that Madison had Carter downstairs. This crowd would have been too much for him. She could work a room alone, and Madison's family was a friendly group who wanted nothing more from her than to figure her out. She had nothing to fear here.

Madison's aunt and cousin from the restaurant showed up a few minutes after introductions, and Jen spent some time talking with them before she checked her watch. Carter had been gone for a half hour and so had Madison. As soon as there was a break in the conversation, she slipped downstairs to check up on them.

She heard shouting from halfway up the stairs. Alarmed at first, she picked up the pace and stepped into the downstairs game room. Carter, Kayla, Madison, and another boy, a few years younger than Carter, were jumping up and down with controllers in their hands, cheering each other on while simultaneously talking smack. A loud roar went up, and several sets of hands flew into the air in both triumph and defeat.

Obviously the winners, Madison high-fived Carter and ruffled his hair. He hugged her. The gesture was so unexpected that Jen didn't know how to react. He was very selective about who he let touch him. He'd picked up his natural reserve from her, and like her, once he let someone in, they were in. Her relationship with Madison had a deeper impact now, and she doubted her decision to let Madison into his life. She'd counted on him being slow to come around. What if she'd made a mistake introducing him too soon?

"Dinner," a voice came from upstairs, interrupting her spiraling thoughts.

Carter saw her first and ran over. "Did you see that? We totally kicked their butts."

She grinned, his enthusiasm a counterbalance to her worry. "I did. Go get something to eat. I'll head up after you." He scrambled past her with the other kid in tow, laughing and rehashing their plays.

Kayla switched off the screens, and on her way by, she touched Jen's shoulder. "He's a great kid. I'm glad you brought him."

Madison walked up and bit her lip, a nervous tick Jen recognized. "How's it going? I'm sorry I abandoned you upstairs."

Jen pulled her close, wanting to express her gratitude at how well Madison had read her son. "This was more important. Your family is great, by the way. And so are you."

Madison blushed and bumped her shoulder. "I didn't want him to feel overwhelmed. I love these people—I really do—but all together, they can be a bit much."

Jen's family and Rachel's family had always been small. Jen's sister had married into a huge extended family and loved it. Jen had never experienced that kind of large family closeness. Growing up an only child was sometimes lonely for Carter. Occasionally, she wished she could give him more. Madison's empathy for her son ticked a box she didn't even know she had. A warm fuzzy spread from her chest to her limbs. She did not want to cry, so she deflected with humor. "Sure. You leave me to the wolves."

Madison pulled her toward the stairs. "Oh, come on. You're not exactly a deer in headlights."

Jen laughed and stopped her on the stairwell. "And that's what keeps you coming back for more."

Madison paused, her eyes serious and intent. "Thank you for coming. And for bringing Carter. I hope you know that I care about him. Like I care about you."

A deeper emotion than desire and lust suffused her body. "I didn't realize this was so important to you."

Madison shook her head. "It's not. You are…I'm mean it is but… you're the first person I've ever brought home to them."

Ah. Jen resisted her urge to deflect and stuck with the moment by acknowledging its importance. "I understand."

"Do you?" Madison seemed to want to say something more.

Whatever she was about to say was interrupted by Kayla's appearance at the top of the stairs. "Hey, are you coming up or what? Food's ready. You know how Dad hates when it gets cold."

Disappointed by the interruption, Jen knew they'd get back to what Madison was trying to say later. Maybe by then, she'd be able to name this pleasant hum of contentment and happiness for what it was.

Halfway through dinner, talk turned to basketball, and Jen listened to Kayla and Tisha go back and forth about the Providence Friars. She spoke up without thinking. "Well, the defense is not what it used to be. That new coach is terrible. What's her name?"

Silence greeted her. Fuck. What did she say? Thankfully, Carter was at the kids' table in another room, watching a movie.

Madison gripped her thigh under the table.

Tisha looked at her. "Janice." The whole room waited for what she'd say next. Jen's heartbeat sped up, and she mentally prepared for the worst. She really wished she knew what she'd said. Waving her fork at Jen, Tisha said, "And that's exactly what I told my cousin."

A collective breath released, and the room visibly relaxed. Madison leaned in and whispered, "Janice is her cousin."

Her fucking cousin. A little warning would have been nice. Jen whispered back. "Next time, I will need a more in-depth brief on your family."

"You got it." Madison kissed her cheek. That delicious shock that came with Madison's kisses traveled through her body.

Kayla groaned. "Oh, gross. Do you have to do that at the table?"

Jen felt her face grow hot, and Madison tossed a roll at her sister, who threw it back.

Xavier put a stop to the volley. "No, none of that. I worked hard on this meal. You all need to eat it, not throw it."

But all of it was said with love in their voices. They adored Madison, and when Jen looked around, she could see it reflected in their faces. This was what family was, and sitting at that table, she longed to be a permanent member.

On the ride home, Carter talked a mile a minute about the games they'd played and what he wanted to do next time. Next time. And there would be a next time. Giddy with the possibilities, Jen reached for Madison's hand, happy and utterly in love.

Chapter Twenty-three

Madison walked the few blocks to Jen's house and headed up the stone path, carrying a gift bag and a bouquet of flowers tucked behind her back. She'd barely knocked before Carter opened the door.

"Mom's upstairs. But I've got something to show you."

He grabbed her hand and pulled her into the living room. A huge Christmas tree occupied the corner, and holiday knickknacks had been placed throughout the room. Putting the bag down by the couch, she stood while he walked her through his latest *Minecraft* design.

"Is that Ms. Hewitt?" Del came through the kitchen carrying a bottle of kombucha.

"I told you, she's dating my mom."

She smiled. "Hi, Del. You can call me Madison outside of school."

Del gave Madison a shy smile, and Carter visibly relaxed.

"What are you two doing tonight?" she asked the pair.

"Staying out of trouble." Jen called from the top of the stairs. Madison looked up, and her breath caught in her throat. Jen wore a mid-length red dress that hung off the shoulder and showed off her long legs; a delicate chain adorned her neck, and jewels winked in her ears. Her tattoos were visible along her back and shoulder.

Madison glanced down at her outfit—a fancy blouse and formfitting black pants—self-conscious.

Jen stepped off the stairs and circled her. "You look nice." Leaning into her, she whispered, "Close your mouth."

Busted ogling her, Madison coughed and cleared her throat. She thrust the flowers out. "These are for you."

Jen smiled. "Thank you."

The doorbell rang, and Carter zipped past them. "Zach's here!"

"That's our sitter." Jen took the flowers to the kitchen and got them settled into a vase. Madison ducked into the living room and pocketed the small gift box she'd brought, leaving the bag behind. Jen brought Zach up to speed, and afterward, both Carter and Del talked at him a mile a minute.

"Now's our chance to escape," Jen said.

"Wait." Madison walked back to the living room and held up the gift bag. "I bought Carter something for Christmas. Do you mind?"

Jen's whole face softened, and she called, "Hey, C, Madison has something for you."

Carter came back from the living room. Madison passed him the bag and said, "I spoke with Kayla. and we'd love to set up a time with you and a couple of your friends. If it's okay with your mom and their parents."

Carter dug into the bag and pulled out two *Star Wars* roleplaying books and a bag of specialty dice. His face brightened as he flipped through the books and hefted the dice. He shot his mother a look. "Can I?"

"Of course." She glanced at one of the books. "Maybe I'll join. Can I play a Jedi?"

"That would be so awesome!" Carter rushed over to show Del the books but stopped halfway there. "Thank you."

Stunned and pleased that Jen would consider joining a game with them, Madison managed, "You're welcome."

Giving her son a quick kiss, Jen slipped her arm around Madison's waist and said, "That was sweet."

Madison followed Jen to the car, happy she'd made the right choice by bringing him a gift. "Would you really play with us?"

Jen opened Madison's door first. "Of course, why not?"

Madison crushed the little voice in her head that said this was too good to be true. Jen did not toss out commitments lightly. If she said it, she meant it. Jen walked around the front of the car, her long jacket wrapping around those legs and that dress. As she folded her body into the driver's seat, Madison followed the line of her leg from floorboard to hip.

"If you keep looking at me like that, we're never going to get to dinner."

"Is that a bad thing?" Madison snaked her hand onto Jen's knee.

Jen started the car and put it into reverse. Throwing her hand behind Madison's head, Jen backed them up but not before stroking the back of Madison's neck. Madison shuddered at the light touch and clenched her thighs together.

"Not necessarily. But I'm hungry." Jen paused, and the look she gave Madison sent a burst of heat through her body. "For food."

Three Rivers was located less than a mile from Jen's house, on the same side of the river. Built inside a converted warehouse, the restaurant occupied the front corner of the building.

Madison took in the small bar and the cozy dining room. "Have you been here before?" Music played amid the muted conversations around them.

"Not often. It's not exactly kid friendly, and it's a little more intimate than I'd like for work purposes."

That made Madison feel special, and when the hostess showed them to their table, Jen even pulled out Madison's chair before seating herself.

"I hope you don't mind. There's only a tasting menu tonight," the hostess informed them before walking away.

Madison leaned in. "Tasting menu?"

"Prix fixe meal." As if that cleared it up for her. Jen must have read her look because she leaned over and said, "I'm sorry. It's a planned menu, appetizers, entree, dessert."

"Oh." She wasn't sure how she felt about not choosing her own dinner.

Jen winked. "Trust me, it's good."

Two cocktails arrived at their table. A pattern was forming, and Madison wasn't sure how she liked it. "Did you order for me?"

Jen shook her head. "Part of the meal."

Madison took a tentative sip. Tangy and sweet with a slight peppery kick. "Is this bourbon?" Jen sipped hers and nodded. If the cocktails were any indication, the rest of the meal would be amazing.

Jen put her hand on the table, an open invitation. Madison interlaced their fingers. They stared at one another while Madison slowly gathered her courage to give her the present.

"What are you thinking?" Jen squeezed her hand and grounded Madison in the here and now.

Her eyes trailed across Jen's body, her desire stirring once again but mixed with awe as well. "How lovely you look tonight."

Jen blushed and laughed. "You know, that's the first time I've heard that and believed it. I don't know why you affect me so much."

"Because I see you." Her desire morphed into a deeper feeling. One that had been creeping into her thoughts about Jen more often than not.

Jen twirled her drink and took a sip. "Hmm. I think you do."

Sensing the moment was right, Madison pulled out the tiny gift box.

"What's that?" Jen smiled.

Madison nudged it toward her. Giving presents made her nervous—Carter had been easy—and she'd spent hours researching this one. "Go ahead. Open it."

Jen hesitated and tapped the box. "I bought something for you, but I didn't bring it. Should we wait?"

Madison was too anxious, and now that she'd given it to Jen, she'd never be able to hold out that long. "No. I don't think I can."

With a slight smile, Jen tilted her head and slipped the lid off. She pulled out a silver and black lure that bent and moved like a real fish. She touched her chest and said, "Oh, Madison."

She beamed inside. It was exactly the response she'd been hoping for. "I hope you don't have one. We didn't really talk about Christmas and gifts, but I wanted to get you a little something. I realized I didn't know what kind of fish you caught and where. So this one works for freshwater and saltwater."

"It's perfect." Jen leaned across the table to kiss her. Madison met her halfway, her heart full and content. She'd made the right choice. "Thank you."

The appetizers arrived, and Madison had no idea what squash blossoms were but loved them stuffed with goat cheese and fried crisp. The oysters and clams were local and fresh, briny and tender.

Her initial nervousness over her present gone, she relaxed into the evening. Conversation had never been an issue for them, and they talked throughout the entire meal. Jen was more present than anyone Madison had ever gone out with. That intensity was only matched by her desire to know more about Jen, who seemed more than willing to open up.

"When did you know you were gay?"

Jen twirled her cocktail before she smiled and said, "I probably knew for a while, but the first time it really stuck, I was in college at a sorority event. There was this girl who'd I'd been talking to on and off all night. She finally pulled me into her room and kissed me."

"What happened?" Madison imagined a younger Jen, less refined but passionate and rash.

Jen laughed and shook her head. "That whole night. That was a thing."

There was a story there, and Madison wanted to know. "And after? Did you date her?"

She laughed harder. "Oh no. She wanted me to do a threesome with her boyfriend. I told her no, but damn, I knew what I wanted after that."

"Did you have other girlfriends before Rachel?"

"A few. One fairly serious before her but she had commitment issues, so we drifted apart. Rachel showed up soon after. What about you? When did you know?"

Madison should have anticipated the question. Jen's compassion and the alcohol dulled the edges of her memory, making it easier to talk about. "High school. My best friend and I started dating. My birth mother threw me out when she found us in bed together."

"Shit. That sucks." Jen's hand wrapped around hers.

She squeezed back, comforted by the touch. "Yeah. She was a winner." She glanced out the window. Muddy snow lined the streets, and a sheen of water coated the asphalt. Cars moved at a steady pace. She'd lost all her stuff back then, clothes, stuffed animals, keepsakes.

She hadn't thought about that day in years. The memories had been so raw for so long.

Jen just held her hand. The silence soothed her while she blinked away the wetness.

"Do you want to talk about something else?"

Slightly embarrassed, she shook her head. "I'm okay. I'm sorry to bring the evening down."

Jen leaned forward and covered both her hands. "No, don't apologize for who you are or what happened to you. Thank you for sharing it with me."

Madison pulled their joined hands together and kissed them. Jen wasn't the only one who felt seen in their relationship. "What are you doing for Christmas?" she blurted before she realized how it sounded. Obviously, she'd be spending it with Carter.

"Well, I wanted to spend it on a tropical island with this incredibly gorgeous and fascinating woman I've met." Jen continued to stroke her hand, moving from comforting to playful.

Imagining just such a scenario made her smile. "Did you ask her?"

Jen's hand stilled, less flirtatious. "Would you go? Not on Christmas, but after?"

Her heart started beating double-time. "Are you asking?"

"Yes. Come away with me."

Something more fundamental was being asked, and Madison replied with all her heart. "Yes."

Dessert arrived, and the conversation continued, with the mood shifting back to playful and flirtatious. But the tension between them was richer and laced with certainty and confidence.

By the time Jen pulled up in front of Madison's apartment and walked her to the door, a different desire gripped her as her eyes raked over Jen's form. "Have I told you how hot you look in this dress?"

Jen leaned in and played with the edge of her collar. "Not in so many words. But I could tell."

Madison slipped her hand down the side and up the slit, touching bare skin. Jen closed her eyes, and Madison shifted closer, her lips ghosting along Jen's mouth. Jen surged forward, and all the emotions of the evening crashed together in an openmouthed kiss.

Pulling away, her own voice breathless to her ears, Madison asked, "Do you want to come inside?"

Jen groaned and flopped her head back. "Yes."

They pushed and pulled at each other's clothing until Madison stood in her living room with her shirt on the floor, watching Jen getting ready to take her dress off. "Wait. Not yet." She bunched her hands in the fabric and hitched it up around Jen's waist. Leaning in, she pushed Jen back to the couch. Jen sprawled backward, and Madison smiled down at her.

Jen tugged on her waist. "Are you just going to look all night? Cause I'm on the clock here."

She laughed. "I didn't know time was money."

"Babysitters are pricey." She flicked open Madison's pants.

"Right." She'd forgotten that Jen couldn't stay the night. A sting of rejection emerged that had nothing to do with Jen and everything to do with that primal part of her that expected her world to crash down when everything was perfect.

Jen traced the edge of her boxers. "Hey, where'd you go?"

Still gripped by her fear, Madison shook her head.

Jen sat up and forced Madison to look at her. "If you don't want this tonight, it's okay."

Madison stumbled over her thoughts, trying to put them into words. "I do. It…it's just, sometimes it feels too good to be true."

Jen stroked her face, drawing Madison's focus toward the here and now and not her internal monologue. "Tell me something. Are you happy?"

More than she could stand, and that was what worried her. "Yes."

Jen wound her hands in Madison's hair and pulled her toward her mouth. "Then give in to that. Fuck the rest."

Closing her eyes, she did just that.

CHAPTER TWENTY-FOUR

"Thank you for coming." Jen linked their arms together as they headed up the stairs to the Biltmore's ballroom and the Providence Preservation Society's Winter Bash.

"No place I'd rather be," Madison said. Which wasn't exactly true. She would have preferred to be several other places with Jen. But this was the first non-family and non-date outing Jen had invited her to, and she wasn't going to pass up the chance to appear in public as Jen's girlfriend. So much of their time together had been on the fringes of their lives that she welcomed this opportunity, even though Jen described it as a charity event for big donors and thus, a work event for her.

Jen looked at her with a slight scowl. "Bullshit. But I appreciate you saying it anyway." Jen handed their invitation over, and the usher allowed them in.

"I'm serious. I just want to spend time with you." She kissed her cheek, but she felt slightly underdressed in a room full of designer clothes. At least it wasn't black tie. She brushed her newly acquired silver necklace—Jen's stunning Christmas gift to her—and took comfort in its feel.

"Unfortunately, this is not going to be the place to do it. But I'll make it up to you," Jen said as she drew them toward the nearest group.

Madison stayed with Jen and listened to her work. Jen knew the personal and professional details of each person she spoke with and asked thoughtful and empathetic questions. Jen told Madison she regularly raised millions of dollars for Brown University, and seeing her in action, Madison could see how. Like most people, Madison had no idea how money was raised. The fundraising she'd done for her lunch program at events like Iron Pour had been nothing compared to what Jen was doing in that room. This wasn't asking for money outright. These people knew Jen and liked her. They trusted her to present a project worthy of their money. She hadn't realized what a gift Jen's time and focus on her project had been.

But as the night wore on, she felt more and more out of place. Jen would introduce her, and she'd answer a few questions about her work before the conversation shifted to people, places, and hobbies well above her income level.

After yet another conversation that left Madison feeling like a plus one, Jen leaned in and said, "I need to talk with someone alone. Would you mind if I sent you off for a bit?"

Madison swallowed her fear at being left alone in this room and said, "Of course."

Jen gave her a brief hug. "You're wonderful. It'll be quick. I promise."

Madison watched her walk away, enjoying the way her ass moved in that dress. She realized that she wasn't the only one looking. Possessiveness rolled through her. Even if she didn't have their trust funds and fancy cars, she did have Jen. She caught one person's eye as they realized they'd been caught. Feeling particularly smug, she winked and turned around. But her confidence was short lived.

Alone in the crowd, she made her way to the bar and ordered a Cosmo. Nursing her drink, she moved to the outer edges of the room against the windows where she could see the first three letters of the big red Biltmore sign. She tensed as a woman split from the crowd and made a beeline toward her. She knew no one here, and she dreaded the idea of making small talk with another stranger.

"You must be Madison." Well-dressed and confident, the woman extended her hand. "Lindsey Blackwell. I've been wanting to meet you."

She had? Madison recognized the name: Jen's alter ego. "You gave Jen the tea box. It's gorgeous, by the way."

Lindsey smiled, and Madison felt at ease. "Thank you. Did she tell you it was a guilt gift, too?"

Madison hesitated because that was what Jen had called it, and she didn't want to make trouble. Lindsey had been the first person interested in her all evening.

"Don't worry. I call it that, too. That's a lovely necklace."

Madison touched its strands for what felt like the hundredth time this evening. "Thank you. Jen bought it for me."

Lindsey nodded. "She has good taste. I wasn't expecting to see you here."

She shrugged. "It was a bit last-minute."

"Me, too. I've been avoiding public appearances, but my mother roped me in." She nodded toward an older woman in the center of the room. Madison recognized her. Senator Blackwell. Even Lindsey belonged here. "You don't mind if I hide over here with you?" She nodded toward the window seats, and they sat. "How did Jen convince you to come to this scintillating soiree?"

Madison laughed. "I volunteered."

"Bet that won't happen again." Lindsey grinned.

Madison laughed with her, but she wasn't sure what she meant. Was it really that obvious that she didn't belong? "She seems to have a lot of these events. They never end."

"I was like that. Working all the time." She chuckled. "Rebekiah would say I'm still like that. When it's meaningful to you, it's hard to put down."

"I'm not sure it is. Meaningful to her." As the words came out of her mouth, she regretted them. It felt like a betrayal of Jen and her trust. "Forget I said that."

Lindsey moved in closer. "No. You're right. She's talked to me about it. I've known her for almost twenty-five years. She has this intense loyalty to what she signs on to, but all that obligation and duty adds up."

She'd seen that loyalty up close.

Lindsey grinned. "That's why I'm glad she met you. When she talks about you, there's a lightness to her."

Madison's heart soared. Knowing that made attending boring functions with people who didn't care about her except for how well-connected she was bearable.

"You're coming to Key West, right?" When Madison didn't answer, Lindsey added, "To my wedding?"

And just as quickly, Madison's doubts returned. So much of Jen's life happened without her. "I didn't know."

Lindsey waved her off. "It's not until April. You've got time."

She told herself it didn't matter. Jen had other things on her mind, and April was several months away. By then, she'd have a better idea where she fit into Jen's life.

Jen kept a discreet eye on Madison until she saw Lindsey approach, and then she finally turned her full attention to the woman in front of her. Marie had caught her halfway toward her original target, and they'd talked shop for a bit. Marie worked at Johnson and Wales in principal gifts.

"Well, if you're ever interested in leaving the Ivy League for something different, let me know."

It was the third job offer this evening. Was there something she was giving off that said, "I'm looking," or was the word out that her new boss was a complete asshole? Maybe it was the normal restructuring opportunities that happened when leadership changed. Jen had spent her career in the Ivy League, fighting among the same set of people. Working outside that circle had a certain appeal right now. She smiled. "That's good to know."

She moved on and took the opportunity Lindsey had given her to speak with someone else. She glanced up and saw the pair laughing. What Jen really wanted to do was clear out her life for Madison and take a vacation. She'd meant it when she'd asked Madison to go away with her. Spring break was coming up in a few months. Maybe she could convince Rachel to take Carter for the week, and then she'd go somewhere warm with Madison. The Caribbean, Mexico, Costa Rica.

She finished her rounds and made her way to the edge of the room. Lindsey stood as she approached and wrapped her in a warm hug. "I'm just keeping her company while you do your thing."

Jen rolled her eyes. "No, you're not. You're avoiding your mother. But thanks anyway." She turned toward Madison, who looked a little wary. Jen went for lighthearted. "Has she been sharing all my awful secrets?"

Lindsey grinned. "Only a few."

She was joking, but Jen could tell something was wrong. Time to make a quick getaway. "I'm done. Can I interest you in a nightcap somewhere far away from here?"

Lindsey shook Madison's hand and said, "It was nice meeting you." To Jen, she said, "Next dinner invite, she's coming with you."

Jen had never really known Lindsey to be that assertive in her personal dealings. Rebekiah must have been wearing off on her. Lindsey headed back into the crowd and left them alone.

Jen held out her hand. "Shall we?"

Madison took it, and they made their way through the crowd with a nod here and there and a couple waves. No one stopped them.

"Are you okay?"

"Yeah." Whatever was going on, Madison seemed to shake it off quickly. Jen didn't push; she'd let her know in her own time.

"Did I tell you how good you look tonight?"

Madison flushed. "No."

Jen stopped them outside the ballroom. "Well, I should have. Those pants are something." She leaned in and kissed her behind the ear. "Because then you'll understand why I need to rip them off you as soon as we get someplace private."

Madison pulled her back and said, "Then screw the nightcap and take me home."

Chapter Twenty-five

Madison lay on her side watching patches of moonlight dance along Jen's curves. She couldn't remember ever feeling this way, her body satiated and her mind quiet. She drifted somewhere between profound and peaceful, just being. These moments alone with Jen were so perfect. When they were together, the outside world faded. But tonight had been hard, and if she didn't face her fears, they'd only get harder. Tomorrow, they'd talk.

"I can feel you watching me." Jen's voice was sleepy, and she started to roll over.

Putting her hand on her back, Madison said, "Stay. Just like that." She moved closer and pulled the white sheet off. She kissed along the pools of moonlight, running her hands beside her lips, stroking her bare skin.

Jen hummed. "Don't stop."

Madison smiled along Jen's skin. "Don't worry. I won't." She ran her tongue along Jen's body, licking and kissing each dimple and dip. Rolling her over, she kissed along her stomach, her breasts, her shoulders, her lips, never staying too long, always moving, always touching.

She drew Jen up slowly to her knees, guiding Jen into her lap. Their faces inches apart, Madison closed the distance and kissed her way up Jen's jaw, caressing her face and moving toward her lips. A gentle pressure moved her closer, and Jen wrapped her legs around Madison's lower back.

Madison caressed the contour of Jen's thigh and slipped between them. Jen inhaled at the first brush of her fingers and moaned when Madison pushed two of them inside. She groaned, and her head fell back. Madison let go of her ass and shifted a hand to cup the back of her head. She held Jen's gaze and started a steady rocking motion, moving Jen up and down on her fingers, keeping her going without letting her get off. Keeping Jen on the edge, Madison didn't expect her to come so quickly, but then Jen's eyes widened, and her hips arched, knocking her off balance and tipping them over onto the bed.

Madison crawled up and over Jen, smiling down at her. Jen opened her eyes and stared. All Madison's emotions boiled to the surface and poured into her awareness. All those moments together, the easy way they fit together. Between this room and the wedding, she had fallen in love. In some ways, it was too soon. But in other ways, it seemed inevitable.

Jen reached up and pulled her down. Their kisses felt more intimate, and when Jen rolled her over to reciprocate, Madison poured all the feelings she had for Jen into their lovemaking, knowing that tomorrow they'd figure it out together.

Madison woke, not sure what time it was, suffering that liminal time displacement of a gray winter day. She grabbed for her phone but came up empty on the side dresser. It must be in her pants on the floor. And where was Jen?

Last night, Jen had come in her lap, so close to her, bodies entwined, their closeness physical and emotional. And when Jen had reciprocated, she had coaxed something quite different from Madison, using her tongue and touch to slowly build, then rip from her depths, emotions that rendered her speechless.

Happiness rose inside her. She was in love with Jen. The little voice in her head laced with self-loathing spoke up, but before it could begin its litany of disaster, she tossed the covers off and got up.

She padded downstairs naked and found Jen stirring something on the stove.

Jen turned and eyed her. "I like the outfit."

Madison ran a hand down her body, brushing along her curls, and the world's cheesiest line came out of her mouth. "I put it on just for you."

Jen switched off the burner and tossed the spatula on the counter. "Did you now?" She stalked across the room and pushed Madison against the wall. It was so cold, she squeaked. Jen covered her open mouth in a ferocious kiss, and Madison felt renewed wetness. She hitched a leg around Jen's waist, causing Jen to murmur, "Hmm. You feel so good."

Madison groaned at her words and nipped at her ear. "So do you. Come back to bed."

Jen needed no further invitation. She chased Madison upstairs and hefted her on to the bed in a move that surprised both of them, and Madison flopped backward.

The door banged open downstairs, and Carter called, "Mom, we're home!"

Jen jumped away. "Fuck."

Carter knew about them, so why was Jen so freaked out? "What's wrong? It's just Carter."

Jen's eyes narrowed, and her expression darkened. "And Rachel."

Madison's inner voice from earlier returned with all its doubts. "I thought you were going to talk to her."

Jen moved around, grabbing her clothes off the floor and getting dressed. "I am, but this is not how I want her to find you." She fixed her with a look. "Do you?"

That broke the mood completely. Madison sat up and rubbed her face.

Jen pointed at her as she closed the door. "Stay here. I'll take care of this."

Madison stared at the door for a half second before she decided to put some clothes on. She got dressed quickly and sat on the edge of the bed, waiting. She could hear feet coming up the stairs and stood. Leaning against the door, she heard Carter talking just outside. Shit. She was stuck. But why? Did Jen really not want her to see Rachel? She could always play it off as visiting. Although she suspected the bed head was a giveaway.

Then she heard another voice. Rachel.

She padded downstairs and spotted Rachel in the entryway, kicking off her boots and hanging up her jacket.

Jen stood in front of her, hands on hips. "You're early. I thought you were coming home tomorrow."

"We caught an earlier flight. What's the big deal?"

"I have plans."

"We'll come."

"No."

"No?"

Even though Jen was handling her right now, Madison realized that long-term, Rachel was not going away, and Jen's reluctance to deal with her made it hard for Madison to trust Jen's commitment. Rachel still treated her like a wife. Why didn't Jen want Rachel to see her there? To protect her or Rachel? She didn't like either answer. Anger and hurt swirled together until she made her choice. She was done hiding, and Jen was going to have to choose.

Bracing for a bit of a blowout, she gathered her courage and stepped out of the kitchen. Jen's face told her she'd made the wrong choice.

"I didn't know you had company." Rachel folded her arms and glared over Jen's shoulder.

Oh, for fuck's sake, why hadn't she stayed in the bedroom? Jen whirled around, wishing telepathy worked. She had to get Madison out of here before she lost control of the whole situation. She could manage Rachel alone but not while Madison was there. "She was just leaving."

Madison clenched her jaw, and her tone dripped icicles. "Yes, of course."

Shit. Jen took two steps, but Madison was already out the door. Jen took off after her and caught her halfway down the driveway. "Wait!"

Madison paused but didn't turn.

"That's not how it sounded." Damn, it was cold without a jacket.

Madison slowly turned. "Really? Because it sounded like you were throwing me out."

Jen reached out, but Madison pulled away. "I was just trying to protect you from her."

Madison crossed her arms. "I don't need protection." Fuck, this was going all sorts of sideways. Before Jen could answer, Madison added, "I can fight my own battles."

Why was Madison making this so hard? She was only trying to make things right. "But Rachel's not yours to deal with."

Madison raised an eyebrow and directed her gaze over Jen's shoulder. "Isn't she?"

She knew without looking that Rachel was watching. "Look. I just need a little more time. Can I call you later?"

Madison's face gave nothing away. "Sure. Whatever."

"I'll fix this, I promise," Jen called after her before she shivered and raced back into the house.

Letting Rachel stay over the holidays had been a mistake. She'd taken Jen's graciousness as a prelude to something more. Time to disabuse her of that notion.

Rachel leaned against the kitchen bar. "Lover's tiff? I hope I didn't—"

"Get out."

"You're kicking me out? But I live here."

Jen nodded. "Yeah, about that. We're going to need to sell this place so that we're no longer sharing it." She'd said it to shock Rachel out of her complacency, but as soon as she mentioned it, the realness of it felt right.

Rachel seemed genuinely perplexed at the turn of events. Jen almost felt sorry for her. That needed to change as well. "But you'd said it was best for Carter."

"I think he's adjusted to life with us apart. It's time to make it official. If you need me to, I'll find my own place, and you can stay here with him. Just not tonight." She handed Rachel her jacket and suitcase. "Here you go." Opening the door, she said, "Come by tomorrow at ten. We can figure out the holiday schedule then. We also need to come up with a better visitation schedule. This coming and going isn't working. Good-bye."

Jen gently pushed her out and closed the door. Rachel had keys, but she wasn't the sort to barge back in when she'd been made to feel unwelcome. That had been the problem all along. Jen had made her feel welcome. She'd been willing to put up with Rachel because she'd felt bad at how things ended, and she'd wanted to keep things civil for Carter. But that civility had cost her. It had to stop.

She went upstairs and knocked on Carter's door. He sat on his bed with his headphones on, reading a book. Jen tapped his knee and sat beside him. He pulled off his headphones and put down his book. "Did Mama leave? We were supposed to go out to dinner tonight."

Her heart hurt for him. Did she run Rachel out for selfish reasons? No, Rachel had fucked things up by coming home too early. She'd changed plans without checking first, and now Jen was left picking up the pieces again. She ignored her anger and opened her arms. "Come here."

Still young enough to seek comfort in her arms, he crawled up beside her. "What's going on with you and Mama?"

She sighed. Best to dive right in. "I think I made a mistake. Do you know how I always tell you how important it is to talk when something's bothering you?" He nodded. "Well, I didn't follow my own advice." In the broadest terms possible, she explained how she had avoided talking with Rachel, and because of that, his other mother had made some assumptions about their future together.

"That's why you're still fighting, isn't it?"

That and your mother's a big asshole. She smiled and said, "Yes. It is." She squeezed him and asked, "How about you and I order some Thai food for lunch and play games after?"

"Sure. Can we play *Fortnite*, too?"

She weighed her reservations about that particular game against his wants. "Sure."

His face lit up, and that alone made her feel less guilty about how things turned out.

"But I need to make a phone call first." Rachel had ruined a wonderful morning that Jen wanted to get back on track.

Chapter Twenty-six

Back at her apartment, Madison's phone dinged, and she glanced at the name, thinking it was Jen. Her breath caught, and her stomach dropped. Erika. She'd been trying to call for a few months, but Madison had deleted the voice mails without listening. She should have blocked her. What was she doing texting? And two days before Christmas? Did she have some sixth sense that knew when to strike Madison at her lowest? Their last contact had been at Jessie's wedding before Jen had intervened.

Swiping it open, she read: *The janitors found this while cleaning my office.*

It was Madison's grandmother's bracelet. She'd lost it several years ago and had spent weeks hunting before she'd finally given it up for lost. Angry at herself for letting the morning with Jen go so wrong, she ignored her better judgment and typed back, *That's great. Where'd they find it?*

Under the couch.

We looked there.

I know. I'm moving offices. It must have fallen out when they took it. Why don't I bring it to you? I'm going to be in Providence the second week of January.

Madison stared at the words. The last thing she wanted was for Erika to come down. She'd always been able to exploit Madison's weaknesses, and she felt too vulnerable in Providence. But she really wanted her bracelet, and knowing it had been found made it much harder to see it sent through the mail. Best to get it over with quickly. *How about now? Where do you want to meet?*

What's your address?

No way. The sting of Jen throwing her out propelled her next words. *I'll come to you. Today. Let's meet at Northampton Coffee. I can be there in two hours.*

Afraid to be alone with me?

Um, kind of, and no way was she going to tell her that. She couldn't tell from the text if Erika was joking or not, but she ignored it anyway. *See you soon.*

She knew she was running away, from Providence and from Jen, but she didn't care. Every instinct in her body was telling her to get out now. They'd moved too fast, too soon. She stood in front of her closet, looking for the perfect outfit. One that said, I'm over you and okay with being alone and not desperate enough to go out with you again. It was a hard look to pull off with her current wardrobe. She finally settled on a professional cardigan, black cords, and her one concession to safety and comfort, winter boots. The winter mix of ice, snow, and slush made walking treacherous. She didn't think a fall in the snow would complement her look at all.

While she drove, her mind played reruns of the morning, and when that got old, it turned to all the other times she'd been with Jen. Sifting and sorting, revising each moment to sync up with Jen's reaction to Rachel's arrival.

Jen called her en route.

Madison picked up on the second ring.

Jen didn't bother with hello. "Can I come over?"

"No. I'm driving to Northampton."

"Oh. Uh, when are you coming back?"

She felt a little bit of satisfaction hearing the disappointment in Jen's voice. "I don't know." She didn't want Jen to think she'd just be waiting around for her.

"Oh, okay. Well…"

"How's Rachel? Did you take care of her?" She heard the nasty tone and hated herself for it.

"Yes." Jen sounded annoyed, but whether it was at Rachel or her, she couldn't tell. She didn't really care. Jen sighed. "This is not how I planned the day to go."

"Yeah, well, me neither."

"I'm sorry."

"I know, but sorry doesn't change what happened." As she said it, she heard how harsh it was. And what had happened? Jen had thrown her out of the house because her ex had come home early. Big deal, and if it was just one instance of Jen making the wrong choice, she'd be more understanding, but it wasn't.

Jen's voice was a quiet whisper, her words curt. "I see."

"I don't think you do. I don't want to be on your list of things to take care of."

"Whoa. That's not fair. I care about you. It's not wrong to do things for the people you love."

Love, caring for, and taking care of were not the same things. Madison felt herself dying inside as she said, "That's not love, Jen. That's obligation." Tears pooled in her eyes, and she pulled off at the next exit, finding a gas station. She didn't want to do this, but she couldn't risk her heart any more than she already had. "I need some space."

There was a moment of silence, then Jen said, "What does that mean?"

"I don't know." She brushed the tears away from her eyes. "I need to sort a few things out before I can talk to you again."

"I don't understand. I thought this was going great."

Madison wanted to scream back at her, "So did I until Rachel showed up, and you threw me out." How did Jen think this was going to go? "You haven't even told Rachel."

Jen exhaled, and her voice sounded rough, like maybe she was crying too. "Well, not yet. I just needed things to settle a bit more."

"I don't think they ever will until you let go. Lindsey was right. You would rather drown in duty than go for what you really want."

Silence greeted her, and then Jen spoke with a choked whisper, "Don't give up on me."

Madison sighed. She'd tried, but she couldn't deal with not knowing who and what she was to Jen anymore. "I'm sorry."

Jen took a breath. "If that's really how you feel..."

Again, Madison wanted to say something like, "No, that's not how I feel. I love you, you idiot, but I can't wait for you to break my heart a little bit at a time while you figure out what you want." But she didn't, and Jen spoke into the silence between them.

"Then I guess we have nothing more to say."

Even though Madison had started this, it still hurt to hear those words come out of Jen's mouth. She'd been hoping for a different response, that some part of Jen would fight for her and refuse to let her get away, but that wasn't what was happening. Jen was letting Madison push her away and in fact, opening the door to let her go. She should consider herself lucky that she was getting out now before her heart broke even more. Her stomach churned, and her eyes burned as she fumbled with the phone and heard the click before she could respond.

Jen chucked her phone across the room and watched it smash against the brick mantel. A spray of glass rained down as it plummeted to the stone hearth. "Fuck." She slumped to the couch and pulled her legs to her chest. "Fuck."

She shook her head and wiped her tears. This was ridiculous. Space? Madison needed space? She'd give her space. And what the fuck had Lindsey said? The urge to call her and bitch her out had Jen getting up and retrieving the bits of her broken phone. One of the sharp edges cut her finger, and she dropped it again. She sighed and picked it up. More glass splinters showered down. Surprisingly, the facial recognition still worked, but the screen was so destroyed, it made using it worthless. She'd have to get a new one.

She picked up the pieces and bandaged her hand while she stewed. She couldn't believe she'd been dumped again. She had been so careful not to do a repeat of Shawn, and yet here she was, picking up the pieces literally and figuratively. What the fuck had she been thinking? Didn't she have enough trouble with Rachel? And this woman was almost a decade younger, without the same life experiences and obligations.

Obligations. Having just proved Madison's point, Jen sat and thought about what had really happened.

None of it made sense. All her arguments couldn't cut through the fear that Madison had. Should she push her way through it? Bully her way back in? But to what end? A reluctant participant in their relationship? Maybe she could win Madison over…no, she *could* win her over. It would take time and effort. Did she have those right now? Did she ever? Perhaps she should just throw in the towel. A relationship with this much work might be the wrong choice at this point in her life.

She wished Madison had voiced these concerns earlier. She would have limited Carter's exposure to her. She would have limited her exposure as well. But she'd been seduced by love again, and now she was paying the price for thinking it could ever work out. And once again, she'd have to live with a very real hole in her heart. Only this time, it hurt so much more.

Fuck.

CHAPTER TWENTY-SEVEN

Madison felt a little numb by the time she rolled into Northampton. She already regretted her rash decision to drive up and meet Erika, but it was done, and she wanted that bracelet back. When she opened the door to Northampton Coffee, Erika was already there in the back, looking at her phone with two cups in front of her. She stood as Madison approached. She seemed genuinely unsure what to do, and Madison felt satisfaction at her indecision.

Madison reached out her hand to forestall a hug. Erika stared for a second before taking it with a half laugh. Madison pointed toward the counter. "I'm going to get something."

Erika pointed toward the second cup. "I bought you a mocha with caramel syrup."

She remembered. Of course she remembered. It was her attention to the detail that had earned her Madison's admiration to begin with. Erika paid attention when it suited her intentions, and right now, Madison suspected that her intentions revolved around her. "Oh, thanks."

She sat and pulled the cup toward her. Erika settled across from her.

The silence was brief before they started speaking at the same time.

Erika said, "How are you?"

"How long are you going to be in Providence?"

Shaking her head, Erika smiled and said, "For the week. I have a conference at Brown. I'm the keynote speaker. I was planning to come down the weekend before."

Of course she was. Madison couldn't resist the urge to needle her. She'd always wanted to get her away for the weekend, but Erika had always said that her wife made it hard to leave. "What does Annelise have to say about that?"

Erika looked at her cup and turned it so the handle faced the opposite direction.

Madison knew that look. She had something to share and wanted a certain outcome but didn't know how to share it, so she was choosing her words carefully. The sudden return to her life, the weekend away in Providence…had she broken up with her wife?

"Annelise left me."

Madison suppressed her laugh. Against her better instincts, she had to know. "Why?"

Erika spread her hands. "I fucked up. She was going through our receipts and found a charge that she couldn't figure out. After all those years with you, and it was a random hookup in Boston that she found out about."

Jealousy that this nameless woman rated a hotel when she had not made her ask, "Did you even know her name?"

Erika's face turned indignant. "Of course I knew her name, but it didn't matter. I think I wanted Annelise to know. After you left, I got careless."

Madison leaned in, furious that Erika had the gall to bring this up. "Careless? You call poisoning every work option for me in Northampton and Boston careless?"

Erika reached out and tried to hold her hands. Madison pulled them back. "I was hurt. And scared. I shouldn't have done that to you."

For so long, she had been desperate for Erika to see her for who she was, but now she didn't care. She was done with her and didn't want to hear any more. "Can I have my bracelet?"

She pulled back. "Uh, it's in my car. I thought we could talk, and I'd go get it."

Madison leaned back, disgusted but not surprised by Erika's tactics. "I can't believe I was ever with you."

"You don't mean that." She reached out again, and Madison recoiled. "What we had was good."

"For you." Everything Erika did was quid pro quo. She took care of Madison for as long as it benefited her, and when it stopped, so did their relationship.

"And you, too. You benefited from it."

"But I never thrived. You held me in place for so long that I forgot I could be anything else."

Was this what her life was like now? Terrible moments with people she didn't like? Jen would never do this. Hold a piece of her life for ransom. On the surface, they were mirrors—age, academic backgrounds—but that was where the similarities ended. How could she have missed that so completely? She had become so used to the idea of second best that it had become her default.

She had assumed the worst intentions because that was what she expected. And now she'd pushed Jen into a similar position, hoping she'd fight for her. But Jen was never going to fight for her because she didn't see her as a possession.

"I'm done here. Let's go get my bracelet."

Erika scrambled to her feet and hurried out to the parking lot. Outside in the bitter wind, Madison hunched into her coat, wondering why she'd come all this way. The bracelet had been missing so long, she'd already accepted its loss. But it'd been a flimsy excuse to get away. And as much as she hated to admit it, seeing Erika cleared away any lingering regrets about losing her. Never had she been more thankful for a direction not taken than when Erika dropped that bracelet in her gloved hand and tried to apologize.

Madison pocketed the bracelet and said something she should have a few years ago. "This is the last time we're going to talk. There's nothing more between us. I don't care if you find another heirloom or missing sock or whatever. We're done. Don't contact me again."

She backed out of the parking lot and drove away feeling better than the last time she'd headed toward Providence. Erika had been the reason she'd met Jen, but Jen wasn't Erika. She knew that now. Too bad it didn't change anything.

CHAPTER TWENTY-EIGHT

Rachel showed up the next morning to take Carter Christmas shopping and didn't come inside. Jen knew she was avoiding her. If she had come in, Jen might have taken all her pain and frustration out on her, and although she'd earned it through the years, this time, it wouldn't be Rachel's fault. Madison had asked for space, but it'd felt like a break up. She was still reeling from the whiplash of the last few days.

While they were out, she took the opportunity to purchase a new phone. With all of her contacts restored, she opened a text message and typed to Lindsey. *We need to talk.*

Jen was back at the house, eating takeout, when Lindsey replied. *What's up?*

What the fuck did you say to Madison? She broke up with me.

What?

Jen waited as three little dots appeared. *I didn't say anything that would have caused that. Why, what did she say?*

That I would rather drown in duty than go for what I wanted.

I did not say that. Jen waited again. *I did say you have a dogged sense of duty that interferes with your relationships, but I also said that meeting her was good for you. Look, I'm sorry. If I can fix it, I will. What's her number?*

Lindsey didn't say anything Jen wouldn't have said in her place. Whatever Madison heard struck a different note. She let Lindsey off the hook. *It's okay. You did nothing wrong. I was surprised, and she mentioned you.*

Are you really okay?

Jen snorted. The first person since Rachel who she'd fallen in love with and felt as if she could build a new life with just dumped her. No. She wasn't okay. *I will be.*

The front door opened and closed before Carter strolled into the kitchen and opened the fridge.

"Is your mama coming in?"

He shrugged.

"Is she still out there?" Jen stood and headed outside.

Rachel was just pulling away from the curb when Jen came out and waved. She pulled out her phone, but Rachel saw her and came back.

Rolling down the passenger window, she said, "What's up?"

Jen opened the car door and got in. "We still need to talk. I want to go back to scheduled visits. These drop-ins aren't working for either of us."

Rachel drummed her fingers on the steering wheel. "Maybe I should call off my tour."

She had no idea where that was coming from. All she wanted to do was hammer out the visitation schedule without having to go back to mediation. "What?"

"You know, take care of things with Carter."

The last thing she needed was for Rachel to be underfoot. "He's okay."

"Selling the house is a big deal. I think I should be here."

Jen wanted to scream, you weren't here when we bought it; why do you need to be here when we sell it?

"What if I just bought it and let you rent it?"

Jen couldn't imagine a worse idea if she tried. "To what end?"

"So Carter would have the house."

"If you really want Carter to have the house, sign the divorce papers and let me buy the other half."

"I don't know. My lawyer says that's a bad idea."

"Is this the same one who told you not to sign the papers? Rachel, I have tried to do this as pleasantly as possible." She was bracing herself for calling the mediator again.

Rachel laughed. "You call breaking up the family and selling the house pleasant?"

"For fuck's sake, Rachel, I need you to let go. For Carter's sake. For my sake. Fuck, for your sake. We all need to move on."

"What's her name?"

"Why does there have to be someone?"

"I saw her in our house."

She had a point. "It's not about her, and you know it."

"I just want things to be the way they were."

Tears streamed down Rachel's face, and Jen felt guilty that it had finally come to this. She softened her tone but spoke the truth. "No, you don't. You love the idea of what we had, but we're not the same people we were."

"I miss us. What happened to us?" Rachel wiped her cheeks.

Jen sighed and looked out the window. "Life. There is no us. We changed. I want different things. You want different things." She turned in the seat and said, "I need you to let go."

Rachel took a shuddering breath. "I know."

"We're in this in-between space where neither of us can move forward. I need you to be the Rachel I once loved and do the courageous thing. Let go." She touched her hand. "Sign the papers. Please." She pulled back and opened the door. "Why don't you come by for brunch tomorrow, and we'll talk schedules then?"

Rachel nodded. "I'll come by around ten-thirty. I promise, we'll talk." Jen closed the door, and Rachel rolled down the passenger window. "I hear you, you know? I just didn't want to listen."

Relief rushed through Jen. Finally.

"Can I ask you a personal question?"

Jen nodded, not surprised but also grateful that Rachel could see boundaries after all.

"Does she make you happy like I did? Back in the beginning?"

She almost didn't answer because it *was* a personal question, and Rachel had no right to an answer. And there was no comparison. Her love for Madison was different than it was for Rachel. Rachel's burned bright and hot. Madison's love was steady and strong. And it was love. Of course it was. The very act of pulling it away revealed it to her so clearly now. She loved her.

"Yes, but it's different. I'm different."

❖

Christmas day, Madison was already having second thoughts about her relationship with Jen. She'd asked for space, and Jen's response had felt pretty final. She'd spent a listless morning cleaning her apartment and watching *Star Trek* before heading over to her parents' house. When she showed up, her mother zeroed in on her mood right away. Taking her to the back porch, she said, "What happened?"

"I broke up with Jen." Saying those words aloud hurt more than she was expecting.

Her mom opened her arms, and she walked into a hug. "I'm so sorry."

She closed her eyes as her mother held her. She spoke into her shoulder. "I really wanted this to work."

Her mom steered her to a bench. "What went wrong?"

Madison sighed. How did she explain a feeling she didn't understand herself? "Nothing. Everything." She told her about Jen not inviting her to Lindsey's wedding and then not telling Rachel about her.

Her mom waited and then said, "That's it?"

She crossed her arms. "It's not like it's really about those two things. You know what it was like with Erika."

She nodded. "Yeah, and that was Erika."

"It's the same thing."

"Is it?" She leaned back and said, "I really wish you had someone before Erika. She totally skewed your idea of a healthy relationship."

She couldn't argue with that. "I sense a but."

Her mom combed back her hair and smiled. "Do you remember Michael?"

A little surprised at the subject change, she flushed at the memory of the dark-haired kid she'd tormented after she'd come back to the house a second time. She exhaled. "I was so mean to him."

"And he still loved you. You know he was here the first time you came to us."

"He was?"

"Yeah, and the two of you were inseparable. People thought you were twins. But when you came back and he was here again, you wanted nothing to do with him."

"I don't remember that. I just remember hating him on sight."

"That's because by eight, your self-protection skills were in full effect. It was safer to keep him at a distance than lose him again. You have this reptilian response whenever you feel vulnerable. You pick up your toys and go home." She paused, her point made.

"Huh." She thought about all her relationships through the years and how superficial most of them had been. Always keeping a part of herself from getting too close. In fact, the only close relationships she had were her adopted family. Erika and Jen had been the exceptions to that rule. Except Erika had first earned her trust professionally. It paved the way for her to earn it personally when their relationship changed. She'd snuck through a back door in her defenses.

"I think your capacity for self-sabotage is pretty good."

Her mouth dropped open.

Apparently, her mother was not done with her point. "And completely justified. I know we don't talk about this because it doesn't matter on a day-to-day basis, but deep in your heart, it's still there. And I think it's not doing you any favors."

"You think I should accept her table scraps." Her parents had always been secure in their love for one another. They'd never come in second best.

Her mom raised a hand in a placating manner. "I think you should examine your reasons for letting her go. She doesn't strike me as a woman who invests her time unwisely."

Kayla barged through the back door and pulled up short. "What? What's going on? Don't shoot the messenger."

Her mother patted Madison's knee and stood. "Think about it." She walked by Kayla, touching her on the way past.

"Do I want to know?" Kayla asked.

Madison curled her lip. "Not really." She didn't have the heart to talk about it again.

"Well, dinner's almost ready." Kayla helped her up, and Madison followed her into the dining room.

They spent the rest of the night laughing and talking about anything and everything but her personal life. She had forgotten how essential they were to her well-being. Those years away had left her adrift, and she didn't even know she'd lost her way until now. Her conversation with her mother resonated, and she left them knowing she had their support no matter what she did.

But had she squandered a good thing hoping for the best thing? And if Jen and her had this deep connection, how could Jen let her go so easily? That said something.

CHAPTER TWENTY-NINE

Jen dropped Carter off and took the long way through the school, hoping to get a glimpse of Madison. It had been two weeks since she'd—they'd—broken it off. Two weeks filled with the shit of her life and no one to really share it with. Her lawyer called mid-week to say that Rachel had signed the papers. The divorce was final, and the house was hers if she'd pay Rachel a dollar. That last part shocked her. She'd been prepared to pay half.

"A dollar? Did she say why?"

Her lawyer said, "No. But I'd recommend you cut a check as soon as possible."

Now the house was hers, and she felt absolutely miserable. She hadn't realized how integrated into her life Madison was until she wasn't. Every day, she woke up, and for one moment, she'd feel all right, then reality would set in, and she'd be stuck with another day going through the motions.

The bagged lunch program was in full swing this semester, with several parents rotating the responsibility of housing and delivering lunches to the kids. A victim of her own efficiency, Jen had created a system that didn't need her or Madison's help. Still, she started to time visits to the school when the chance of overlap would be high, the urge to see Madison so great. She couldn't bring herself to text or call, but she'd managed to convince herself that she was still respecting Madison's boundaries if she accidentally bumped into her at school. The cruel irony was, she saw Shawn more instead.

She left school with no sightings and, feeling sorry for herself, called in sick to work. She drove over to Olneyville and pulled into Nat's garage.

Nat was standing under the hydraulic lift with her hands buried in the undercarriage of an Aston Martin. Jen leaned against the wall and watched her work without a word of greeting.

Nat spoke without looking her way or stopping. "Are you just going to stand there all day?"

Loath to get rid of the silence and yet eager for the companionship, Jen sighed and pushed off the wall. "I was thinking about heading to the shore to do some surf casting."

Nat pulled her hands away from her work and wiped them on the rag hanging out of her back pocket. She hitched an eyebrow. "Awfully cold day for it. No work?"

Jen grinned. "No work."

"Forecast calls for snow."

Jen shrugged. "Then I leave."

Nat searched her as if for the meaning behind the words. "What happened?"

Her question punched through her shields and scored a direct hit at Jen's heart. Shoving a fist against her mouth, she held in her tears. "She left me."

"Oh." Nat walked over. "I'm sorry. What did you do?" She said it without malice, but the implication that it was somehow Jen's fault hit her hard.

She sank to the floor and choked on her tears. "Nothing. Everything."

Nat followed her, their knees touching.

"Why do you think it's my fault?"

"I didn't say that."

Jen stared at her, surprised that she'd deny it so quickly. "What did you do?"

Nat moved her head side to side. "Well, when you say it like that, it does sound like your fault. But that's not how I meant it. Tell me what happened."

And she did.

Everything that happened, including the divorce.

Nat's only comment came at the end. "She's right."

"Rachel?"

Nat made a face. "No. Madison."

"About what?"

"Taking care of her."

Those words stirred up the anger and hurt she'd felt the first time she'd heard them. "I do. I did take care of her."

Nat leveled a look at her. "But did she need you to?"

Jen opened her mouth, but no words came out.

Nat shook her head. "You spend all your time making sure everyone is taken care of that you don't pay attention to what's happening inside you."

"But I thought you said I should be careful with her?" She racked her brain trying to figure out Nat's angle in all this.

"I did. But that was for your sake and not hers. She's not the one who needs to be rescued. You are."

My track record's a little damaged.

But you're not.

And that's what it boiled down to. She took care of things so she wouldn't have to take care of herself. Madison had seen right through her act and had called her on it.

"I'm just saying, if you want her back, you need to show her that she's your equal and not another responsibility."

Jen took a deep breath and wiped her tears away. Nat waited until she had pulled herself together before patting her on the knee and getting up. She hauled herself up and brushed her hands on her pants. She felt hollow inside but better, like the first good day after a long illness.

With a tilt of her head, Nat said, "I can't go today, but this Sunday I've got time."

Jen nodded. "I'm going to head out anyway."

Nat went back to work, and Jen went to the back room to gather her gear. When she came back out, Nat had already attached the rack to her roof and held out her hand for her pole.

"I'm glad she signed the papers. I never liked her."

She'd always assumed that Nat's personal distance had to do with her own innate need for solitude and not because of the company Jen kept. "Why didn't you say something?"

She shrugged. "You weren't ready to hear it." She tugged on the fasteners and stepped back. "Keep the gear if you want, but text me when you get home so I know you're okay."

Jen gave Nat a brief hug and headed down to the south shore. She wasn't expecting to catch much; both the time of day and year conspired against her. But as she cast her line into the surf and started reeling it back in the cold January sun, she felt the peace that the action and the ocean gave her. A sea otter's head bobbed along the waves, indicating that the sea bass she was looking for were out there. She got a pull on the line and tugged. It tugged back. She reeled it in slow and steady and pulled in an empty line.

She checked her lure—the one that Madison had given her for Christmas—and cast back again. While she tracked the oncoming storm, her mind replayed the last few months. She'd tried so hard to fit into the molds she'd created. Good wife, good parent, good employee, that she'd forgotten what she wanted in life.

All this time, she'd thought it was Rachel holding her back. And in some ways, it was. But really, it was her own grief at the dissolution of their family. She was holding them together and not letting any of them grow. Carter needed to establish his own life with Rachel. Rachel had always been a capable parent, but Jen had interfered and put her own stamp on all their interactions together. She needed to back off. Carter had already accepted the split and was done living his life in one house.

As much as she railed about the nesting agreement, it was her who had been afraid to let go of that. It would mean that the relationship was truly over, and she had failed to make it work. And that was the real kicker for her. Failure. She'd failed to fix her marriage.

Her mother had always wanted her a certain way, and even though she'd loved Rachel, Rachel had been her mother's wish for Jen. Madison was her own choice for her own self, independent of expectations and obligations. What was she afraid of? Not that she'd say no but that she'd say yes. Yes to a lifetime together to the ups and downs that she'd always thought she'd share with Rachel but never had.

Madison was the first person to see her as she was, not who she could be. She didn't know she needed that until Madison came, and now that she wanted it, it was gone. If she'd been the cause of their breakup, she could have salvaged it and made it work. She always had. But it was Madison who'd pulled the plug, and there was no going back from that.

She lost track of how many times she'd thrown the line and reeled it back in as the snow started to fall. She quickly packed up and headed to the parking lot, alone and empty-handed.

Chapter Thirty

Madison tracked a particularly rowdy group of boys and another set of girls. The edges of their play touched but didn't cross over. Carter and Del sat together on the ground between the two groups. It was the second week back at school, and the kids hadn't settled down yet from their winter break.

She'd been hoping to catch sight of Jen at pickup or drop-off, but so far, she'd missed her. She didn't want to call or text, afraid that Jen would just ghost her. For some reason, not knowing how Jen would react versus having it confirmed seemed easier to cope with. If she could just catch a glimpse or speak to her, however briefly, she could decide if it was worth the risk. And there were plenty of risks.

She'd had a lot of time for introspection over the holidays. Her mother had been right. Seeing Erika again had reopened all her failed relationships, and she'd gone over and over them trying to figure out how and why they ended, and she kept coming up with the same answer. It was always her. She ended it before it could get too serious. She wasn't afraid of being alone; she just didn't want to be left. And that fear had made her world very small.

Lost in thought, she heard shouts, and then one of the boys pushed another into Del. Del stood and swung.

Things escalated quickly, and by the time she got over there, Carter was already on top of another kid, arms swinging. Madison reached into the middle. She hauled him back just as he was swinging, and he clocked her in the face. She staggered back at his yowl of pain while her own mouth started to throb. Carter dropped to the ground and curled up around his hand.

She followed him down. "Are you okay? Where's it hurt?"

He cradled his hand in his lap, tears streaming down his cheeks. More teachers arrived, rounded up the perpetrators, and dispersed the crowd. She got to her feet, using her body to shield Carter from the group. She scanned the adults and waved Eamon over. "I need to take him to the nurse. Can you—"

As he got closer, Eamon's eyes went wide. He pointed at her face. "Are you okay?"

Madison tilted her head and touched her fingers to her lips. They came away red. She grimaced. "Yeah, I'm fine. Help me with him."

Heading back into the building, she could feel her lip starting to swell. Carter whimpered when the nurse touched his hand. "We should get this checked out." She made eye contact with him. "You need X-rays, honey. I'm going to call your parents."

Carter shifted and said, "Please don't. She's going to be mad."

The nurse paused. "She needs to know what's going on, Carter."

He pointed to Madison. "She can tell her."

The nurse turned and cocked an eyebrow. "It's up to you."

The last time she'd spoke with Jen had been to break up with her. As much as she wanted to talk to her again, she wasn't sure what kind of reception she'd get, and she was not looking forward to that cold, professional tone. Carter's whole face pleaded with her, and her resolve crumbled.

"She's not going to be mad at you. She might be worried, and she might be upset you used your fists instead of your words. But she's not going to be mad. She loves you."

She started to pull away, but Carter called her back. "I'm sorry I hit you."

She knelt without touching him and said, "I know. I'll be right back."

His voice trembled. "Will you stay with me if she's angry?"

Her heart went out to him, and she said, "Of course. Even if she isn't."

She didn't have to be with Jen to be there for him. Even though Madison was willing to admit that she wanted to be there for Jen as well.

❖

Jen's cell rang in the middle of her staff retreat. Her boss glared at the intrusion. She glanced at the number and ducked out of the conference room. "Madison?" It was the first time they'd spoken since Madison had called it off. Her stomach dropped. She could think of only one reason she'd call in the middle of a school day. Carter. "What's wrong?"

"Carter's okay, but we'd like to take him to the ER."

Thoughts of broken bones and unexpected seizures appeared in her head. "What? What happened?"

"He got in a fight with a couple classmates. His hand is swollen. We're not sure if it's broken."

Madison filled her in as Jen walked back into the room to pack up. She scribbled a note and passed it to her boss. She didn't even bother waiting for his reaction. If he had an issue with her leaving, he could fuck right off.

"Over what?" Her son had never been in a physical fight. His karate teacher had drilled the idea that an actual fight was a last resort, and he believed it.

"I think some words were spoken. I suspect transphobic because Del threw the first punch. Carter just backed him up."

Jen suppressed a smile. Now that sounded like her son. She hit the button to the elevator and asked, "Can you stay with him? At the hospital? I'm in New York City." Her car was in Providence, three hours away. "I need to get to Penn Station. Can I call you back?"

She stepped out in the street and pulled up her train app. She'd just missed one heading east and needed to haul ass eight blocks to catch the next one. She considered catching a cab but didn't think it would get her there any faster. She hurried through the streets, switching her ticket on route. She just made the last call for the next train and slipped into the mostly empty business class cabin. Taking off her backpack, she leaned against the seat and closed her eyes. The adrenaline rush was crashing, leaving her cold and shaky. Of all the days to have something happen, she had to be three hours away.

Taking a deep breath, she called Madison back. "How's he doing?"

"Good. We're at the ER and waiting for the doctor."

"Can I talk to him?"

"Sure." She heard the phone being passed over.

"Hi, Mom." His voice said he knew he was in trouble.

She spoke gently. "How are you feeling?"

"It hurts."

"I know, baby. Are you okay with Madison being there? I could get Aunt Elizabeth."

"No. I'm good. She's good."

"Do you want to tell me what happened?"

Carter shared more details until he said, "I gotta go," and handed the phone back.

"Jen?" The business tone was gone, and Madison spoke in a softer voice. One Jen hadn't heard for almost a month and had missed every day since.

She swallowed her sadness and said, "I'm here."

"How are you doing?"

"Wishing I wasn't stuck on a fucking train." She glanced around, realizing how loud she'd been.

"It's going to be okay. I've got him."

There were so many words she wanted to say, but all that came out was, "Thank you."

"I can take him home after this. What time will you be back?"

"Around six. But I can call my sister if you need to go home."

"Do you want me to go home?"

"No!" That came out more emphatic than she meant it to. "I mean no, not unless you want to go home." Why the fuck was she so wishy-washy? She blew out a breath and finally said what she meant. "I want you there. I trust you with him."

There was a slight intake of breath, and then Madison said, "Thank you."

Silence hung between them while Jen struggled for something more to say. She didn't want to break the fragile connection they'd just made.

"I should go. There're taking him to X-ray now, and I should pay attention for you."

"Right. Let me know what happens. And thank you again."

"See you soon."

While she waited to hear back, she called Rachel and filled her in. Rachel responded appropriately, even offering to come home.

"I don't think that's necessary."

"Well, I'm here if you need me." Carter might, but Jen didn't.

"Thanks. I'll let you know what happens."

Forty minutes later, Jen breathed a sigh of relief when Madison texted.

Just a sprain. Getting discharged soon.

Despite leaving on time, the train stopped for an hour and a half on the tracks, and it was almost nine by the time she walked into her house. Most of the lights were off. Only a small set of track lights in the kitchen and the foyer were on. The living room glowed blue from the television, and two figures were curled up on opposite ends of the couch, fast asleep.

Her heart softened, and she sighed. Nat was right. She had needed to be rescued. When she'd first met Madison, she'd been trapped in a web of responsibilities that had all but drowned her. Each step with Madison had helped her recognize those ties. She'd never be free of them, but she could choose how they affected her.

Madison woke up, her lip swollen and sore, before she saw Jen standing in the doorway, lit from behind. She didn't mean to fall asleep. Stifling a yawn, she shifted her body, and Carter stirred. "Mom?"

Madison rubbed her hand against his hand and whispered, "She's here."

Jen walked in and knelt next to her sleepy son. "Hey, honey. How're you doing?"

Carter yawned. "Mmm. Okay. Sleepy."

Jen kissed his forehead and then scooped him up in her arms. She groaned and put him back down. "Shit. He's really too big for this."

Carter plopped back on the couch, and Jen nudged him. "Come on, buddy. Let's go upstairs."

They steadied him and led him up the stairs and to his bedroom. Not sure if she was needed, Madison hung by the door and watched Jen tuck him into bed. She waited as Jen sat on the edge of the bed, rubbing his forehead until his breath evened out. Madison turned, expecting Jen to follow, but she didn't.

Jen sat with her head bowed and her shoulders slumped. Nothing had changed between them. They still hadn't talked, but Madison's heart went out to her. Jen looked so defeated that she covered the room in two steps and pulled her into a hug.

Jen sagged against her, and Madison could feel tears on her neck. She'd never felt more vital and needed than in this moment with Jen. All this time, she'd been looking for always, and she'd missed right now. She'd been looking for declarations and gestures when all along, Jen was communicating through the quiet moments to her.

With a sniff, Jen finally pulled away, and Madison helped her to her feet. She quietly closed the door and led Jen into the hallway. She let go of her hand, not sure where they stood and not wanting to push her luck. Jen might have let her comfort her in the dark, but that was not a license for something more.

In the dim light, Madison could just barely see her face. "You must be exhausted."

Jen murmured her agreement but said, "And hungry."

"Come on. There are leftovers in the fridge."

Downstairs, Jen moved toward the fridge, but Madison put her hand on her shoulder. "Sit. I've got it."

Not bothering to switch on the lights, she gathered the chicken and rice she'd made for Carter and herself a few hours ago. She fixed a plate and put it in the microwave.

"You don't have to do this."

She glanced up. Jen sat with her head propped in her hand and with a slight smile and a curious expression. "I don't mind. You've had a long day, and someone should look after you." She spoke without thinking. After all her insistence on not wanting to be rescued, here she was doing it to Jen. Her face burned, and she started to backtrack.

"I know things have been tense between us, and I didn't mean to imply that you couldn't. If you want me to go—"

The microwave dinged, and she set the plate down in front of her. Unable to keep from looking, she was caught by Jen's gentle expression.

Jen stood, her chair scraping along the floor, and grabbed her hand. "I don't want you to go anywhere."

Madison turned. Jen gasped and flipped on the overhead lights. "Did Carter do that?"

Madison reached up and touched the cut. "What? Oh, yeah, but not on purpose. I got caught in the fray."

Jen brushed Madison's fingers aside and moved closer. She traced the cut's contours, the edges still raw. "Does it hurt?"

Madison shook her head, closing her eyes at the gentle touch. "Not really."

Jen pursed her lips and looked like she might say something more, but instead she guided them back to the island. Relieved and nervous, Madison sat next to her and watched her eat.

"Mmm. This is good. Thank you." In between bites, she asked, "How was he?"

"Tired. Worried. He did really well at the ER, but he's scared about how you'll react."

She sighed. "I bet. I got a message from Kathleen. Two days suspension. Were you there? Did you see anything?"

Madison filled her in on the details, omitting names, but Jen pressed her.

"Did he say anything else?"

"Not much. Mainly, he was concerned about your reaction."

Jen took her last bite and leaned back.

Madison grabbed the plate, but Jen put her hand on its edge. "I've got it. You don't have to clean up after me."

Madison let go and moved back. "Just how much trouble is he in?"

Jen shrugged and stood. She poured herself a glass of water and offered one to Madison. "I'm not sure. I don't want to encourage him, but sometimes, you need to stand up to bullies and bigots."

"I've got a couple books that might help." She felt slightly awkward offering Jen parental advice, but it was actually part of her professional wheelhouse.

Leaning against the sink, Jen smiled. Her whole face reflected her gratitude. "That would be really nice. I'm a little out of my depth these last two years. And Rachel is no help."

"You're doing a great job."

"It doesn't feel like it. I just can't seem to get ahead of anything. Carter, my job—" She stopped, and Madison knew what she was going to say.

"Me."

"You." Jen folded her arms. "I'm not trying to rescue you."

This conversation had been simmering beneath the surface since Jen had come home. This was it. If Madison left now, they'd never have another moment like this. "I was wrong."

Jen raised an eyebrow. "About?"

Madison chuckled. "Everything. You, Erika, me. I thought if I really mattered to you, you'd fight for me. And you didn't."

Jen sputtered. "You told me you needed space. I'm not going to chase you down."

She held up her hands in surrender. "I know that." Smiling, she shook her head. "Now."

The track lights cast half of Jen's face in shadow, making her expression hard to read. "I thought we were done."

Madison stood and moved closer. Jen's eyes burned in the darkness. She'd been selfish and rash, not understanding just how much Jen had opened up her life for her. "I'm sorry I gave up on us too soon. I gave up on you."

Jen locked eyes with her and held her there. "If this is going to work, you need to talk to me. You can't just run away."

Hope swelled up inside Madison, and she reached out for Jen. "And you. You can't just take care of it. Fix everything. Let me help you."

Jen wiped the corners of her eyes. "I know. I'll try."

"That's all I ask." She pulled Jen toward her.

"Don't give up on me," Jen whispered fiercely.

Madison held her. "I won't."

Chapter Thirty-one

Jen slowly pulled back and rested her forehead against Madison's. "Will you stay?"

Madison nodded, and Jen felt her heart settle into place. She didn't want to think what no might have meant. Something had changed, and there was no going back. She locked up and took her upstairs.

In the bedroom, uncertainty gripped her, and she started opening drawers. "I don't know what you want to wear. I've got shorts, T-shirts. I'm not sure if my underwear would work." She kept talking, not even listening to herself until Madison's arms wrapped around her. She closed her eyes at her touch.

"You're nervous. You're cute when you're nervous."

Jen turned in her arms and stared at her lip. "I can't believe I missed it."

Madison smiled and angled her head to give her better access. "You had other things to think about."

Jen touched her face. "Still it looks like it hurts."

Closing her eyes, Madison hummed at her touch. "It doesn't. I can barely feel it."

"Would you feel it if I did this?" She leaned in and brought their lips together, gently, gingerly.

Madison jumped and yelped. "Ow."

"I'm so sorry. I should have asked." She pulled back, but Madison held her in place.

Shaking her head, Madison said, "No, it's not that." She smiled and then winced. "Apparently, it does hurt, but don't stop." She peppered light kisses around her lips. "Just. Be. Gentle."

The kisses continued, growing more intimate while shirts and socks, bras and pants slowly fell to the floor. Jen gently pushed Madison back until she lay naked across her bed. Jen paused and looked at her, really looked at her. From the beginning, Madison had seen so clearly who Jen was. But Jen's own vision had missed what was right in front of her.

Madison opened her eyes. "What?"

"I love you."

Madison's face flushed, and she reached for Jen. "I love you, too."

Jen kissed her with greater urgency until words became secondary to touch.

A few hours later, Madison got up to pee and padded back into the bedroom. She snuggled down next to Jen and burrowed into place, enjoying the rightness of holding Jen close.

"Comfy?" Jen rolled over in her arms.

With a sigh, Madison slung another arm around her and squeezed. "Very."

"You know you were right."

"About?"

"I was avoiding telling Rachel."

"You were?" She wasn't sure how she felt about being right on that one.

"I didn't want to deal with the fallout. I'd been living for her needs and not mine for so long that I forgot about myself."

She chuckled.

Jen poked her. "That wasn't supposed to be funny."

"I thought the same thing about Erika."

Jen propped herself up on her elbow. "Really?"

"I saw her a couple weeks ago." She paused and then added, "The day we broke up."

Jen's eyebrow shot up, and her mouth twisted. "Really? I'd wondered."

She got a tiny thrill at the jealousy coming off her. "Seeing her again highlighted how little she valued my needs. I didn't know I'd taken that as a default until I started seeing you. I created the same pattern with you that I had with her."

"Are you saying I'm like her?" Jen's voice rose an octave.

Madison sat up and held her. "No. You're nothing like her. But I didn't know that until I saw her again."

Jen's features relaxed into a smile, but her shoulders were still tight. "Hmm."

The tilt of Jen's head and the tense set of her mouth caused Madison's desire to flame up again. She shifted positions and slowly pushed Jen onto her back. Hovering over her, she said, "You look pretty hot when you're jealous."

Jen's eyes narrowed, and she said with mock sincerity, "I'm not jealous. I'm possessive."

Madison laughed. That statement couldn't be further from the truth. Jen was the personification of, if you love something, set it free. Madison had learned that the hard way, and she wasn't likely to forget it anytime soon. Nor did she want to.

Jen leaned in and nipped her shoulder. "Oh, you think that's funny. Let's see if you're still laughing when I'm done with you." Another bite and Madison's laughter became a gasp. "Yeah, that's what I thought."

For the rest of the night, they made love, dozing on and off, confessing their hopes and fears in the dark.

Just before dawn, Madison spoke her deepest fear. "Where do we go from here?"

Jen smiled at her. "Wherever we want."

"How can you be so sure?"

"I'm not. But I've got you, and that's all I need." Jen yawned before she dozed off again.

Warm light poured through the bedroom windows and woke Madison again. She lay on her side, watching patches of sunlight dance along Jen's curves, remembering when moonlight touched those same spots before everything changed.

"I can feel you watching me." The same words and sleepy voice from the last time.

Putting her hand on Jen's back, Madison said, "Stay. I like the way the light hits you from this window." Madison moved closer and pulled the white sheet off. She kissed along the pools of sunlight, running her hands beside her lips, stroking Jen's bare skin.

Jen turned. "Come here."

Madison crawled into her arms, and Jen kissed her awake.

"How're you feeling?"

Unable to hide from her emotions anymore, she answered with the truth. "Happy. Scared. Tired. You?"

Jen yawned. "Tired. Happy."

"Scared?"

Jen shook her head. "I told you last night. No need. I've got you." She kissed along the edge of Madison's collarbone.

In the light of day, Madison heard her words and took them at face value. She could hold on to her fears, or she could trust Jen and stop running.

Jen poked her head up. "Still scared?"

"A little. But I'll get over it."

Jen dipped her head a little lower, and Madison hummed. "Don't stop."

She heard the smile in her voice as Jen's lips brushed along her skin. "Don't worry. I won't."

Epilogue

Nine months later

"Carter!" Putting her coffee cup in the dishwasher, Jen checked her watch and called up the stairs. "We're going to be late."

"I can't find my laptop." He clomped down the stairs. It looked like a comb had barely touched his hair. But the rest of his clothes matched and were relatively wrinkle free. Even his red Converse were tied or whatever passed for tied in that complicated laced up look. She could see the teenager starting to emerge from her eleven-year-old.

"Where did you have it last?" Madison walked into the kitchen and started shuffling papers on the kitchen bar. She hauled out a red laptop bag and passed it to him. "You mean this one?"

He grinned and stuffed it in his backpack. "Thanks."

Jen walked over and kissed her cheek before giving Carter a once over. "Did you brush your teeth?"

He rolled his eyes and hefted his backpack. "Mom…"

She turned and headed toward the side door. "Fine. But don't blame me when the girls or boys don't want to go anywhere near you." Sending him out the door, she headed to the car while Madison set the alarm and locked up behind them.

Carter piled into the back. "Why do I always have to ride in back? I'm getting kind of squished back here."

Jen glanced at him. He'd grown an inch and a half in the last year, and it wasn't the first time he'd complained.

The ride to school was relatively quiet. As she pulled into the parking lot, she took in the progress on Hutchinson's newest building, a fully funded cafeteria. They'd broken ground on it two weeks ago, and it was scheduled to open next year.

Pulling into a parking spot, Jen opened her door and flipped her seat up so her son could clamber out. He gave her a one-armed hug and a quick kiss on the cheek. "I'll see you later. Don't forget Eli's picking you up after school."

He waved at Madison as she got out on the other side. Jen watched him open the school door and disappear.

Madison cut her a look. "He's got a point. Maybe we should start taking my car."

Jen rolled her head toward her. "Uh, no."

Madison slung her bag over her shoulder and walked around the front of the Porsche.

Jen met her in front of her hood. "He's getting older. Maybe I should buy his car early and let you drive it."

"I don't think so," Madison replied with the ease of a repeated conversation.

Jen leaned into her personal space. "Eventually, I'll catch you in a moment of weakness, and you'll surrender."

Madison kissed her cheek. "Not likely but keep trying. I like to see you work for it."

Jen grabbed her hand as she pulled away and brought her in for a quick kiss. Her toes tingled, and her nerves lit up, just like the first time. Shaking her head, she pulled away, slightly breathless. "Wow."

Madison opened her eyes and smiled. "Wow." She reached out and fixed Jen's collar. "Go. I'll see you tonight."

Blown away by the whirlwind events on the last year, Jen called out. "Hey."

Madison turned.

"Thanks for not giving up on me."

"Always." Madison winked.

Jen let that word reverberate for a moment. Always. It wasn't the word that had scared her but the work behind it. She'd done always before and failed. But that didn't mean she shouldn't try it. Always needed someone willing to go the distance and do the work. She'd thought that was Rachel, and for a time, it was, and then it wasn't. She'd been stuck in limbo for so long that she'd forgotten what always felt like. Always was a promise to pick up the pieces and work together. Always was what Madison had to give.

"I love you."

"Love you, too." Madison waved good-bye.

Jen got in her car and watched Madison's ass move in those tight pants across the parking lot. She could have sworn there was a bit more sway to it. And then Madison stopped at the door and turned. She flashed her a smile that said she knew Jen had been watching her all along.

Madison finished the dishes and headed out to the back porch while Jen was upstairs with Carter. October was next week, and she could feel the slight chill of fall in the warm night. She bundled up and moved away from the house and its ambient light as one or two stars emerged in the night sky. They already had a series of events scheduled for the month that included a ghost tour and Iron Pour. Her life was busier than it had ever been, and she loved it.

She'd given up her lease a month ago and moved in. After spending six nights out of seven at her house, Jen had suggested they make it permanent. She'd been worried it was too soon and the house too small, but Jen had come back to her in a week with architectural plans and a timeline to renovate her garage to accommodate a second story apartment.

She couldn't really argue with that, and so she moved in. Construction crews came three weeks later. Besides, it did feel better knowing that she had a place to go to if she needed space.

She came back to the porch and sat, listening to the night sounds. Behind her, the French doors opened, and Jen's hand skimmed along her neck. "Aren't you cold?"

She huddled a little in her sweatshirt. "Kind of. But it's too nice to go in."

Jen tapped her lap. "You mind?"

Madison opened up her arms and helped Jen settle in next to her. "Still reading?"

Jen rested her head against Madison's shoulder. "Yeah. But he's tired."

She smiled. "I bet."

Jen took a deep breath. "I could get use to this."

Madison kissed her forehead and pulled her in. "I already have."

Jen hummed and snuggled closer, and they sat in the semi-dark.

Closing her eyes, Madison soaked up Jen's warmth and listened to her breathe until it shifted and gradually evened out. Madison moved slightly and gently nudged her. "Are you falling asleep on me?"

"Hmm…maybe."

"Are you happy?"

Jen lifted her head and smiled. She kissed Madison by way of answer before she pulled back and said, "Yes. Are you?"

Madison leaned in and returned her kiss. "Very."

About the Author

Leigh wrote her first story in a spiral notebook at the age of five and she never stopped pretending. She grew up in three of the four corners of the US before heading to college. Despite the warnings that doing so would make her a lesbian, she went to a women's college.

She lives and works in upstate New York with her wife, son, and two Siamese cats, Percival and Galahad. When she's not writing, reading, or parenting, she's tabletop gaming with a crew of like-minded nerds.

Books Available from Bold Strokes Books

Aurora by Emma L McGeown. After a traumatic accident, Elena Ricci is stricken with amnesia leaving her with no recollection of the last eight years, including her wife and son. (978-1-63555-824-1)

Avenging Avery by Sheri Lewis Wohl. Revenge against a vengeful vampire unites Isa Meyer and Jeni Denton, but it's love that heals them. (978-1-63555-622-3)

Bulletproof by Maggie Cummings. For Dylan Prescott and Briana Logan, the complicated NYC criminal justice system doesn't leave room for love, but where the heart is concerned, no one is bulletproof. (978-1-63555-771-8)

Her Lady to Love by Jane Walsh. A shy wallflower joins forces with the most popular woman in Regency London on a quest to catch a husband, only to discover a wild passion for each other that far eclipses their interest for the Marriage Mart. (978-1-63555-809-8)

No Regrets by Joy Argento. For Jodi and Beth, the possibility of losing their future will force them to decide what is really important. (978-1-63555-751-0)

The Holiday Treatment by Elle Spencer. Who doesn't want a gay Christmas movie? Holly Hudson asks herself that question and discovers that happy endings aren't only for the movies. (978-1-63555-660-5)

Too Good to be True by Leigh Hays. Can the promise of love survive the realities of life for Madison and Jen, or is it too good to be true? (978-1-63555-715-2)

Treacherous Seas by Radclyffe. When the choice comes down to the lives of her officers against the promise she made to her wife, Reese Conlon puts everything she cares about on the line. (978-1-63555-778-7)

Two to Tangle by Melissa Brayden. Ryan Jacks has been a player all her life, but the new chef at Tangle Valley Vineyard changes everything. If only she wasn't off the menu. (978-1-63555-747-3)

When Sparks Fly by Annie McDonald. Will the devastating incident that first brought Dr. Daniella Waveny and hockey coach Luca McCaffrey together on frozen ice now force them apart, or will their secrets and fears thaw enough for them to create sparks? (978-1-63555-782-4)

Best Practice by Carsen Taite. When attorney Grace Maldonado agrees to mentor her best friend's little sister, she's prepared to confront Perry's rebellious nature, but she isn't prepared to fall in love. Legal Affairs: one law firm, three best friends, three chances to fall in love. (978-1-63555-361-1)

Home by Kris Bryant. Natalie and Sarah discover that anything is possible when love takes the long way home. (978-1-63555-853-1)

Keeper by Sydney Quinne. With a new charge under her reluctant wing—feisty, highly intelligent math wizard Isabelle Templeton—Keeper Andy Bouchard has to prevent a murder or die trying. (978-1-63555-852-4)

One More Chance by Ali Vali. Harry Basantes planned a future with Desi Thompson until the day Desi disappeared without a word, only to walk back into her life sixteen years later. (978-1-63555-536-3)

Renegade's War by Gun Brooke. Freedom fighter Aurelia DeCallum regrets saving the woman called Blue. She fears it will jeopardize her mission, and secretly, Blue might end up breaking Aurelia's heart. (978-1-63555-484-7)

The Other Women by Erin Zak. What happens in Vegas should stay in Vegas, but what do you do when the love you find in Vegas changes your life forever? (978-1-63555-741-1)

The Sea Within by Missouri Vaun. Time is running out for Dr. Elle Graham to convince Captain Jackson Drake that the only thing that can save future Earth resides in the past, and rescue her broken heart in the process. (978-1-63555-568-4)

To Sleep With Reindeer by Justine Saracen. In Norway under Nazi occupation, Maarit, an Indigenous woman; and Kirsten, a Norwegian resister, join forces to stop the development of an atomic weapon. (978-1-63555-735-0)

Twice Shy by Aurora Rey. Having an ex with benefits isn't all it's cracked up to be. Will Amanda Russo learn that lesson in time to take a chance on love with Quinn Sullivan? (978-1-63555-737-4)

Z-Town by Eden Darry. Forced to work together to stay alive, Meg and Lane must find the centuries-old treasure before the zombies find them first. (978-1-63555-743-5)

Bet Against Me by Fiona Riley. In the high stakes luxury real estate market, everything has a price, and as rival Realtors Trina Lee and Kendall Yates find out, that means their hearts and souls, too. (978-1-63555-729-9)

Broken Reign by Sam Ledel. Together on an epic journey in search of a mysterious cure, a princess and a village outcast must overcome life-threatening challenges and their own prejudice if they want to survive. (978-1-63555-739-8)

Just One Taste by CJ Birch. For Lauren, it only took one taste to start trusting in love again. (978-1-63555-772-5)

Lady of Stone by Barbara Ann Wright. Sparks fly as a magical emergency forces a noble embarrassed by her ability to submit to a low-born teacher who resents everything about her. (978-1-63555-607-0)

Last Resort by Angie Williams. Katie and Rhys are about to find out what happens when you meet the girl of your dreams but you aren't looking for a happily ever after. (978-1-63555-774-9)

Longing for You by Jenny Frame. When Debrek housekeeper Katie Brekman is attacked amid a burgeoning vampire-witch war, Alexis Villiers must go against everything her clan believes in to save her. (978-1-63555-658-2)

Money Creek by Anne Laughlin. Clare Lehane is a troubled lawyer from Chicago who tries to make her way in a rural town full of secrets and deceptions. (978-1-63555-795-4)

Passion's Sweet Surrender by Ronica Black. Cam and Blake are unable to deny their passion for each other, but surrendering to love is a whole different matter. (978-1-63555-703-9)

The Holiday Detour by Jane Kolven. It will take everything going wrong to make Dana and Charlie see how right they are for each other. (978-1-63555-720-6)

Too Hot to Ride by Andrews & Austin. World famous cutting horse champion and industry legend Jane Barrow is knockdown sexy in the way she moves, talks, and rides, and Rae Starr is determined not to get involved with this womanizing gambler. (978-1-63555-776-3)

A Love that Leads to Home by Ronica Black. For Carla Sims and Janice Carpenter, home isn't about location, it's where your heart is. (978-1-63555-675-9)

Blades of Bluegrass by D. Jackson Leigh. A US Army occupational therapist must rehab a bitter veteran who is a ticking political time bomb the military is desperate to disarm. (978-1-63555-637-7)

Guarding Hearts by Jaycie Morrison. As treachery and temptation threaten the women of the Women's Army Corps, who will risk it all for love? (978-1-63555-806-7)

Hopeless Romantic by Georgia Beers. Can a jaded wedding planner and an optimistic divorce attorney possibly find a future together? (978-1-63555-650-6)

Hopes and Dreams by PJ Trebelhorn. Movie theater manager Riley Warren is forced to face her high school crush and tormentor, wealthy socialite Victoria Thayer, at their twentieth reunion. (978-1-63555-670-4)

In the Cards by Kimberly Cooper Griffin. Daria and Phaedra are about to discover that love finds a way, especially when powers outside their control are at play. (978-1-63555-717-6)

Moon Fever by Ileandra Young. SPEAR agent Danika Karson must clear her werewolf friend of multiple false charges while teaching her vampire girlfriend to resist the blood mania brought on by a full moon. (978-1-63555-603-2)

Quake City by St John Karp. Can Andre find his best friend Amy before the night devolves into a nightmare of broken hearts, malevolent drag queens, and spontaneous human combustion? Or has it always happened this way, every night, at Aunty Bob's Quake City Club? (978-1-63555-723-7)

Serenity by Jesse J. Thoma. For Kit Marsden, there are many things in life she cannot change. Serenity is in the acceptance. (978-1-63555-713-8)

Sylver and Gold by Michelle Larkin. Working feverishly to find a killer before he strikes again, Boston Homicide Detective Reid Sylver and rookie cop London Gold are blindsided by their chemistry and developing attraction. (978-1-63555-611-7)

Trade Secrets by Kathleen Knowles. In Silicon Valley, love and business are a volatile mix for clinical lab scientist Tony Leung and venture capitalist Sheila Graham. (978-1-63555-642-1)

Death Overdue by David S. Pederson. Did Heath turn to murder in an alcohol induced haze to solve the problem of his blackmailer, or was it someone else who brought about a death overdue? (978-1-63555-711-4)

Entangled by Melissa Brayden. Becca Crawford is the perfect person to head up the Jade Hotel, if only the captivating owner of the local vineyard would get on board with her plan and stop badmouthing the hotel to everyone in town. (978-1-63555-709-1)

First Do No Harm by Emily Smith. Pierce and Cassidy are about to discover that when it comes to love, sometimes you have to risk it all to have it all. (978-1-63555-699-5)

Kiss Me Every Day by Dena Blake. For Wynn Evans, wishing for a do-over with Carly Jamison was a long shot, actually getting one was a game changer. (978-1-63555-551-6)

Olivia by Genevieve McCluer. In this lesbian Shakespeare adaptation with vampires, Olivia is a centuries old vampire who must fight a strange figure from her past if she wants a chance at happiness. (978-1-63555-701-5)

One Woman's Treasure by Jean Copeland. Daphne's search for discarded antiques and treasures leads to an embarrassing misunderstanding, and ultimately, the opportunity for the romance of a lifetime with Nina. (978-1-63555-652-0)

Silver Ravens by Jane Fletcher. Lori has lost her girlfriend, her home, and her job. Things don't improve when she's kidnapped and taken to fairyland. (978-1-63555-631-5)

Still Not Over You by Jenny Frame, Carsen Taite, Ali Vali. Old flames die hard in these tales of a second chance at love with the ex you're still not over. Stories by award winning authors Jenny Frame, Carsen Taite, and Ali Vali. (978-1-63555-516-5)

Storm Lines by Jessica L. Webb. Devon is a psychologist who likes rules. Marley is a cop who doesn't. They don't always agree, but both fight to protect a girl immersed in a street drug ring. (978-1-63555-626-1)

The Politics of Love by Jen Jensen. Is it possible to love across the political divide in a hostile world? Conservative Shelley Whitmore and liberal Rand Thomas are about to find out. (978-1-63555-693-3)